In-Laws and Outlaws

Kate Fulford

This first edition published in 2017 by:

Thistle Publishing
36 Great Smith Street
London
SW1P 3BU

www.thistlepublishing.co.uk

Chapter 1

"I'm a writer." I said in reply to Marjorie's enquiry. I'm not, but I have done the occasional bit of copywriting. I once did a poster for a friend of mine who has a fruit and veg stall on Chiswick High Road. It said 'Mangoes Bananas' next to a picture of a man who clearly had mental health issues. Alf thought it was very funny and put it on the side of his van. Unfortunately the Advertising Standards Authority found it rather less amusing but for a while I was one of the most widely read writers in that neck of the woods.

"Anything I might have read?" Marjorie asked, although not with any particular enthusiasm. I had the distinct impression that, despite her follow up question, Marjorie wasn't in the least bit interested in my answer. She had asked me all sorts of questions in the short time I had spent with her but she did so, I felt, more in an attempt to unsettle me and not because she had any desire to get to know me better. I should explain that I was a few months into a relationship with Marjorie's son, Gideon (excellent name, excellent man), and this was my first meeting with his parents.

"Oh, I doubt it," I replied, "my work is very... niche." I like to keep things quite vague, too much certainty not being a good thing in my view. People who are very certain about things aren't usually very interesting, as Marjorie was in the process of proving.

I had been in Marjorie's house, which I had thought was in Sheen, for about half an hour by the time of this exchange, and I felt as if I were lurching down one disastrous conversational cul-de-sac after another. The first had involved, as it happens, the location of Marjorie's house. It wasn't, she had assured me and in contradiction to all the available facts, in Sheen at all.

"Richmond borders," she had said in a way that brooked no opposition. "We have a Sheen postcode because of those idiots at the Post Office, but it's actually Richmond borders."

"Is that an official place then, like the Scottish Borders?" I had foolishly thought she was making a joke and responded in kind.

"No." Marjorie replied, without even the merest hint of a smile. She was, it would seem, in deadly earnest.

"Oh, I see." I didn't see at all. I had ended up in this position due to a clearly futile attempt to ingratiate myself with my boyfriend's mother. Having believed myself to be in Sheen I had told Marjorie that I had once had a friend who lived there, to which she responded with an icy "and what has that got to do with me?"

I had soldiered on, not having encountered such a response before and therefore not having seen the warning signs that indicated I was digging a hole for myself. I had told Marjorie that I knew Sheen quite well on account of this friend that had lived there. I had embellished the story of my friendship somewhat (I hadn't known the subject of my story since primary school for example, and neither had we ever gone to Zumba classes together) but I was simply trying to find some common ground, as one does in conversations. The whole exchange had left me wishing I had never heard of Sheen let alone had a passing acquaintance with someone who had once lived there. And now I was burbling on about being a writer. Would I never learn? Luckily I was saved from having to conjure up answers to any more of Marjorie's questions by Gideon's father.

"Drink, anyone?" asked Malcolm. He was standing in the doorway of what Gideon's mother, I had learnt, called the lounge shaking a bottle of sweet sherry at us. He had taken Gideon off somewhere not long after our arrival leaving me alone with Marjorie, so I was inordinately pleased to see him back as it presumably meant Gideon was not far behind.

"Lovely," I heard myself say, despite never having been especially fond of sherry, sweet or otherwise.

The house in which I found myself sitting, very uncomfortably at that moment, was a half-timbered, mock Tudor beast in a street of similarly beastly houses. It had, as Marjorie had been quick to point out, five bedrooms and three (count them!) bathrooms. She had imparted this information as we made our way from the front door to the lounge, and in such a way that one might have assumed I was an estate agent or even a prospective buyer. I half expected her to give me a brochure so keen was she to extol the virtues of her home.

I am, as a general rule, very interested in other people's houses but this place was a very dull affair. Everything about it was done in the kind of good taste that it is difficult to dislike but which it is, at the same time, impossible to love. I was, however, trying my very hardest to love it. These people and their home were, I very much hoped, about to become my people and their home a second home to me. I was quite determined to make a good impression, but I didn't seem to have got off to a very good start.

Meeting someone's parents shouldn't, by the time one is of a certain age (and I am of a certain age), matter but it does, I suppose, indicate that you are part of a 'couple'. I must confess to being permanently confused by the rules that surround sexual pairings. At fifteen one could find oneself 'going steady' on the basis of a single kiss. By eighteen sleeping with someone was no guarantee that you were an item. Once into one's twenties the idea of 'meeting the parents' became a useful shorthand for knowing where one stood. At this stage I was at something of a disadvantage, lacking parents whom boyfriends could meet, but until her premature death I had occasionally used my Aunt Audrey as an analogue for them. Once one passes thirty (and thirty is an ever smaller dot in my rear view mirror) the whole thing becomes, theoretically at least, somewhat less important, as people, one would hope, move beyond needing parental approval for their relationships. Even so, these people might one day be one's own family and making a good impression is therefore to be desired.

I had approached meeting Gideon's parents with some trepidation. I don't have a great track record with families generally, not having had much practice, and so my trepidation had only increased when he had hinted that there might be quite a lot more riding on it than I might have wished.

"Mum's amazing," Gideon had told me, "we're very close. I really trust her judgement." This is not what anyone wants to hear when on the verge of meeting a prospective life partner's mother. What one wants to hear is that she will love anyone that one's prospective life partner loves or (even better) that one's partner doesn't care what his (or her) mother thinks. That Gideon seemed to care what his mother thought was therefore a bit of a blow and I was sent into something of a spin following Gideon's suggestion that he and I have Sunday lunch at his parents' home. They did, however, live quite close by, about halfway between the flat that I was by that time gradually moving out of, and Gideon's home, which I was gradually moving into, so I couldn't really come up with a reasonable excuse not to go. And it was just a Sunday lunch, a perfectly normal, casual Sunday lunch of the sort that families all over the country routinely enjoy. But however much I tried to convince myself that it was just a meal I couldn't rid myself of an uncomfortable feeling in the pit of my stomach. What if they (and by 'they' I meant his mother) took a dislike to me and convinced Gideon that he should dislike me too? What if I made a fool of myself? What if I broke something? What if...?

"Stop it Eve, I'm sure they're perfectly nice people who will be delighted to meet you. They will only want Gideon to be happy, and as you make him happy it'll be fine." I had shared my fears with my friend Claire and she had done her best to reassure me. "Just be yourself and I'm sure they'll warm to you," she had said. So here I was, trying my best to impersonate someone who was just being herself, and yet waves of chilliness were coming off Gideon's mother much as if she were a portable air conditioning unit.

"So how do you like London?" Marjorie was looking at me blankly despite having asked me a question, another in a long line of non sequiturs that had left me all at sea and rudderless, conversation-wise. She reinforced my perception that she was uninterested in my response by turning away from me as soon as she had finished speaking to stare intently at the huge diamond that adorned her ring finger.

"Oh, I love it." I said. "Always have done. Although I have heard that there are some other excellent cities."

"So you don't prefer the North?" Marjorie didn't look up as she spoke, she just kept fiddling with her ring, which was, as I'm sure she meant it to be, rather disconcerting.

I carried on regardless. Why she thought I should prefer the North (I could tell from her tone that she was using a capital N), by which I presumed she meant the north of England, I had no idea, but I would be charm on a stick whatever this woman threw at me.

"Well, the countryside is very lovely," I said, "but it's a long way from London." At this point Malcolm brought me a gin and tonic (I don't know what happened to the sweet sherry, perhaps Gideon, wherever he was, had had a word). It was warm and the tonic was flat, but I wasn't about to complain. This meeting was all about making a good impression and complaining about one's drink didn't come into that category.

"It must have been interesting," I ventured, "living all over the world?" As Marjorie had expressed an interest in my thoughts on the North I thought this was a reasonable gambit, my attempts at finding common ground over Sheen having failed so spectacularly. She and Malcolm had, so Gideon told me, lived in various exotic locations courtesy of Malcolm's career (he was now retired) as a legal something or other working for a multinational company that did something I can never quite recall.

We were by now seated in the dining room. Marjorie had demanded that we all head in there almost the very moment Malcolm had brought me my drink so I hadn't even had a chance to take a swig of gin in the hope it might take the edge off things a bit, but at least Gideon was now back on the scene.

Once seated Marjorie had placed a pre-loaded plate of Sunday lunch in front of each of us, something that I found a little intimidating as mine contained far more than I could comfortably eat at one sitting. The only thing over which the diner had any portion control was the gravy, which sat in splendid isolation in an ornate gravy boat in the very centre of the vast table, just out of everyone's reach.

"Not particularly," replied Marjorie taking her seat. Before picking up her knife and fork she placed her hands, palms together and fingers lightly touching, just above her plate. For a moment I thought she was going to say grace and wondered if I should bow my head, but instead she glared into the middle distance and simply said "eat". Neither Malcolm nor Gideon seemed to think this was odd and simply chowed down. I, somewhat gratefully, did the same as at least it meant that any attempts at conversation could, for the time being at least, be abandoned. I felt very much as rats must when they are put into mazes by people in white coats. However hard I tried I couldn't find any subject on which Marjorie and I could have a normal discourse. Every possible conversational route led to a dead end.

"This is delicious," I said, having shovelled down a few mouthfuls of the enormous mountain of food in front of me. It wasn't. It looked and tasted like a pub roast meal, the kind where you can only tell what the meat is based on whether you are served apple, mint, or horseradish sauce. I assumed that the slab of grey protein on my plate was probably beef as it was accompanied by a square of barely cooked batter that I could only assume was meant to be Yorkshire pudding. There was no horseradish.

"I'd like some mustard." Malcolm announced getting up from the table, "Anyone else want mustard?"

"You and your mustard," hissed Marjorie, "why you have to slather good food with that muck I don't know. I spend hours slaving in the kitchen and then you go and cover everything with mustard." I had been about to say that I would also like some mustard but Marjorie's antipathy towards it indicated to me that it would be politic to go without.

"Oh Mum, let him eat what he wants, he's the one abusing his taste buds." Gideon smiled broadly at his mother as he spoke and I saw her soften under his gaze. She clearly adored him. Upon our arrival Marjorie had hugged Gideon to her and made a grimace that implied his arrival might offer some blessed relief from the awfulness of her existence. She had refused to meet my eye. She had, rather, looked me up and down while adjusting her cardigan, a neat little affair in navy blue with gold buttons and a vaguely military epaulette on each shoulder. She had then extended her hand such a very small way that I practically fell over the threshold in an attempt to get close enough to grasp the very end of her fingers in a limp handshake. I now looked back on that experience as something of a highlight, so difficult had been everything since then.

"Yes, Ian, you're quite right. Let him suffer!" Marjorie actually smiled as she watched Malcolm head off on his mustard mission. I had wondered if she had some sort of muscle problem that made her unable to smile as up to this point she had worn only a pinched expression that could have been annoyance, unhappiness, displeasure, or all three combined.

"Ian?" I blurted out. "Your name is Ian?"

"Mum's always called me Ian," Gideon explained. "She's never liked the name Gideon. I started using it when I was about thirteen because I thought it was cooler and it sort of stuck."

"So your name isn't really Gideon?" I felt vaguely cheated as I liked the name Gideon. It is interesting and unusual and I was disappointed to discover that it was simply a teenage affectation. I often tell people that Eve is short for Evangeline, when in fact it says Evelyn on my birth certificate. Gideon had enthused about the name Evangeline when I had told him, so it would have been a shame if we had both been going by aliases.

"His name is Gideon. It's a name that has been in my family for generations and which Marjorie accepted at the time of his birth." Malcolm made this rather dramatic statement as he returned from the kitchen carrying a very small jar of sludgy brown mustard. I was even gladder I hadn't said I wanted any.

"I did not accept it at the time," countered Marjorie, in what was clearly a well-worn argument. "I was not given any choice. My child, my first born and I wasn't even allowed to name him myself." Any hint of a smile was long gone.

"Now Mum, it doesn't really matter what I'm called does it? I'm still your first born, aren't I?" Gideon stretched across the vast expanse of table and rubbed his mother's arm while surreptitiously winking at me. She put her hand over his and took a deep breath as if the heavy burdens she carried (whatever these burdens might be) had been momentarily lifted by her son's gesture.

I valiantly fought my way through the plate of food I had been allotted (although I noticed that Marjorie left most of hers while Malcolm could clearly have eaten twice as much, he only just stopped short of actually picking up his plate and licking it) but it left me feeling even more uncomfortable than I had before lunch. I hate feeling overfull. I think that being hungry is an altogether more pleasurable experience. The difference, I think, is that hunger is easily remedied while feeling overfull can take hours to wear off. So there I was, feeling overfull, and not even as the result of a delicious meal, when Marjorie asked who wanted pudding, or sweet as she called it.

"I bought a caramel cheesecake," she announced "from that baker on the corner, you know the one Ian." The look

Gideon gave me suggested that he didn't. "I'll cut it into quarters." Oh my god, a quarter of a caramel cheesecake. I don't have a sweet tooth so the thought of eating twenty five percent of a caramel cheesecake when I was already full to bursting made me feel physically sick.

"Oh, not for me thanks." I said. "That was delicious but I couldn't eat another thing." I hoped I sounded sincere.

"I'll pass as well Mum, but that was great." Gideon tapped his stomach as if to prove his sincerity. We couldn't have been more sincere.

"Your father and I can eat it tomorrow I suppose," Marjorie huffed, "if it hasn't gone off by then. Pass your plates." The look on Malcolm's face spoke clearly of his disappointment. He had not had enough main course and was now to be denied pudding. I on the other hand was even more relieved that I had refused. A cheesecake so dangerously close to going off was best avoided, even if one were hungry.

"Oh no," I urged, "you go ahead. It's just that I don't often eat pudd... sweet. I..." I wasn't sure how to continue, but felt as if I should try to rescue a situation which seemed to have made both Gideon's parents dislike me at the same time.

"It's no inconvenience at all," said Marjorie in a tone that indicated that it was an inconvenience, although why someone not wanting pudding should be inconvenient I had no idea, "we'll do whatever you want."

I bridled, internally at least, at the injustice of Marjorie's statement. I hadn't asked anyone else to do what I wanted, I'd simply refused the offer of a quarter of a caramel cheesecake because I was full and because it sounded revolting, but I had made no mention of this second reason. Neither had I demanded that everyone else follow suit.

"I'm going to show Eve the garden, OK Mum?" Gideon came to my rescue. I was only too eager to leave the room without a backward glance, but I couldn't help noticing the look of disdain on Marjorie's face as she took in the napkin I had flung untidily on to the table. Everyone else had folded theirs neatly. That is it, I thought, she hates me.

"So what do you think of them?" Gideon asked once we were safely in the garden and out of earshot. If I had, even for a moment, considered being truthful his next question would have stymied the impulse. "Mum's great, isn't she?"

No, I wanted to reply, she's a bitch of the first order. "Well," I replied, "she's certainly a character."

"She can be a bit tricky but she has a lot to put up with." Gideon continued. "Dad's not the easiest of men to live with and sometimes it gets the better of her. That's why I left you two alone together, to give you a chance to get to know each other without Dad being there."

Thanks a bunch, I didn't say. Nor did I add that neither of Gideon's parents had struck me as particularly easy people but from what I had observed it looked as if it was Malcolm rather than Marjorie who had the most to put up with. But Gideon clearly knew them far better than I did so I felt that I should, for the moment at least, accept his assessment of the situation. "She's a pussycat really," he went on, "she just doesn't know much about you yet." Pussycat my arse. Unless of course she was like my Aunt Audrey's cat, Tassita, a truly despicable creature that had hated everyone, including my aunt. I had only known Gideon for a few months but until today he had struck me as a very perceptive man. We had shared long conversations in which he had illustrated that he understood a great deal about the human condition, which as a professor of psychology he jolly well should, but now I wasn't so sure. How could he believe that the woman I had just met was a pussycat? We had, by now, wandered over to stand under a small apple tree to shelter from the drizzle that had been gently but persistently falling all day.

"I should probably have offered to help with the washing up." I said, reaching up to pull an apple from the branch above my head.

"Oh no, she wouldn't have liked that at all!" Gideon sounded quite horrified. "She's what you might call house-proud," he continued. "She likes everything to be done her way. Did you see that rug in the hall?"

"The one with the tassels all around the edge?" I asked. See it? I had almost tripped over it in my haste to escape the dining room.

"Mum has a rake she uses to keep the tassels straight. I'm telling you, she wouldn't thank you for helping in the kitchen." Gideon laughed at what he saw as his mother's little foible. I, on the other hand, found the idea of raking rug tassels extremely sinister. It's the kind of thing that I'm pretty sure serial killers do. If asked my opinion in respect of people who rake rug tassels it would be to treat them with the utmost caution.

"So," I said, returning to the subject at hand, "the problem is that she doesn't know much about me?"

"Yes," Gideon replied, "that is correct."

"So, what does she know about me?" I asked. "What have you told her?"

"That you're a friend of mine."

"Is that it?" I was a little taken aback.

"Yes." Gideon, like so many of his sex, while useful in all sorts ways can, I'm afraid, be utterly hopeless in others.

"So she has no idea that we are a couple?" I exclaimed. "She has no idea that you won't let me put my shoes in your wardrobe when I come over due to your seemingly limitless pairs of nearly identical boots taking up all the available space?"

"The thing is you should never wear the same pair of boots two days in a row so it's always best to ..." he began.

"Not really the point I'm making right now." I interrupted the boot story, which I had now heard at least four times, in an attempt to get things back on track. "She doesn't know that we're a couple?"

"Not exactly. When I split up with Nicole Mum said it would be good for me to have some time to myself and she was quite excited at the idea that she and I could spend more time together. I didn't like to upset her." Nicole had been Gideon's partner when he had met me, so that had meant curtains for Nicole (or at least for her relationship with Gideon, I didn't kill her). "I just thought it was a better strategy," Gideon continued, "to let Mum get to know you and like you before I told her about us." Gideon shrugged as if all this was perfectly normal. If there had been a klaxon of some sort in the garden designed to warn of imminent danger it would undoubtedly have gone off at this point. The garden, however, contained no such a device and I had, by this point, grown pretty fond of Gideon so there's every chance I wouldn't have heeded it anyway.

"Really?" I said. "So you lie to your mother to make your life easier? That's appalling." I often lie to make my life easier, but that doesn't mean that I condone lying in others. I had by now separated the apple from its branch (they had been quite reluctant to part but I had persisted) and was about to sink my teeth into it.

"Best not do that, they're really sharp, and Mum doesn't like her fruit being messed with, not by strange women anyway." Gideon nudged me affectionately. He is not a man given to effusive apologies but I think he realised that I was feeling a little uncomfortable with the situation he had put me in. Here I was thinking that I was being introduced to his parents as his new partner, while they thought that I was simply a friend. "I will tell her, I promise. But not this afternoon, I'll call her in the week and have a chat. It'll be fine. Let's go in, I think she's got Dad making coffee."

"I don't drink coffee in the afternoon," I said, slightly sulkily.

"Well," said Gideon, taking hold of both my shoulders so that I had to turn and face him, "you better had today or we'll all have to go without. And I like caramel cheesecake."

"Really?" I said again.

"Yes, really. Now let's go in, it's getting chilly out here."

Once inside I had to sit, or rather perch, on the edge of Marjorie's very uncomfortable and overstuffed sofa for what seemed like an age before Malcolm came in bearing a tray on which were placed four tiny cups of coffee. He had been banging and crashing around in the kitchen for much longer than seemed entirely necessary for the task in hand while a coffee machine intermittently made loud hissing and sploshing noises. He was now looking remarkably pleased with himself for a man who had simply made a hot beverage.

"I couldn't find any cake." he said as he crossed the room, slopping much of the coffee that it had taken him so long to make into the saucers as he did so.

"That's because there isn't any." Marjorie snapped back.

"Oh," said Malcolm, looking somewhat downcast. He perked up, however, as he looked down lovingly at the coffee he had just made.

"Nothing like a good cup of coffee," he announced, setting the tray down and handing each of us a cup. And, to use a well-worn joke, it was nothing like a good cup of coffee, being both tasteless and lukewarm. Marjorie clearly thought it was acceptable though, and it seemed to loosen her up somewhat.

"You know," she began, looking straight at me, the hint of a smile playing around her lips, "I'm very good with accents and I can hear yours quite clearly. I have a very good ear."

I looked at her, bemused. I had lived in Norwich between the ages of six and sixteen but had not developed even so much as a hint of a Norfolk accent, so I really had no idea what she was talking about.

"I'm sorry?" I looked to Gideon for some clarification.

"What do you mean Mum?" he said. "What accent?"

"A northern accent of course!" Marjorie exclaimed. "You said Eve was from Blackpool and I was just saying that she doesn't have a very strong accent but with my ear I can pick it up."

"But I'm not from Blackpool," I blurted out, "I'm from..." where was I from? Not Norwich, not really. If I was from anywhere I supposed I was from London as I had been born there and lived more of my life there than anywhere else, "... here. I've lived in London virtually all my life. I have been to Blackpool but I can't imagine that I picked up much of an accent in a weekend." I must confess I laughed at this point, but as soon as I did I felt that it was the wrong thing to have done.

"Gideon never said she was from Blackpool," Malcolm said, smiling at me. It was the first time I had seen him smile properly and it transformed his face. He actually looked quite friendly, and I could see the resemblance between him and his son which up till then had been obscured by Malcolm's scowl. "Eve hasn't got even the merest trace of a northern accent," Malcolm continued. "Gideon said that they met in Blackpool. It's not the same thing as coming from Blackpool, not the same thing at all. I think you must be mistaken Marjorie." Gideon and I hadn't exactly met in Blackpool but it had been at a conference held there that we had, so to speak, cemented our relationship.

I watched Marjorie closely waiting to see how she would react. I was worried that my lack of a northern accent would make her dislike me even more than she already seemed to. I felt that by not being from Blackpool she might feel that I had, in some way, humiliated her.

"Oh, silly me," said Marjorie, smiling broadly for the first time that day. "I must, as you say Malcolm, have been mistaken." I think I might have actually let out an audible sigh of relief. Perhaps all was not lost and I could make Gideon's mother like me. I certainly hoped I could as it would make life so much easier. I have come up against mothers before and, in my experience, getting on the right side of them is, if not exactly crucial, then very much to be desired.

Chapter 2

My experience of families has been quite varied but it has rarely been satisfactory. My own little nuclear unit came to an abrupt end when I was six and for reasons I have never fully fathomed I went to live with my Aunt Audrey in the aforementioned Norwich. Despite being a social worker specialising in child care Audrey was spectacularly ill equipped to act in loco parentis. The principal recollection I have of her home was how it was both silent and extremely noisy at the same time. It lacked any of the sounds I associated with family life (laughter, conversation, singing, crying, arguing) but this absence was filled with the sounds of inanimate objects coming into contact with each other in a way that seemed to indicate that they were not well suited to share a house. It was, most certainly, a cacophonous metaphor for the relationship between my aunt and me.

Audrey had lived in a tiny terraced house that comprised two small rooms downstairs with a kitchen and bathroom tacked on the back, and two equally teeny tiny bedrooms upstairs. There were no carpets or rugs anywhere. Downstairs the floors were stone and upstairs there were bare floorboards. Every time either Audrey or I moved around the house, or moved anything within it, the sound would ricochet around the small space. To add to this soundscape Audrey was a big fan of pottery. Every meal was accompanied by the scraping of cutlery on earthenware crockery. All of this would have been bad enough, but Audrey seemed unaware that her interior design choices when combined with a child would militate against the quietude she professed to need so that she could, as she frequently reminded me, think. I was forever being admonished to be quiet, but however hard I tried I could not interact with Audrey's home (I never once thought of it as my home) without noisily drawing attention to myself. The situation was made worse by the fact that the bedrooms were interconnected, making it necessary to go through the back bedroom to get to the one at the front. Audrey, because of her need for quiet, insisted on sleeping in the back one, away from the road (which was, as it happens, very quiet). Whenever I needed the loo in the night, which I often did largely because of the fear engendered by worrying about how much noise I would make should I need to go, I had to pass through Audrey's bedroom. I quickly learnt every creak and squeak of the journey and would freeze, like a rabbit confronted by a fox, at every sound to assure myself that Audrey was still asleep and not about to bellow at me. Descending a wooden staircase can still fill me with the unreasonable fear that I am about to be shouted at, as well as a vague desire to pee. This makes it all sound very grim, and in many ways it was but, on the upside, Audrey did leave me alone a lot.

Family life with Aunt Audrey having been so very far from what I assume is the norm one of my chief ambitions in life has been to create a secure, happy, and settled home life for myself. I have always been open to ideas about what that family might comprise. I am not in the least hung up on the notion of a nuclear family, so long it's secure, happy, and settled that'll do me. By the time I met Gideon I think it's fair to say that I had not been as successful as I might have hoped when lying in my bed as a child fervently wishing for a family (and a pony, which didn't turn out very well either) very different to the one of which I was notionally a part. Having said that, it isn't entirely true to say that I completely lack family, I do have a younger brother, Dominic, but sometimes (quite often in fact) I wish I didn't.

A few days after meeting the 'amazing' Marjorie I was back at my old flat, where I had gone to pick up my few remaining belongings. I hadn't specifically told Gideon that I was moving into his flat at this point but I was sure I would be able to work out the finer details when the time came and so had pushed ahead with the move regardless. It was just as I opened the front door that my phone rang. Dropping my keys on the hall table I scrabbled to retrieve it from my bag. I didn't get to it in time but could see that I had missed a call from Dominic.

"Hi Sis," said the voice mail he had left for me, "I really need to talk to you. Something's happened and I need your help." My heart sank, which I know it shouldn't on hearing from one's brother, but Dominic only ever seems to call me when he wants 'something' or 'something' has happened. This might lead one to conclude that I don't hear from him very often but this is not, unfortunately, the case.

"So what's happened?" I asked when I finally spoke to Dominic a few hours later. He had, as per usual, turned his phone off almost as soon as he left the message for me, or had put it on silent, or forgotten that he had called me and was ignoring my incoming calls, or was trying to avoid someone else and was inadvertently ignoring me at the same time. Any of these scenarios was equally likely and all had occurred in the past. I could have done without talking to my brother that day as I had had a rather unpleasant conversation with my now ex landlady (and flatmate) just after I got his message. I had given her my notice with immediate effect and she had been rather difficult about returning my deposit as the washing machine had just broken and she wanted me to contribute to its repair. I didn't think I should have to contribute as I hadn't used it in months, having been using Gideon's. She also said that I would have to continue paying rent until she could find a new lodger, which I felt was wholly unreasonable. I told her that a death in the family necessitated my abrupt departure but she was unswayed by my loss. I had been quite upset by her behaviour as we had always got on quite well, and if I had just lost a family member I would have found her attitude very hurtful indeed. It seemed a shame that several years of harmonious co habitation should end on such a duff note. It was just my bad luck, I suppose, that I had to deal with Dominic and an unreasonable landlady all in the same day.

"Why do you always think something has happened?" Dominic demanded to know. Because you said so in your voicemail was the obvious answer but there was no point in saying it. "Can't I call my sister just to talk?" Yes, Dominic, you can, I also didn't say, but you never do. "So how are things with you?" he asked. I knew he didn't care how things were with me but I was going to tell him anyway.

"Really good actually. Gideon has asked me to move in." I was keen to share the good news that, on hearing I had been evicted by my unreasonable landlady with immediate effect, Gideon had offered me a home seeing as, in his words, "you practically live with me anyway", but that was as far as I got.

"Yeah, great. Anyway, you will not believe what that... what Sophie has done now..." Sophie had been the love of my brother's life for a short time ten years previously.

Had it ended there she would no doubt be a mere footnote in my brother's truly epic list of ex-lovers (he's not particular good looking but he has a boyish charm that infuriates me but which brings out the mothering instinct in far too many women). That Sophie still got airtime was due to a split condom (I know it's not romantic and is definitely too much information, but such is the miracle of life) which resulted in Pixie, my niece and only other extant relative.

While I had been brought up by our father's sister, the aforementioned Audrey, Dominic had been farmed out to our mother's brother and his wife (they are still alive as far as I know but have, for reasons Dominic has never explained, cut off all contact with him, and never really had any with me), and we rarely saw each other until our late teens. When we reconnected I had been keen to develop a relationship with my estranged brother. This was, I felt, my chance to develop a truly satisfying familial relationship. Fat chance.

"She won't let me see Pixie." Dominic continued.

"Oh," I replied, as non-committally as I could. Dominic and Sophie had split up before Pixie was born, but they had been using the poor child as a proxy for their animosity towards each other ever since.

"What did you do?" I asked, although I knew I shouldn't have said it even before the words were out, but it was a natural assumption to make. Sophie may not be perfect but she does (pretty much) always put Pixie first. Dominic, on the other hand, seems far more concerned with asserting his rights as a father than with his daughter's well-being. On more than one occasion I have met up with the pair of them, father and daughter, and he has all but ignored Pixie in order to give me a blow by blow account of how hard he had to fight to get access to a child in whom he seems to have no interest.

"Why do you always think it's me that's done something?" Dominic angrily demanded to know. If Dominic wasn't my brother or if I had wider pool of relatives with whom to interact I'm pretty sure that I would have as little as possible to do with him, but there is something about the relationship I can't give up on. I remember the little boy I once knew and while it wouldn't be true to say my heart melts, my shields lower and I find myself sucked into situations I would rather avoid.

"I didn't mean you, in the singular, I meant you as in you and Sophie," I clarified. I had meant Dominic in the singular, but there was no mileage in pointing this out. "What's happened?"

"Why do you always assume something's happened? It could just be that Sophie is being bloody minded." He can go on like this for hours. It's very wearing.

"Is she just being bloody minded?" I asked as noncommittally as I could.

"Kind of." Dominic replied evasively.

"Mmm," I said.

"We had an argument about me seeing Pixie and now she won't let me see her at all."

"Not at all?" I asked.

"Not overnight. She says it's what Pixie wants, but I know she's lying. So I'm going to take her to court and I need your help."

"You're taking Pixie to court?" I asked.

"Not Pixie, Sophie. Only an idiot would imagine I would be taking a nine year old to court."

"Why do you want my help if I'm an idiot?"

"Is that a joke?" Dominic doesn't really have a sense of humour. That is another reason why his success with the opposite sex is so difficult to fathom.

"So is that all there is to it? You can't have Pixie overnight," I knew for a fact that Dominic didn't like having Pixie overnight, but he conveniently forgets the facts when there is a principle at stake, "and you want to take Sophie to court over it?"

"All there is to it? That I am being denied access to my daughter!" Dominic exclaimed. "I might have known you wouldn't understand, not being a parent." My brother loves saying this. He is very attached to his role as a father. Not because he has played any active part in Pixie's upbringing, but because he believes that simply having had a stray sperm hit the target makes him morally superior to anyone who hasn't reproduced. The only difference between me and my brother is a failure of birth control. He has literally done no more actual parenting than I have. Less probably, as I reckon I have had Pixie on my own far more times than he has. Sophie is an actress and while this means she is usually on benefits or working in a cafe, it also means that she needs childcare at short notice and at odd times of the day, when she has auditions for example, or the very occasional acting job. Dominic is a teacher and while one might think this would give him lots of free time to care for his child, particularly in the school holidays, one would be wrong. Sophie's parents emigrated to Canada when she was at drama school, taking her younger siblings with them, so she has no family over here. So, as the only relative either of them has access to, I have all too frequently had to step into the breach. It's not that I dislike Pixie, I am actually quite fond of her, but I have never wanted children (having my own has never figured in any of my family scenarios although I have toyed with the idea of being a fabulously fun stepmother, so long as the children lived with their mother) and am constantly amazed at how they can be so utterly exhausting and so extremely boring at the same time. It's got better as Pixie has got older, and now she is nine I am coming to enjoy my time with her more, but nothing about the experience of being an aunt has made me think that motherhood would have been preferable.

"It was in the street, and Pixie was there." Dominic continued.

"What was in the street?" I was getting a bit lost.

"The argument, about access to Pixie. Sophie started screaming about how I was never there for Pixie." Sophie had a point. "And then she said Pixie didn't want to see me." This was perfectly possible. Whenever I spent time with Pixie and Dominic the child seemed to get no particular pleasure from her father's company. I could sense, however, that Dominic was trying very hard to make himself the victim of this story. It was proving a struggle even for someone as sure of his own essential victimhood as my brother.

"Mmm," I said for a second time.

"This upset me so much that it's just possible I might have pushed Sophie." This was so clearly disingenuous I was amazed that my brother could bring himself to say it. He had obviously thought long and hard about the form of words he would use but they sounded as natural coming from him as it would to hear a dog asking you to please stop throwing that stick as they would rather read a good book, thank you very much.

"Pushed her? Pushed her how?" I asked.

"Shoved her. In the shoulder," Dominic continued. "She was saying, screaming," he quickly corrected himself, "that I was a crap father and that Pixie didn't want to stay over anymore and then she came up and shouted right in my face and I shoved her away." I have known Sophie for a long time and I have rarely heard her raise her voice, and then only if she thinks Pixie is about to come to harm. She doesn't strike me as a shouter, and Dominic had never mentioned any previous incidents of Sophie shouting.

"And then what happened?" I prompted.

"She says I can't be trusted with Pixie."

"That's very disappointing for you," I said briskly, "but I'm afraid I can't talk now, Gideon has just come in. Hi Gideon," I called to the empty flat. Gideon was actually out for the evening at some academic thing. He'd asked if I wanted to go too but I can only really take professors one at a time so had declined.

"The thing is I need you to be a character witness for me." Dominic said in a wheedling tone that set my teeth on edge.

"Really?" I couldn't see any upside for me in doing what my brother wanted. If Sophie didn't want him to have Pixie overnight I felt that was very much up to her. Not only had he given Sophie very little help bringing up their child, he had even gone so far as to intimate on occasion (usually when Sophie needed money) that he couldn't be absolutely sure Pixie was his, although he'd never pushed it so far as to get DNA test. While I would be sorry if the fallout between Sophie and Dominic led to me not seeing Pixie, the one way I could see of making certain I wouldn't get to see my niece would be to side with my brother in a case he would probably lose. I really couldn't see how committing perjury on Dominic's behalf could benefit me at all.

"So you'll need to go and see my solicitor," Dominic continued. "I'll send you the details."

"I didn't say I'd do it." I replied.

"Yes you did." Dominic sounded so affronted that I wondered for a moment if I had acquiesced without realising it. My brother can do that to you.

"I really do have to go," I said, "OK Gideon, I'm coming," I shouted to a still absent Gideon. "Look, Dominic, I'll call you tomorrow. Oh, and I had to change my email again so there's no point in sending anything until I give you the new one. It might not be secure." I knew this would ensure that I got no emails from Dominic. My brother is a world class conspiracy theorist. He is absolutely convinced that there are powers at large that control everything through a vast web of informants and henchmen, but despite the huge power this cabal wields they are unaccountably concerned with what a geography teacher at a failing east London school thinks and says about them. "What was that?" I added, just to ram the point home. "Did you hear a click on the line?" As it happens I had heard a faint click, but it was probably just static.

"Yeah, bye. Speak soon." Dominic hung up with indecent haste, and mercifully just before I let out a snort of laughter.

Chapter 3

Gideon had described his mother as 'amazing', and while it was true that I had been amazed by her behaviour in the short time I had known her, I didn't think it was in the way that Gideon meant. I must, I thought, be missing something. I therefore decided to call on the expertise of my friend Claire, who is training to be a clinical psychologist and so knows a thing or two about human behaviour, to try to get a better understanding of what was going on in Marjorie's head. It was through Claire that I had met Gideon so she did, I felt, have some responsibility for ensuring that things turned out well.

I remember the first time I clapped eyes on Gideon with great clarity. I had met up with Claire at the university at which she was studying and we were in the post graduate cafe. It was just before Halloween, I remember this especially clearly because the cafe was selling cupcakes decorated with spider's web motifs in black icing, one of which I had foolishly purchased. The very moment I first saw Gideon my mouth was filled with the most cloying buttercream concoction and I'm pretty sure that my teeth were blackened by the spider's web icing. Of all the types of cake available cup cakes are among my least favourite, but everyone else had bought one and so I had felt that I ought to do the same, especially as I shouldn't really have been there, not being either a post or even an undergraduate at the university.

Gideon's presence was brought to my attention by one of Claire's fellow students, Theresa, to whom I had taken an instant and initially unaccountable dislike, and who also had black icing on her teeth, which only confirms my belief that I was highly likely to have had some on mine.

"Oh my god, it's Professor Rowe," Theresa hissed excitedly, spraying a light shower of cupcake spittle onto the table. Everyone else seemed to know what this meant and clearly shared her excitement.

"Who?" I asked.

"Professor Rowe!" exclaimed Claire, clearly aghast at my ignorance.

"Who?" I asked again, as I felt that simply repeating the professor's name, however emphatically, fell well below Claire's usual explanatory powers.

"He was in a documentary on BBC4, and we're just about to go to his first lecture." Claire was watching Professor Rowe intently throughout this explanation. "He's a bit of a superstar at this place, not that that means much." I like Claire a lot but she is a bit of an academic snob. She went to Oxford, or possibly Cambridge (for many years I had thought she went to Oxbridge but it turns out there's no such place), one of the two anyway, and got a first in something extremely brainy before going on to do a PhD in something even brainier. She never let an opportunity pass to point out that she was slumming it at the University of the Arse End of Nowhere, as she liked to call the institution in which we were now sitting eating Halloween cupcakes.

"He isn't as good looking in real life as he is on television." Theresa added, rather sniffily I thought. Following her eye line, and that of pretty much everyone else in the room, I took my first look at Professor Gideon Rowe. I could only wonder how good looking he had appeared to be on television as in the flesh he was one of the best looking men I had ever seen. I should say at this point that I don't believe in fate and I don't think that the universe has been ordered to please me. If it had it would most certainly have been very different in very many ways. It follows, therefore, that I don't believe there is such a thing as a soul mate, one person specifically designed for each of us. If there were what would be the chances, realistically, of ever meeting that person? If one's soul mate happened to be a llama farmer in the Andes while one was based in west London and had no particular interest in llamas this would surely prove an insurmountable barrier to true love. When I saw Professor Gideon Rowe, however, I felt an instant and very strong connection with him. It was almost as if I recognised him, despite not having seen the BBC4 documentary referred to by Claire. It was simply that he looked familiar, as if he were an old friend that I simply hadn't come across yet. It was as if, I suppose, he were family, but in a good way.

"This lecture you're going to," I asked Claire as we left the cafe, "what's it about?"

"Perception and memory," she snapped as she struggled to get her coat on while not dropping her book filled bag. Claire is very clever but she is a bit inept in some of the more basic motor skills.

"Let me carry that," I said taking the bag from her. "Perception and memory you say? Sounds fascinating, mind if I tag along?" It sounded boring, but I wanted to see this Professor Rowe in action.

"No it doesn't," she replied, "not to you anyway. And as you so clearly want to ogle Professor Rowe I don't suppose I could stop you anyway." Claire stalked off down the corridor with me tripping along behind, looking rather as Quasimodo must have tripping around Notre Dame as Claire's incredibly heavy bag dragged my shoulder down.

I had no idea how I was going to bring myself to the professor's attention but where there is a will there is, in my experience, generally a way. As it happened the way involved signing up for a psychology conference in Blackpool (the things we do for love or whatever you want to call it) that I could ill afford, and finding out far more about perception and memory than I ever wished to know. But the upshot was that I was now living in the gorgeous Prof's gorgeous flat in gorgeous Chiswick.

I had always thought that it was rather mercenary of Lizzie Bennet to only realise that she fancied the britches off Darcy once she had seen Pemberley, but I have since learnt the wisdom of her point of view. A good man is a good thing, a good man with a good property, well that puts him in another league quite frankly, and while Gideon's home isn't exactly Pemberley it's still a pretty impressive abode. He bought the flat, which is on the top floor of an Edwardian Mansion block, many years ago when mortgages could be obtained by five year olds with only a handful of Lego and some soft toys in lieu of a deposit. It has three bedrooms (one of which Gideon uses as a study), a sitting room, and a very large kitchen. It does, unfortunately, have a bus terminus in front and an industrial estate behind, but I'm sure that Elizabeth found things about Pemberley that were not entirely to her taste once she moved in. It also looks very much like a flat in which a man with no interest in interior design has lived alone for many years, but these are minor quibbles when set against the fact that it is in Chiswick, which is somewhere I have long wanted to live. I have hopped around west London over the years, circling the prize if you will, but now I had finally landed and living here was even nicer than I had anticipated. So everything on that front was just peachy, even if Marjorie was in danger of taking the bloom off my wonderful new life somewhat.

Having met up with Claire for a coffee I explained in some detail what had been going on with Marjorie since I had first met this 'amazing' woman.

"Don't you think you might be overreacting slightly?" Claire suggested. "Do you think that you are, perhaps, judging Marcia's..."

"Marjorie's." I corrected her.

"...Marjorie's behaviour by your own? Just because you engineer situations to get what you want doesn't mean that everyone else behaves in the same way." Claire looked at me thoughtfully over the top of her coffee cup. We were in a cafe on the top floor of a department store on the King's Road. Claire, having completed the course at the jumped up sixth form college (her words, not mine) where Gideon worked, had begun studying for a doctorate in counselling. I had thought that perhaps this might be a possible new career for me, to become a counsellor, mainly because I enjoy telling people what to do and generally think that I know what's best for them. It turns out, however, that this isn't what being a counsellor entails at all. It takes an absolute age to become one, costs a fortune, and you have to listen non judgementally to people moaning on about their miserable lives (and I already had enough of that from Dominic), so that was the end of that.

"I don't know what you mean, when have I ever engineered a situation?" I replied huffily.

"Oh come off it Eve, do you really think I didn't see through your machinations over Gideon when we went to

Blackpool? All that nonsense about my having to arrive at exactly ... well at exactly the time it was you told me to arrive."

The Blackpool trip which had marked the start of my relationship with Gideon had taken some engineering, it was true. Theresa also had her eye on my (as I already thought of him) professor and had planned to use the journey up north to get to know him better. But as she, along with Claire and Gideon, had travelled together to Blackpool in my car I had managed to ensure that Gideon sat in the front with me, and the rest, as they say, is history.

"So you're saying I am only with Gideon because I engineered, allegedly engineered, the seating arrangements on a car journey?" I tried my best to sound affronted.

"Of course not. Once you had decided you were going to have Gideon Theresa never stood a chance ..." Claire continued.

"Because of my machinations ..." I interrupted, indignant at the aspersions Claire was casting on my relationship.

"Yes, because of your machinations. If only you would use your powers for the good of humanity, imagine what you might achieve." Claire replied calmly. Claire is almost always calm. "The point is that Gideon was in your thrall from the moment you two met. Theresa couldn't compete."

"What do you mean, couldn't compete? Her father's very rich you know, and a doctor." I had lost count of the times Theresa had casually dropped this information into conversation on the way to and from Blackpool (I had managed to pretty much avoid her while in Blackpool but she was difficult to get away from in a car).

"Oh do shut up," said Claire, but she did smile. "You know exactly what I'm talking about." What she was talking about was my supposed looks. People have been telling me that I'm good looking, beautiful even, all my adult life.

I was, as my school photos attest, an ugly child but something happened in my teenage years that changed the way that other people viewed my features. I, on the other hand, still think I'm pretty ugly. I'm not being modest, I just don't see what others see in my features. I have huge bug eyes, a snub nose and fat lips. I do have good cheek bones, but that's about it. I prefer to believe that it is my sparkling personality that men find attractive. "Theresa is a very fragile woman," Claire continued, "She just wants to be loved."

"Don't we all?" I responded.

"Yes, but Theresa is more needy than most. She comes from a very high achieving family."

"Really?" I said, rather archly. "She's never mentioned that."

"And again, shut up," said Claire. "She admires you, you know. You should be kinder to her."

"Admires me? Why?" I was somewhat taken aback. My dislike of Theresa was so visceral that I was surprised to find she felt anything but antipathy toward me.

"Goodness only knows. She says she likes the fact that you don't seem to care much what anyone thinks of you."

"I do care what people think of me!"

"You care that they think what you want them to think of you, it's not the same thing," Claire explained. "And she would love to have what you and Gideon have. You've formed a strong bond with him that seems to be based on a relatively clear eyed assessment of each other's strengths and weaknesses."

"You old romantic." I said. "How do you know so much about how Theresa feels anyway?"

"Other people do exist when you're not with them Eve." Claire replied.

"I know that!" I said, rather too emphatically. I do know it but I'm not sure that I entirely believe it. Doesn't everyone believe that everyone else only truly exists when they are in one's presence? "So how's she getting on, with her course that is?" I added, to display that I really did know that Theresa existed when I wasn't there. She was, I knew, studying for a doctorate at some weird sounding psychological institute. The application process had, apparently, been long and difficult. I had received a blow by blow account of how brilliantly she had done to secure a place at what she assured me was a world renowned centre for something that escapes me right now when I had run into her in a coffee shop in Chiswick a few weeks earlier (the only downside to living in Chiswick being that Theresa lives there too).

"It's not going very well unfortunately." Claire explained.

"Oh, that's a shame, but back to me and my life." I said before finishing the very last piece of my fruit tart. I might not be a big cake fan but I do like a good, French patisserie style fruit tart, and all the tastier for being paid for by someone else, in this case Claire.

"She's had to take on a job to make ends meet," said Claire. "The bursary she was hoping for fell through and her father won't pay as he doesn't think what she's doing is worthwhile." She obviously wasn't finished with Theresa, even if I was.

"So she's got to work! How appalling for her. Do you think we should organise a fund raiser? I could make muffins!" I have always had to work, from long before I left school, to have any money at all so forgive me if I couldn't summon up much sympathy for Theresa.

"There's no need for that," Claire chided me. I don't really know how Claire and I have maintained our friendship for so long as she disapproves of almost everything I say and do. I think I like her because she is a better person than I am and having her as a friend makes me feel like a slightly better person than I know myself to be. What she sees in me is an enduring mystery. Perhaps she thinks she will one day save my soul (she is a Born Again Christian, which is like a normal Christian but with full fat milk and an extra shot), although what one does with saved souls I am unsure. "So she is under a lot of pressure as she has no time to study and is too tired to be effective at work." Claire concluded.

"Oh, that's a pity." I said. "Anyway, back to me and my problems."

"Yes, Eve, back to you and your problems."

"What's so funny?" I demanded to know as Claire unaccountably let out a hoot of laughter.

"Nothing, my dear Eve, nothing. So, do you really think the whole thing was engineered by Marjorie because she wants to upset you or," Claire looked at me pointedly, "are you perhaps guilty of the fundamental attribution error?"

"Is that the one where you can't see the camel in the rich man's eye because of the plank in your own?" I asked. Psychologists, I had learnt in one of the lectures I sneaked into while stalking (for want of a better word) Gideon, have discovered that there are simply hundreds of errors in the way we humans think. I could have told them that without all the dubious experiments.

"No, that's from the Bible, sort of. The one I'm referring to is the one where we assume that the actions of others are due to their disposition while our own actions are caused by circumstances."

"So you're saying that I'm looking for some sinister motive to explain why Marjorie should want to ruin my birthday when in fact she was really just locked out?"

I should explain what we were talking about. Since my initial meeting with Marjorie she had positively showered Gideon and me with invitations to Sunday lunch and various other gatherings. I, for reasons with which any one in a new relationship might sympathise, didn't wish to spend half of almost every weekend with Gideon's parents. With a little ingenuity and only a very few untruths, I had therefore managed to head off a large number of these invitations and by the time my birthday came around it had been nearly two months since we had seen Marjorie and Malcolm. I'm not usually a great one for celebrating birthdays, but it was my first since meeting Gideon and coincided with our nine month anniversary, so I had decided to push the boat out a bit.

"That smells good," Gideon announced as he came in the front door that evening, "I could smell it all the way up the stairs."

"We're having potted shrimps with melba toast to start," I told him, "followed by roast chicken with mushrooms. It's supposed to be guinea fowl with porcini but they both cost a fortune and I had already spent a bundle on the shrimps, and then we're having a surprise pudding."

"What's the surprise?" Gideon asked.

"That there is no pudding, as we'll be stuffed by then, but there is cheese and fruit." There was going to be pudding, a chocolate fondant which is Gideon's favourite but which I was afraid might be my culinary Waterloo and so had decided not to get his hopes up at this point. "And," I said, thrusting a bottle towards him, "there's champagne!" It was actually sparkling wine, but it was very good for the price.

"I'll go and get changed and then I'll be right with you," he said, heading off down the hall towards the bedroom while I returned to my labours in the kitchen.

Amongst many other things living with Gideon had enabled me to rekindle my lifelong love affair with cooking. When you're only cooking for yourself it's difficult to get very excited about it. A big part of the pleasure I get from cooking is the pleasure it gives to others, and when cooking for one it is also difficult not to cook too much. However delicious any meal might be on its first outing, it rather loses its appeal by day three.

One of the very few memories I retain from my childhood, before I was orphaned (I know it's perverse but I quite like the word orphan, it sounds romantic and vaguely Victorian, plus orphans often do pretty well in literature), is not so much a memory as an emotion, and it is of family meals. Not weekday teatime, but Saturday and Sunday lunch. I have a very strong sense of my family home being enveloped in a warm fug of cooking smells at weekends, smells that told me I was safe and loved. Aunt Audrey wasn't at all interested in cooking, so much of the food I ate until I taught myself to cook was either boiled in a bag or rehydrated. I think I learnt how to cook so that I could create my own warm fug of love, and now I had someone with whom to share that fug. Gideon's flat also had a very lovely and well equipped kitchen (it was the one room on which he had lavished any attention as he is also quite a keen cook) so I was able to go into warm fug overdrive.

It was as I did a final check on everything that the phone rang. I ignored it, as I often do if I am otherwise occupied. I can't see why I should always leap to it whenever someone calls, it's not as if I'm an emergency service. After a few rings it went to the machine and I forgot all about it. Having done all I could in the kitchen for the time being I wandered down the hall to the sitting room carrying two glasses of Cava. It was early October but already quite cold, so I had lit the gas effect fire earlier to take the chill off the room. Gideon says it is the equivalent of throwing tenners up the chimney but he had it fitted, presumably at some expense, so I think it would be equally wasteful not to use it. I had also bought some candles for added atmosphere and so, having put the glasses down, I set about lighting them too. The room looked absolutely beautiful, aglow with soft light and dancing shadows. In truth it looks best of all like this as the harsh light of day only serves to highlight the poor quality of the decorating and the very much past their prime soft furnishings. I turned on the radio and couldn't quite believe it when I heard a piece of music issuing from it of which I am particularly fond. I have no idea what it's called (I think it's something to do with a bird, possibly a lark, but I'm not sure) as despite many years listening to Radio 3 I have failed miserably to learn anything about classical music. If I am ever asked to be a guest on Desert Island Discs (unlikely I know, but one should be prepared) I'll have a hell of a job humming tunes to mystified researchers in the hope of identifying my eight pieces. No matter, everything was perfect, just perfect.

"That was Mum on the phone." Gideon poked his head around the sitting room door, clearly not intending to come in. "I have to go round there I'm afraid. I won't be long."

"What are you talking about? What's happened?" I was genuinely alarmed. Something deeply important must have occurred or why would Gideon be leaving me, and on my birthday, to go to his mother?

"It won't take long. She's locked out and Dad's at a golf club thing," he explained. "I'll take my spare keys round, let her in and be back before you know it." He was already halfway down the hall as he said this last bit. "See you later."

"Isn't there a spare key somewhere she can use?" I called after him.

"Yes... no. I'll explain when I get back. Bye."

I was in bed, although not asleep, by the time Gideon returned at around ten thirty. I had eaten the potted shrimps and put the chicken in the fridge while the chocolate fondant, or at least the ingredients for it, were in the bin. I hate waste but I had thrown them away in a fit of rage after a fourth, ill advised, glass of sparkling wine. I had received regular text updates during the evening but they had done little to enhance my mood.

Marjorie had been so upset, so she claimed, by the loss of her keys that Gideon had had to stay with her until his father's return. The spare keys had, it transpired, been in the shed where they were always kept but Marjorie had been unable, in her panic, to find them. Having gained entry to her house she claimed that she was worried that her keys might have been stolen rather than lost and that someone might try to enter the house. She had therefore insisted (or Gideon had offered, but I'm sure it was at her insistence) that Gideon stay with her.

I pretended to be asleep as Gideon slipped quietly into bed beside me. I thought this was for the best as I was quite certain that I wouldn't be able to control my still simmering rage and I wasn't really sure who I was most angry with. I was angry with Gideon for not coming back all evening and I was angry with his mother for ruining my birthday with her pathetic inability to find a key to, or be alone in, her own house. I knew, however, that I couldn't justify my feelings to Gideon. I was, I feared, behaving like a spoilt child because my birthday had been ruined and it was hardly fair that I should seek to blame someone else for this when it was no one's fault. And yet I was still angry and I couldn't help but feel that Marjorie should shoulder most of the blame. She must, I reasoned, have engineered the whole thing. She must be trying to get back at me for all the Sunday lunch invitations I had refused and taken her revenge by ruining my birthday dinner.

"She may have unconsciously engineered the situation, I suppose." Claire mused. "Her son hasn't been in a cohabiting relationship for some years and she had become used to spending parental time with him. She is, by your assessment, in an unhappy pair bond..."

"Marriage," I interrupted, "it's a marriage." Claire does sometimes take the psychology speak a little too far.

"Yes, marriage. But she isn't getting what she wants from Gideon's proximity since he became your, as you might say, boyfriend." Claire concluded.

"So Marjorie is unconsciously engineering situations to spend time with Gideon without me or Malcolm being present?" I summarised what Claire seemed to be saying. "It's not that she hates me? It's possible I suppose," I mused, "but if that's the case what do you make of this?" I then related an incident that had happened only a few minutes before I had met with Claire that morning.

I was on one of the up escalators that slice through the middle of Peter Jones (it's the name of the store, not a person) on my way to meet Claire when I saw Marjorie on one of the down ones. We were looking directly at one another. She couldn't have failed to see me. I smiled and waved. She looked at me, a puzzled frown on her face. I returned the puzzled frown, assuming that she was signalling her puzzlement at seeing me here, although why this should have been quite so puzzling I was unsure as I am free to move around London as I wish. I signalled that I would follow her down the escalator, which I did, expecting to find her waiting for me at the bottom. I didn't really want to see her, but I thought it would appear rude not to at least have a few minutes chat. When I got to the bottom of the escalator however, she was nowhere to be seen. I tried to pick her out from the hordes of shoppers circulating in the store and had almost given up when I caught a glimpse of her over by the lifts. She looked a little flustered as she waited, jabbing furiously at the button, presumably in the mistaken belief that this might make the lift arrive more quickly than it otherwise would. I waved frantically but failed to attract her attention as she turned back to the lift, the door of which was just opening, and stepped in.

"So, Claire," I said, somewhat triumphantly, "what do you make of that?"

"I strongly suspect," said Claire, wiping the last crumbs of a pain au raisin from her mouth, "that she didn't see you."

Chapter 4

It was only a matter of days after my meeting with Claire that I had reason to concur with her assessment of Marjorie's behaviour. I had cycled over to Richmond to buy some jars of a particular brand of olives that Gideon can't, apparently, imagine life without and which aren't to be found anywhere in Chiswick. Buying them involved a roundtrip of several miles on my bike (such devotion). I was standing at the till explaining to a very chatty check out assistant why I had eight jars of olives when I was assailed by a very loud 'cooee'. Not realising that the 'cooee' was directed at me – why should it be? I was far from home, and south of the river – I ignored it. I carried on ignoring it even as it got louder and louder until finally I heard my name being called in between the cooees.

"Cooee, Eve, cooee. It's me, Marjorie. I'm over here." And, sure enough, over there was Marjorie. "You must come home with me for a coffee," she said, grabbing my wrist as soon as she was in reaching distance. I do not like being forcibly made to go anywhere but I felt that I couldn't snatch my hand back without appearing rude. I therefore had to stand for several uncomfortable moments with my wrist held tight in Marjorie's diamond encrusted claw like grip. "I insist," she said, before finally releasing me when I nodded my assent.

Traffic being what it is in London my bike and I arrived at Marjorie's house several minutes before she turned up in what I noticed was a brand new sports car. I have no idea what it was, I know very little about cars, but even I could tell it had probably cost rather a lot of money.

"It's lovely isn't it?" Marjorie said, simpering at the great hunk of metal as if it were a puppy. "Malcolm said I didn't need a new car, but the old one had done over ten thousand miles, so it was time for a change." My own car had done close to two hundred thousand miles but was not about to be replaced. I didn't mention this. "And anyway," she continued, "I bought it with my money, so it's not up to him, is it?" She looked at me coyly in the sort of 'we girls must stick together' way that I have always disliked. I have never felt a particular affinity with anyone based purely on their gender and, in my experience, women prone to this sort of gesture are those least likely to stick up for other women. All right for some, I thought as Marjorie opened the garage for me to stow my bike. She had looked at me rather askance when I suggested that I didn't want to leave it outside where there was nothing to lock it to.

"You really think that anyone would want to steal that?" she had said, dismissing my trusty steed. I know it wasn't a brand new car and she did have a point, but even so it seemed a little rude. I said nothing however and simply followed her through the front door, waiting patiently as she punched the code into the alarm system. So it was dangerous enough around here for her to have to protect her things but mine, it seemed, not so much.

"Now," said Marjorie once we were ensconced in her huge kitchen with a cup of coffee in front of each of us (she had made instant, the coffee machine was clearly Malcolm's domain), "I want to know all about you. Every little detail.

Ian and I are very, very close and he has always shared everything with me. He has hardly told me anything about you though," she let out a little laugh, "and I am dying to know all there is."

Where on earth do you start when someone asks such a thing of you? Marjorie's question was a bit like being asked to recite all the facts that you know about everything. What should I tell and what should I withhold? Where to begin? Where to end? My mind went blank.

"Well, I, that is, I..." I muttered. Thankfully I was saved from going any further as, just at that moment, Marjorie let out a blood curdling shriek.

"Get down!" she ordered. It took me a moment to realise that she was talking to me. I had presumed that an animal of some sort had come into the room. I realised what she meant, however, when she threw herself under the kitchen table at which we had been sitting before grabbing my arm from below to make sure that I did the same.

"Did you see her?" Marjorie gasped as we huddled on the floor beneath the table. This was not at all what I had been expecting when she had invited me back for a coffee.

"See who?" I asked.

"Meryl bloody Streep." As the only view from the kitchen was of Marjorie's garden I was rather bemused.

"Meryl Streep is in your garden?" I asked.

"In next door's garden," Marjorie hissed through gritted teeth. "She's looking over the fence. Can you see her?"

I poked my head above the level of the table just far enough so that I could see, but hopefully not be seen by, whoever was looking over Marjorie's fence (while she had said it was Meryl Streep I thought this was unlikely). I could just make out a figure peering through the hedge on the left hand side of the garden.

"Yes," I hissed back, "she's still there."

"I'll tell you a funny story about her." Thank goodness there was a funny story associated with this as otherwise it would seem very odd to be cowering under a table with one's partner's mother in an effort to avoid Meryl 'bloody' Streep. Marjorie launched into her story while the pair of us crouched on the floor.

"She came here for coffee once, along with some of the other girls, you know." I didn't know who the girls where, but I nodded as if I did. "She sat here, at this very table," Marjorie pointed to the table above our heads, as if I needed clarification. "She was sitting exactly where you were just sitting, and chatting away to me as if butter wouldn't melt." Where, I wondered, was this going? "Then, no more than a year later, she moved in next door and do you know what she said to me?" Of course I didn't. " 'Hello', she said, 'I don't think we've met.' Don't think we've met, I ask you! And to think, she had been a guest in my home. My home! Can you believe the rudeness of the woman? She should have got an Oscar for that performance." The Meryl Streep reference finally made sense. "Such an affected woman," Marjorie continued. "No class at all. Not an ounce. All brass and no class, that's what she is. Has she gone?" I peered over the edge of the table once again and was able to confirm that Meryl had now, indeed, gone.

"Oh, that's better," said Marjorie as we resumed our seats. "Now," she said, smiling at me broadly as if nothing out of the ordinary had occurred, "where were we?"

After quite lot of general chit chat about me and my background (I focused heavily on having been orphaned and rather less on my adult life, and got the expected response) and with Marjorie slightly moist eyed at the trauma I had been through as a young girl, I announced that I really had to go. While I was glad to have had the chance to spend some time with Gideon's mother, and while I felt that it had gone reasonably well, I couldn't imagine wanting to spend a great deal more time with her, especially not alone. The truth was that she wasn't a very engaging conversationalist even when she was trying to be pleasant. She asked endless questions to the point where I felt as if I was being interrogated and she had nothing particularly interesting to say herself. But she didn't have to be interesting, she simply had to not actively dislike me. As we seemed to have got on well enough it was, I thought, mission accomplished.

"I really must get back Marjorie," I said, smiling broadly at her, "but this has been lovely, really lovely, we must do it again sometime."

"Oh, must you go so soon?" Marjorie looked as if she was about to grasp my wrist again but I managed to move it out of the way this time without appearing to be avoiding physical contact. Had she really, I thought, not had enough of me? I had been there over an hour, and I had certainly had enough of her.

"I've been asked to help with a friend's daughter's birthday party," I said, "so I really must get back. Lots to do!" Nice touch that, I thought. I didn't add that I had excused myself from helping at the party itself, or that it wasn't for another three days anyway. All I had to do was make a cake that I would deliver before the arrival of any children, which suited me fine. I don't dislike my friend's daughter, but she is a handful on her own so the idea of being trapped in a room with her and ten others of the same age (three) was not very appealing.

"One last thing," Marjorie said over her shoulder as she carried our empty coffee cups to the sink. "I know what you've been up to. You might fool Gideon, but you don't fool me, you naughty girl." Having placed the cups in the sink she turned to look at me, her right index finger wagging from side to side and a knowing smile playing around her lips. I was unsure whether the smile was sinister or conspiratorial. I opened my eyes wide to indicate a complete lack of guile and waited to see which way this was going to go. "You buy cake mixes don't you, you naughty girl." Oh thank goodness.

"You won't tell him will you?" I opened my eyes even wider, a look of apprehension on my face, and took the opportunity to grab her wrist, squeezing it possibly a little harder than necessary. "It's just that I've never really mastered baking."

Marjorie must have observed me putting a box of cake mix into my basket when we were at the supermarket. How long, I wondered, had she been watching me before she began cooing from across the store?

"Don't worry Eve," Marjorie said, patting the hand with which I was still holding her wrist. "Your secret is safe with me. But you can give these to Ian." I released her as she turned to pick up plastic box that had been sitting on the worktop behind her. "Tell him I made them for him specially. Or tell him you did, if you'd prefer, I won't tell." She tapped the side of her nose before adding "We women will have our little secrets, won't we? They're flapjacks," she continued. "Ian adores flapjacks. Try one. They are delicious." She opened the box and pushed its contents towards me.

"No thanks. No really," I said as she positioned the box directly under my nose as if it were a nosebag and I a horse.

"Go on," she insisted, "it'll give you energy for the ride home."

"No, I really can't." I averred. She had pushed the box so close by now I was practically inhaling its contents. "I can't eat oats," I explained, "I can't digest them." It's true. For many years I ate porridge for breakfast, day in, day out, all year round. Turns out it's not as good for one's insides as people would have you believe, or at least not for mine. The merest hint of an oat these days and I get the most horrendous indigestion.

"Really? You can't eat oats? How odd," said Marjorie looking dumbfounded. "Well, take them for Ian anyway."

I gingerly took the proffered box and cycled off homeward. Claire, I realised, was quite right. It was possible that Marjorie hadn't engineered the ruination of my birthday and she may not have seen me in Peter Jones. We could, I was sure, develop a perfectly acceptable working relationship. I had, I was now almost sure, been fretting over nothing.

Chapter 5

Having made some headway in my relationship with Gideon's mother (Malcolm didn't really count as it was clear where the power lay in that marriage) I felt that I was ready to delve a little further into his family. I was not that perturbed, therefore, when Gideon suggested we pay a visit to his sister and her family.

I knew very little about Helen other than that she was two years, to the day, younger than Gideon, that she was married, and that she had a lot of children. Unlike her brother and parents she was not London based but lived near East Grinstead which is not, as I had assumed, a grimy northern mining town, but a pretty half-timbered sort of a place in West Sussex.

"Is this really the way?" I asked Gideon as wc bumped along a farm track that appeared to stretch to infinity. I have been to the countryside before but I had no idea that people really lived down farm tracks, so far from anything that might come under the heading of civilisation.

"Bizarre though it may sound I do know where my own sister lives. I have been here before you know." Gideon replied, somewhat tersely. Tersely is not generally a nice way to be spoken to, but I could forgive him as I had asked a lot of questions on the journey down. While I hadn't been perturbed when Gideon suggested the visit I had become increasingly perturbed the closer we got to his sister's home. As a consequence I had been trying to establish as much as I could about where we were going and what reception I might expect to receive when we got there. It was through this questioning that I had established the bare facts detailed above. The response to most of my questions had been either "why don't you wait and see when we get there?" or, as Gideon's patience ran out "how the hell am I supposed to know that?" I think that my question regarding whether Gideon was really sure we were going the right way was the final straw, questionwise, and as we were nearly there I realised that I might as well, as he had advised, put a sock in it.

Despite his terseness in the face of my barrage of questions, or perhaps because of it, the more I got to know Gideon the more I liked him. Long term exposure to another person usually only serves to highlight that person's faults but, so far, Gideon had only gone up in my estimation, and he seemed pretty keen on me too. We just sort of clicked. I had never felt as comfortable with anyone as I did with him and, while I still fully expected everything to go horribly wrong (this being the statistically probable outcome) so far we seemed to be defying the odds.

"Seriously?" I yelped. "Are you sure you haven't brought me here to murder me?" My yelp was due to the fact that Gideon had just told me that I had to get out of the car and open the farm gate that was blocking our path. After travelling for simply ages along the farm track we had finally come to an actual farm yard but this was not, it seemed, our ultimate destination and we were to continue yet further into the wilderness. I simply couldn't keep quiet in the face of such madness.

"If you think that's a real possibility then I suggest you make a run for it now. If not," Gideon continued, "you need to shut this gate behind me and then open the one on the other side of the yard."

"She lives the other side of a farmyard?" I was flabbergasted.

"Yup, as do the rest of her family."

"How very odd, when there are so many towns they could live in." I observed.

After all the farm track, farm gate and farm yard business I was fully expecting to see a farm house awaiting us – it seemed the only logical conclusion to the journey. I was a little disappointed, therefore, to be faced with a rather unprepossessing house built, I guessed, in the late sixties or early seventies. It looked like a council office that had been mistakenly plonked down in the middle of a field instead of by a roundabout on a ring road. If the house was a surprise, then the woman that came to the door was a revelation.

I had no real idea what Helen might look like (Gideon having been monumentally vague in response to my questions) but I suppose I had thought she might be a younger version of her mother. I couldn't have been more wrong. The first thing that struck me was Helen's hair. It was stupendous. It was very thick, very wavy, and ran in a golden river down her back. Marjorie had thin, completely white hair that she wore in a rather masculine crop and Malcolm had what looked like an old scouring pad on his head. Even Gideon doesn't have amazing hair. He has perfectly acceptable hair, but it wouldn't trend on twitter. Helen had clearly got the entire store of good hair genes originally assigned for the whole family. What her home lacked in fairy-tale wonderfulness her hair certainly made up for.

The rest of Helen didn't, if one was being entirely truthful, quite live up to the hair. She had a perfectly pleasant face, but if she had got the hair Gideon had certainly got the looks, and while he is tall and athletic looking Helen is a little on the plump side, rather like a cottage loaf to his baguette if you will. In addition to her hair being nothing like her mother's, her personal style was also the very antithesis of Marjorie's, who favoured neat, vaguely military cardigans worn over sweaters if it was cool and plain blouses in pink, pale blue, or white in more clement weather. She also perennially wore what I believe are called slacks (I am unclear on the distinction between slacks and trousers, but you know it when you see it), in taupe or navy. I don't think I saw her in a skirt more than once or twice in our whole acquaintance.

Helen, on the other hand was a far less buttoned up dresser. On this occasion she had on a floaty, peasant style skirt and a thick, possibly hand knitted, jumper. She didn't appear to be wearing any make up, except for possibly a little Vaseline on her lips. She was that sort of a girl. She did however, once one got past the hair and clothing, bear quite a strong facial resemblance to Marjorie which I had never perceived in Gideon. It was slightly unnerving.

"You made it!" she exclaimed, folding her brother into a hug before doing the same to me. She made me feel like a giantess as, like her mother, she is quite a lot shorter than I, and I'm not particularly tall. It was a lovely hug nonetheless. "Come in, come in, Joe'll be home soon and then we can have supper, you must be starving."

Once inside the house I could see immediately that it was the complete opposite of its exterior, and of Marjorie's home. Where the outside was comprised of unyielding straight lines, unattractive dirty grey bricks, and metal window frames, inside it was warm (figuratively and actually) and inviting. It also positively vibrated with life, as well it might as Helen and Joe had, I now learned, four children.

"This is Martha, and this is Ruby," said Helen as two tousle haired blonde girls appeared by her side. They must have been around ten or eleven and I realised, on closer inspection, that they were identical. While their hair and clothes were completely different, one had short hair and the other long, one wore trousers while the other was in a skirt very like her mother's, their faces were exactly the same. "Yes," said Helen in response to my unspoken question, "they're twins, as are Hector and Jake." Two boys of about thirteen had appeared from upstairs. "And this," said Helen, as a young woman came from the direction of the kitchen, "is Celeste."

Celeste was attired very differently from the rest of the family, who were all dressed in very much the same hippy-ish style as Helen. She had cropped, peroxided hair, and looked extremely chic in skinny black jeans and a black roll neck jumper. I initially assumed she was yet another of Helen's children but when she spoke she had a distinct French accent. Unless she was one of these people who start speaking with a foreign accent following a bump on the head, which seemed unlikely, I had clearly assumed wrong.

" 'Allo, 'ow lurvly to meet wis ewe boat." Celeste extended a slender, elegant hand with which she gave first me and then Gideon a very firm handshake.

"Celeste is the ... she's the daughter of a ... of a family I spent a year with ... in France ... when I was a teenager. She's here to ... um ... help the children and me, I suppose, with our ... with our .... French." Helen stuttered and stumbled her way through this explanation. She was clearly lying, although what she was lying about was less clear.

"I thought young French people came here to improve their English." I observed.

"Yes," Helen concurred, "that would make more sense, but I suppose she can do that too."

"De ewe speck Frenshh?" Celeste looked at me with a steady gaze. She was clearly a very self-possessed young woman.

"Oh, I was a complete dunce at languages at school." I replied, unwilling to meet her eye. She struck me as one of those people who take life very seriously, and who believe that truthfulness is of paramount importance at all times. I find this type of individual disconcerting, and for a moment I felt extremely uncomfortable. People who never tell lies have that effect on me.

"So that's everyone apart from Joe, and he'll be back soon." Helen said, snapping me back into the moment. "Let's have a cup of tea and you lot," she made shooing gestures with her hands towards the children, "find something to do while the grownups talk. You can watch Only Fools and Horses!" Helen was obviously trying to whip up some enthusiasm for Only Fools and Horses, but the children weren't buying it. After a short impassioned protest from the boys they did, however, trudge off, along with Celeste, into what I assumed to be the sitting room, while Gideon and I followed Helen into the kitchen.

"We can't get anything here, no television, no broadband, no mobile phones, it's because we're in a valley." Helen explained as Gideon and I sat down at the big farm house style table (at last, something farm like!) that dominated the room. "But we do have a DVD player and Joe picked up a box set of Only Fools and Horses at a car boot last weekend, so that'll keep them occupied." The countryside was, it would seem, even worse than I had feared.

"So how are you all?" Gideon asked once we were ensconced at the huge table, a mug of tea in front of each of us.

"We are all fantastic, as you would know if you phoned me occasionally." Helen replied, giving me a theatrical wink.

"You just said you don't have any phones." Gideon pointed out.

"We have a landline." Helen countered.

"You can call me then, can't you?" Gideon responded with a smile.

"I shall do just that then, you see if I don't." Helen replied laughing. She really was nothing like her mother, which was, in truth, an immense relief. "And how are Mum and Dad?"

"They're well," said Gideon. "You should get up to town and see them more often."

"It's difficult for us to get away what with the animals and the children, and Mum doesn't particularly like coming to the country so ..." Helen's voice trailed off.

"Well, they send their regards," said Gideon.

"Their regards! Oh my, that is thoughtful of them." I could sense there was something unspoken beneath this exchange, but it was clearly going to remain that way, for the time being at least. "But that's enough about us, I want to know about Eve." Helen turned to me. "Eve," she said, cupping her face in her hands, "what do you think of our family?" We were still laughing when an unfamiliar voice with a strong Australian accent boomed out from behind me.

"What's so bloody funny?" the voice demanded to know. I turned to see someone who I very much hoped was Helen's husband Joe as whoever it was had a shotgun slung over his arm. You really don't want strangers brandishing firearms demanding to know what you're laughing at, especially not when you are in the middle of nowhere with no mobile phone coverage and a landline that could easily have been cut. Joe, for thankfully it was he, was very tall, very well built, and very hairy (hair was clearly a big thing in this neck of the woods). He sported a thick beard as well as wavy hair down to his shoulders. He was an impressive sight, even more so as in addition to the shotgun he had a brace of what I assumed were pheasants thrown casually over his shoulder. He also had a very large, very muddy black hound that wouldn't have disgraced the name of Baskerville standing obediently at his side. "I hope you're not scaring Eve off with stories about your family. You all right Gid mate?"

"Eve doesn't look like the sort that scares easily," said Helen. "You're not easily scared are you Eve?" She looked at me enquiringly.

"I don't think so," I said, wondering where all this was going.

"I expect Mum adores Eve, doesn't she Gid?" Helen shot a mischievous look at her brother.

"Of course she does. She and Mum get on really, really well." One 'really' would have been overplaying it, but I had perhaps been more effusive in my praise of Gideon's mother than I really, really thought she merited.

"Well, that's good, that's great in fact." Helen gave me a little pat on the arm. She seemed to feel that I needed reassurance that all was well, which had the complete opposite effect to that intended. Why, I wondered, was it necessary to reassure me that it was great news that I got on with Marjorie, unless getting on with Marjorie was of the utmost importance?

"Is there any tea in that pot, I'm parched?" asked Joe who, having dropped the pheasants onto the kitchen worktop, had walked over to stand behind Helen's chair. The hound, now presumably off duty, was settling itself in a huge basket by the Aga (of course they had an Aga), preparing itself, I assumed, for a lie down. I had never knowingly spent a night in a house that contained both firearms and a hound of such monstrous proportions and I wasn't sure whether it made me feel very safe or quite the opposite.

"I don't think so," Helen replied to Joe's enquiry. "I can make you some more," she said, making as if to get up.

"No, you stay there love, I'll do it," Joe replied, laying a hand on her shoulder. She reached up and covered his hand with her own and they shared a brief glance. If Marjorie and Malcolm had left me feeling that Gideon's family was rather less than I might have hoped for, it looked as if Helen and Joe might more than make up for their deficiencies, guns, dogs, and a total lack of twenty first century technology notwithstanding.

"So you've passed the test then Eve?" Joe called over his shoulder from where he was filling the kettle.

"What test?" I asked.

"The Marjorie test," Joe explained. "Marjorie, you see, has very strong views on her son's girlfriends. Who was that girl? Red hair, came from Carlisle. Marjorie tried to..."

"Shut up Joe," said Helen, interrupting Joe's reminiscences. "I'm sure that Eve doesn't want to talk about Gideon's old girlfriends. And we haven't got time to go through all of them, not in a single weekend anyway." She ruffled her brother's hair as she spoke and he responded by poking her in the ribs. They were clearly very fond of each other.

"Didn't she tell you that one of them was a junkie, Hels?" Joe continued as he came and sat at the table with his tea.

"I told you to shut up Joe," Helen said firmly, "and I meant it."

"And that girl Nicole," Joe was clearly as determined to keep the conversation going as his wife was to end it. "She really got it in the neck, poor cow."

"It's true that she wasn't particularly fond of Nic." Gideon conceded.

"Why didn't she like Nicole?" I asked.

"Marjorie said she looked odd." Joe explained.

"In what way odd?" I was keen to get to the bottom of this as Marjorie had recently made much of the fact that I reminded her of Nicole. "When I saw you standing on our doorstep the first time we met I really thought it was Nicole for a moment," she had said. "I said to you, didn't I Malcolm, I said 'don't you think she has a look of Nicole about her', didn't I Malcolm? So similar." Neither Malcolm nor Gideon had passed any comment and the conversation had moved on. I had been a little put out as I didn't want to think that I was simply a type that Gideon routinely picked up. Gideon had assured me, however, that I looked nothing like Nicole and that I shouldn't give it another thought.

"She said," Joe continued, "that Nicole always looked as if she was up to something, and as if she needed a good wash. She used to call her Dirty Nicole, and not in a good way." He gave a throaty laugh.

"I think that really is enough about Gideon's past girlfriends, don't you?" Helen gave Joe a look that clearly implied he had gone too far.

"Don't worry about it, Hels," said Gideon, putting his hand over mine, "All Eve needs to know is that I'm going to marry her, aren't I Eve?" Gideon looked at me for confirmation.

"Yes, you are, you most certainly are." I concurred.

"Wow! Really? You're finally going to get married? Joe, I think we need something stronger than tea!" Helen looked thrilled, although I wasn't so sure that Joe shared her delight. It was difficult to tell, what with all the hair, but it looked to me as if he was unsure whether or not this was a good idea.

"Keep it to yourselves though will you? I haven't told Mum and Dad yet." Gideon continued.

"Oh, good luck with that then," said Joe, winking at me, and thereby confirming my suspicions that he didn't think this was unalloyed good news.

"Oh shut up you," said Helen, "I'm sure it'll be fine."

"And that's what you think people wear in the country?" Joe was looking at me appraisingly as we stood by the back door the next morning.

"Isn't it?" I replied, somewhat taken aback. I had put quite a lot of thought into my sartorial choices for this weekend and I felt that I had pretty much nailed it.

"Well," he said, clearly unimpressed my attire, "it'll have to do."

I had, in preparation for my countryside sojourn, visited a wide range of charity shops in and around Chiswick and finally come across a quite stunning waxed coat. It was almost floor length and had an extra flappy cape bit that covered my shoulders. It also had more pockets than all the other coats I had ever owned combined. I presumed they were for putting the kind of things in that people in the countryside routinely need to have about their person, what with their being so far from shops so much of the time. What these things might be I had no idea, but should I ever find out I would certainly have the pockets for them. The coat was a little on the roomy side, but you can't have everything. I had teamed it with some black wellies borrowed from Claire, whose feet are only marginally bigger than mine so a thick pair of socks almost made up the deficit, and a very fetching, if also rather over large, waterproof hat that I had found abandoned in Richmond Park some months previously. I was, I will admit, quite pleased with my ensemble. I looked every inch, or so I had believed, the countrywoman.

"Come on then," said Joe, "we've got provisions to get. See you guys later." This last remark was directed towards Helen and Gideon who were sitting at the table, which still contained the detritus of breakfast. The plan was that Joe and I would go and obtain the necessaries for supper while Gideon and Helen had some quality sibling time together. I had readily agreed to Joe's suggestion as I felt that he had things to tell me that he didn't feel could be said in front of Helen. So here I was heading off in my rather oversized country attire, to get provisions.

"Aren't we driving?" I asked as Joe strode passed the mud encrusted Land Rover (what else?) parked outside.

"No. We're heading this away." Joe pointed to what looked like a very dense forest that covered the hillside behind the house.

"Oh," I replied, "I see." I didn't see, but followed Joe anyway, running slightly to keep up. Gideon walks fast and so, as general rule, do I. I have to run for a few steps occasionally to keep up with him, but it's never been a problem for me. I am fit and healthy and well able to manage. This was, however, something else altogether. For a start the hill was rather steep and my socks weren't quite thick enough so my boots threatened to come off with every step. On top of this my lovely coat not only weighed a ton, it also made me substantially wider than normal so I kept getting caught on branches whilst trying to get through gaps I would usually have been able to negotiate with ease. As a result keeping up with Joe proved rather more challenging than I might have hoped, and he made me no concessions, striding on ahead at an Olympian pace. Having fought my way through what seemed like several miles of forest we came to the top of the hill. Joe looked as if he wasn't going to stop so I managed to indicate that I would like to take a moment to admire the view. I had to do this largely through sign language as I was too breathless to speak, and when I did turn around to see how far we had come I was disappointed to note the house was only a few hundred yards below us.

"How… how… how… much further?" I finally managed to gasp, having pushed my hat back so that I could see Joe, as it had the unfortunate habit of falling over my eyes if I didn't keep regularly adjusting it.

"Just over the next rise," he assured me, pointing to another hill that must have been at least thirty miles away. It was almost obscured by the curvature of the earth.

"Oh, great." I muttered.

"Right, now I've got you alone, we need to have a little talk." Joe had begun walking again, so I had no choice but to do the same, much though I longed to collapse in a heap on the ground.

"Do we?" I asked.

"Now, Eve," Joe began, "Any idiot can see that you and Gideon are very happy."

"Yes, we are," I concurred.

"And that's great, really great, but I have to warn you, you don't know what you're getting into." Joe continued.

"Don't I?" I responded.

"The thing is that Marjorie, well Marjorie is a very strong willed woman."

"Is she?" I asked, disingenuously.

"Yes, Eve, I'm afraid she bloody is. And she thinks that she knows what's best for everyone, especially her children." Joe continued.

"Does she? Think she knows what's best I mean, rather than actually knowing what's best." I could see that Joe was quite angry but at least he wasn't armed, although Baskerville (turned out that was actually the hound's name) was with us.

"If I didn't love Helen so bloody much she might have scared me off." Joe continued. "Why do you think we live out here, in the middle of nowhere?"

"Because you like it?" I ventured, unlikely though this seemed.

"Yeah, there is that, but it's also because Marjorie doesn't like it. She and Hels, well they... to be honest Marjorie can be a first class bitch. If it was up to me we'd never have anything to do with her, but Helen, well, she just keeps going back for more, whatever I say. Hels says she's not going to put up with her mother anymore, and then ... well, she does, Put up with her that is."

"What does Marjorie do?" I asked, intrigued.

"She uses Hels." Joe sounded quite angry.

"What do you mean, uses her?"

"If Marjorie wants to play happy families, then she's all over us, but then she'll be so bloody critical she makes Hels feel like shit. Marjorie knows better about everything and is quite happy to say so. She criticises where we live, how we live, how we're bringing up the kids, everything." Joe was on a roll now, and really quite furious, but he had stopped walking to vent his anger so I could have a little rest and catch my breath. "Once, when they came for the weekend, she even brought her own sheets because she said Helen didn't use the right conditioner on ours. Can you believe that? Anyway," he continued, "I've tried to get her to cut the old bitch out of our lives, but she won't. I've no idea why. It's the only thing we ever argue about."

"Oh." I said. "And what about Gideon?"

"He's the golden boy, isn't he? Marjorie's perfect son." Joe had resumed walking at a cracking pace but the trees had thinned and the ground levelled so I could almost keep up. "Look," he said, "you must have wondered why he's never married? Good looking, if that wussy metropolitan look's your thing, financially solvent. Never married."

"Well," I said, silently cursing my coat for being so damned heavy, and I didn't even have anything in the pockets, "he'd never met me."

"There's that of course. But it might also be that he's never married because Marjorie has stuck her oar in every time. She might just think he ought to marry you," Joe let out a huge 'ha' which made me think he thought this unlikely, "but if she doesn't then I would suggest that you..."

"That I what?"

"Just watch your back," Joe said, "that's all I'm saying."

"But she can't stop him marrying me," I said, "he's a grown man."

"Maybe, maybe not. Just watch yourself, that really is all I'm saying." It clearly wasn't all he was saying, but it was also all he was going to say. "Not far now," he assured me, as we plunged into another densely wooded area, the subject of Marjorie clearly closed. Where the hell, I wondered, were we going, and what sort of 'provisions' were we going to find when we got there? Perhaps Joe had set snares for rabbits, or we were going to pick mushrooms from the forest floor, who knew?

"There," Joe said, pointing at something in the distance. "Can you see it yet?"

"See what?" I asked, peering through the trees with no idea what I was looking for.

"Tesco's. Now where," he said, patting his numerous pockets, "did I put the shopping list?"

"Mum and Sasha were thick as thieves, for a while at least." Helen said in reply to my question. We were doing the washing up after dinner (they didn't have a dishwasher, obviously) and I had been quizzing Helen, as subtly as I could manage, about Gideon's past girlfriends. "But then," she continued, "it all went very frosty, and not long after that Gideon and Sasha split up."

"What went wrong? Weren't she and Gideon engaged?" I prompted. Gideon had told me about Sasha leading me to admit that I too had once been engaged, but as the fact that my engagement had led to marriage wasn't relevant to the conversation I hadn't felt the need to mention it. It wasn't as if I was married to anyone else when Gideon and I decided to wed, and that's all that really matters, isn't it?

"They were," Helen confirmed, "not that I thought they were as well suited as you two." Helen paused as she scrubbed at an already spotless casserole dish. "I really mean that you know," she continued, "I'm not just saying it. Well I am just saying it, obviously, but that doesn't mean it's not true."

"Thanks Helen, that's really nice to know." I replied, taking the dish from her. "Do you think your mother had anything to do with their relationship ending?" I threw this in as casually as I could. While I already liked Helen and sensed that she wasn't as enamoured of her mother as was Gideon there was, I felt, no need to signal how interested I might be in her answer.

"Well ... the thing is, I suppose ... well to put it another way," said Helen, not having put it any way at all yet. "Sasha, well, she dumped Gideon, not the other way round ... so that's not very likely is it?" Helen was lying again, that was the second time since I had arrived. Why do so many people lie, I wondered, especially when they are so bad at it? I know that sounds hypocritical, but really.

"But you suspect that your mother had something to do with it?" I asked, adopting just the right tone, I hoped, of incredulity.

"Oh no," said Helen, far too emphatically. "Sasha just got cold feet I suppose. That must have been it. Cold feet. Nothing more to it than that. Absolutely a case of cold feet, nothing more." Helen was trying to sound casual, off hand even, but she wouldn't meet my eye and kept scrubbing at another, also clearly spotless, dish. She was a bad, bad liar. "Isn't it cold for the time of year?" she said, apparently signalling an end to the previous conversation. "I mean really cold. I'll get you an extra blanket for your bed. I wouldn't want you and Gideon to get chilly in the night."

The washing up finished and my mind slightly unsettled, we joined Gideon and Joe in the dishevelled but homely sitting room. As if it wasn't untidy enough already the two of them were sprawled on the floor looking through some old photographs they had strewn haphazardly across the floor. I squatted down next to Joe to take a look.

"Oh my god, is that really you?" I exclaimed. The photo that had elicited this response was of a very young but still recognisable Joe and Helen. "How old were you?"

"Fifteen," Helen replied, "at least I was, Joe was seventeen. That was only about a week after we first met."

"You met as teenagers?" I said. "Wow." Gideon had told me that Joe and Helen had been together a long time, but not quite how long.

"My dad brought us over for a year to experience the old country." Joe explained. "Helen was the first girl I saw when I rocked up at school, and that was that, there's never been anyone else, not for either of us."

"But then his Dad took them back to Sydney and we didn't actually see each other for another three years until Joe came back when he was twenty." Helen continued the story.

"But we wrote to each other a lot..." Joe said. "Or at least I did. Hels wrote about three times, and one of those was a postcard. I thought she'd forgotten me."

"As if!" Helen exclaimed vehemently.

"But we got through that and we've been together ever since." Joe concluded. He and Helen shared a smile that hinted at a depth of relationship that only many years together can create. I felt a twinge of jealousy. I didn't resent their happiness and things were going really well between Gideon and me, but I always think there is something arrogant about new relationships. Love that lasts is infinitely more to be admired than the infatuation of the early months as it is far, far easier to fall in love than it is to stay in love. Helen and Joe seemed to have managed both.

Joe carried on sifting through the huge pile of photos that littered the floor. There were lots of Gideon and Helen as children alongside Malcolm and Marjorie on various family holidays or days out. One photograph in particular caught my eye. In all the previous pictures Marjorie had looked rather stiff and uncomfortable as if she had been drafted in to play the role of mother to this family, and not very convincingly at that. In this photograph however she was laying on the lawn of what looked like the garden of the Sheen house, propped up on her elbows, a hand on either side of her face and a look of theatrical shock on her face. Helen and Gideon were either side of her in the same pose. It looked as if they were having a great time.

"This is a lovely photo," I said picking it up. Helen's unsettling comments seemed ridiculous in the face of a picture of such familial bliss.

"Let me see," said Helen taking the photo from me. "Oh, that's not Mum." I didn't know what she was talking about, it was clearly her mother. "No," she said, conclusively, "that is our aunt, Meg."

"Huh?" I queried.

"Yes," confirmed Gideon as he took the photo from his sister, "that's Meg all right. She's Mum's twin. Identical twin," he added as if that could possibly have been in doubt. "Twins run in our family," he went on, "as you might have noticed. She was great fun wasn't she?" He looked to Helen for confirmation. She nodded, a sad smile on her face.

"Is she dead?" I asked, not unreasonably given that he had referred to Meg in the past tense and I had never heard her mentioned before.

"No," volunteered Helen, "we just haven't seen her for a very long time. She suffers from depression, amongst other things. Mum sees her from time to time and tells me how she is, but she's not really up to seeing anyone else." Helen had taken the photo back and was gazing at it lovingly. "God, I adored Auntie Meg. She was so lovely. A bit of a ditz it has to be said, but very sweet and funny, even if she didn't always mean to be. It's so sad that the children have never met her, she'd have adored them, but Mum says she's something of a recluse these days. Rarely goes out." Helen looked wistfully at the photo in her hand. "She used to take us swimming every Saturday, remember Gid?"

"God, yes! Mum hates the water so she'd never even come to the pool with us when we were kids. Meg couldn't swim either, but she still took us along, week in, week out. She would sit and watch while we had swimming lessons."

"Where did she live?" I asked, remembering my strange encounter with Marjorie in Peter Jones the morning I had met Claire for coffee.

"Somewhere off the King's Road, near World's End." Helen replied. "I guess she's still there, Mum's never mentioned a move. She had a funny little rented bedsit. I'm afraid I lost the address years ago though." She was still looking wistfully at the photo. "Why do you ask?"

"Oh, you know what..." I was about to blurt out the details of my encounter with the woman I was almost certain must have been Meg, but something made me stop. The woman I had seen didn't match the description Marjorie had given Helen of her aunt at all. Although I had only seen her from afar, the Meg I had seen looked to have all her faculties working perfectly. If Marjorie had some reason for keeping her sister away from the rest of her family, and it wasn't the reason she had given, then it might prove useful to me to find out more. Knowledge is, so they say, power. I had learnt enough about Marjorie one way or another to make me realise that I would have to find some way to manage her. I had no idea whether or not Meg could be of any use, but until I knew more I felt it best to keep my own counsel.

"What?" asked Gideon.

"I fancy another glass of wine, that's what. Anyone else join me?" I would pay for that little lie in the morning when I woke feeling less than chipper, but right then it was the only thing I could come up with.

Chapter 6

Meeting Helen and Joe and their children had, despite what I had learned about Marjorie's ability to interfere in her children's relationships, lifted my spirits enormously. They felt like the kind of family I might like to have, which is something that I have rarely experienced. Part of the problem, I think, is that I have no memories at all, not a one, of my parents. I don't even have a very clear idea of what they looked like, as whatever family photo albums there may have been somehow managed to get lost when my parents' home was dismantled (by whom I have no idea, I only know that it was).

I have come up with various reimaginings of what my parents may have been like but how close these are to the truth I do not know. I remember bits and pieces about my life before their deaths, but where my parents should be there is just a blank. I know more about how they died than I do about how they lived. They were killed in a head on collision while on their way back from somewhere, possibly a party. They were hit by a van driven by a man who had, in all probability, fallen asleep at the wheel and drifted across in front of their car too late, presumably, for whichever one of my parents was driving to take evasive action.

I had, at the time of their death, been asleep for several hours, even though I had tried to stay awake until they came in. I do remember that I always did the same thing whenever they went out. I would press my right cheek against my bedroom window so that I could see the main road at the end of our road and watch for their car. If my parents were not in the first car that passed I would wait for another three cars. If they still failed to return I would allow myself another three, and so on until either Tessa (the teenaged babysitter who was watching over me and Dominic while our parents were out somewhere, dying) came to check on me or I got too tired and was forced to give up. I have never been able to shake off the feeling that, had I waited longer that night, I might have averted the whole awful tragedy. The idea that anything in this world or the wider universe can be controlled by our thoughts alone is ridiculous, and yet I still cling to the idea that somehow, at that moment, I could have been omnipotent if only I could have stayed awake.

At six years old I obviously didn't really understand what had happened. Had I been asked I would have presumed, if six year olds can presume, that my life would go on much as before in the absence of my parents. My brother and I would carry on living in our house with, perhaps, Tessa to look after us. I found out quite quickly however, that my presumption was very, very wrong.

The first, totally unexpected and very unwelcome, consequence of my parents' death was that my ballet teacher, who happened to be a neighbour and one of my least favourite people in the whole world, was unaccountably put in charge. I had been on the receiving end of Mrs Green's discipline more than once, and it had never been a pleasant experience. First, I had got into terrible trouble for refusing to dance at the back in a concert given by my ballet class. I was a short child and couldn't be seen if I was hidden at the back and, as I had a rather higher estimation of my dancing ability than Mrs Green, this led to some friction. Second, Mrs Green had once tried to imprison me in her garden following an incident involving her daughter Susan and a swing. The swing was one of those triangular framed ones and it wasn't attached to the ground properly. Mrs Green's husband had just run off with the art teacher at the school where he taught (I only learnt about Mr Green's infidelity much later, from Susan. She wrote to me every month for the next ten years without ever once receiving a reply, which I think says quite a lot about both of us). Mrs Green had therefore put the swing up by herself when she was probably in no fit state to be doing DIY. As a result when Susan and I began to swing on it rather too enthusiastically (probably at my instigation as Susan was not a natural thrill seeker, unlike her father) the whole edifice toppled over hitting Susan on the back of the head on its way down. Having seen events unfold from her kitchen window Mrs Green came running to Susan's aid. Thinking that this would be a suitable time for me to leave I began sidling across the garden towards the side passage with the intention of making my exit to the street beyond. Mrs Green was not having any of it.

"And where do you think you're going?" she had thundered. I was rendered completely speechless, never having been shouted at by another child's parent before. "You will stay here while I see to Susan. You," Mrs Green said, pointing at me accusingly, "are completely responsible for what's happened." I didn't even to stop to remonstrate with her about the unfairness of this assertion (it probably wasn't unfair, but at six you think most things are unfair), but used the head start I had to outrun her and leg it down the side of the house to freedom, my promising career as a ballerina coming to an abrupt end in the process.

You can imagine my horror therefore, on coming down to breakfast on the morning in question, when I found that not only were my parents missing, they had been replaced by a tear stained Mrs Green. Many years later I would reflect that Mrs Green was actually in a very bad place at this point in her life and that she did a sterling job in taking on the task of looking after two bewildered children. She did a much better job, in truth, than our own relatives, who arrived shortly afterwards, supposedly to take over. At the time I was incapable of such clear thinking however and was simply appalled.

The first relative to appear was Aunt Audrey, our father's sister. She had not played a major part in my life up to this point and, despite the fact that I would go on to live with her for the next ten years, she never did play a major role. Following close on the heels of Aunt Audrey were Uncle Mike and Aunt Karen, the brother and sister-in-law respectively of our mother. We still had two of our four grandparents living, but they had fallen out with our mother when she married our father and they had never reconciled, even following the births of their grandchildren. Being people of principle they clearly didn't think they should change their stance just because there had now also been some deaths in the family.

The next few days were the most confusing and difficult that I have ever experienced, and I have had quite a few confusing and difficult times so I know of what I speak. The adults who were supposed to be in charge kept disappearing behind closed doors and shouting. Dominic had no real idea what was going on and kept asking where our mother was and looking for her in the most unlikely places. He became fixated on the idea that she was hidden behind the wardrobe in my bedroom. It was in an alcove and there was barely room for a toddler to squeeze down the side of it, let alone a full grown woman. But no matter how many times I tried to tell him that the only thing to be found behind the wardrobe was a collection of half eaten biscuits that I had thrown there when my eyes proved to be bigger than my stomach, Dominic would still sit for hours on the floor of my room, waiting for our mother to come out from behind the closet. He was, however, quite happy to believe that our father was at work and so did not feel the need to hold a vigil for him. I've sometimes wondered if Dominic's belief in all sorts of things that are clearly impossible are predicated on his clearly impossible belief that our mother was hiding behind my wardrobe. Perhaps if one of his other bonkers theories is proved true he believes she'll finally reappear.

After several days of shouting and crying behind closed doors the adults seemed to come to some sort of agreement and within a few hours of the last bellow from Uncle Mike we were whisked away. Dominic was bundled into a car with Uncle Mike and Aunt Karen, but it would appear that they didn't have room for me (that I was, as I have already mentioned, a very ugly child while Dominic was quite cute may have had something to do with their decision), and I found myself in the back of Aunt Audrey's Hillman Imp heading for somewhere called Norwich.

As I was driven away I could see Mrs Green waving goodbye from their front room window. Susan, who was standing next to her mother, couldn't wave as she was clutching my only recently acquired cat, Mr Perkins, to her chest and nuzzling his head. In all the shouting about which child would go where the only thing on which they all agreed was that Mr Perkins was staying put. It was this that finally caused my tears to fall. My parents, wherever they had gone were, I was quite certain, together, but I was all alone and seeing Mr Perkins sitting contentedly in Susan's arms was just too much. I cried solidly all the way to Norwich, which only served to annoy Aunt Audrey and didn't make me feel any better, or bring about the return of Mr Perkins.

Chapter 7

"Mum's invited us for Burns' Night," Gideon announced over breakfast one morning in early January.

"Really?" I tried not to sound too incredulous. After all that had happened over Christmas I was surprised to be invited back into Marjorie's home so soon, but I took it as a positive sign that recent events were to be consigned to history.

I should explain that my first Christmas with Gideon had not gone exactly as I might have wished. I had thought that we would have a quiet Christmas, just the two of us, but Marjorie had decreed that we were to have lunch at her house. I had been reluctant to go as a day spent in the company of Marjorie was, in my estimation at least, a day that could have been better spent doing almost anything else. But Helen, Joe, and their numerous children would also be in attendance so that made the prospect altogether more bearable. It might even be fun. I envisaged family board games perhaps or even, in my wilder imaginings, Twister.

The first intimations that all might not go well came a few days before the day itself, when I had to ask Gideon a huge favour regarding Dominic. Gideon and I were Christmas shopping at the time, trying and so far failing, to find a present for Marjorie.

"How about this?" I said pointing to a piece of glass shaped like an owl. It was hideous but Marjorie had lots of similarly ghastly ornaments dotted around her home so it seemed a reasonable choice.

"Maybe, but Mum is quite hard to please, present wise. She might not like it." Gideon picked up the lump of owl shaped glass. "What is it anyway?"

"How could she not like it? What's not to like?" I replied. There was a lot not to like about this hideous object but having already proffered countless potential gifts, none of which Gideon felt would pass muster with his mother, I was prepared to throw almost anything in his path if it would bring this hellish experience to an end. "It's an owl." I added.

"Mmm, an owl," Gideon said thoughtfully. "It might do." He held it gingerly between his thumb and forefinger and turned his hand so that he could look at it from various angles as if this might help him to come to a decision on its worthiness. "But then again, she might not like it."

"Surely she'd like anything you bought her?" I said. I thought that's what mothers did, accept any old tat from their children with protestations of great joy. While I had no recollection of ever buying my mother a present, I'm sure I must have given her at least one or two in the six years we spent together. I'm equally sure that she would have professed to love whatever it was that I had given her.

"Mum knows what she likes," Gideon said. "I got her a lovely piece once. An abstract sculpture made from driftwood. I saw it in a gallery on the Suffolk coast, but a few days later I got it back in the post. It came with a note from Dad saying that she didn't want it in the house."

"Is that the thing on the hall table? Looks like a petrified penis?" Gideon nodded in confirmation. I couldn't help but have some sympathy with Marjorie's position. It was a uniquely horrid object. "Christmas," I said grabbing Gideon's free arm and snuggling up to him in what I hoped was a charming manner, "it really is a time for families, isn't it?"

"I suppose so." Gideon pulled his arm away and returned the owl to its place on the shelf before picking up a sculpture of a couple of cats nuzzling one another.

"Oh," I said as if the thought had taken me by surprise and was quite inconsequential. "I don't think I told you, but Dominic needs somewhere to stay over Christmas. I said he could come to us." I tried to sound bright and breezy, as if it were the most natural thing in the world that my brother should spend Christmas with his sister, which in a normal family it would have been.

The thing is that I was pretty sure that Gideon would not be happy. He and Dominic had not exactly hit it off on the one occasion they had met. Dominic had decided to launch an attack on the proliferation of universities (like the one at which Gideon taught). He went on to explain, at some length, that these places were cynical money making machines providing a second rate education to young people who had been carefully nurtured by devoted teachers (like him) in secondary education. Such institutions did nothing to expand these youngsters' minds, gave them no real career prospects, and left them saddled with debt. "It's not your fault," he had assured Gideon, "I'm sure you try your best, but the whole system stinks."

"Why can't he stay in his own flat at Christmas?" Gideon replied, replacing the nuzzling cats on the shelf.

"It's being fumigated apparently." I explained.

"That figures," he continued. "Isn't there somewhere else he could go?"

"You know there isn't." I said.

"No, I don't suppose there is," said Gideon with weary resignation. It was hardly a fulsome invitation and made clear his feelings for Dominic. A few days later however, I realised that I had misjudged him. He's almost too good a man sometimes.

"Mum insists that Dominic come with us," he said, over dinner one evening. "She said that she couldn't live with herself if she knew your brother was at home alone while we tucked into our Christmas dinner. She is amazing, don't you think?"

"Yup, amazing, absolutely amazing." I concurred, not quite truthfully.

On reflection I should have gone with my instinct, which was to keep Dominic as far as possible from Gideon's family, and most definitely at Christmas. I would happily have left him behind with a pizza, a bottle of whiskey, and a box set of Breaking Bad (I think he hopes one day to do for geography teachers what Walter White did for chemistry teachers), but I could hardly refuse the invitation without it looking odd.

The sad truth is that I don't really trust Dominic around people, at least not ones that are anything to do with me. All I could do was hope that he would behave well for the few hours we would spend in Marjorie and Malcolm's home. As it happens my hope was misplaced and the fallout from Christmas was both swift and dramatic. On Boxing Day, around mid-afternoon, Gideon received a phone call from his father. Marjorie, Malcolm said, had been crying pretty much nonstop since we had left the day before. She couldn't believe that my brother and I had come to her home only to ruin the Christmas she had so lovingly planned. Marjorie, Malcolm went on, had begged him not to say anything as she had no desire to cause any trouble between Gideon and me, but he, Malcolm, couldn't stay silent. It was possible, Malcolm conceded, that Dominic was not aware of what he was doing, but as for my attempts to make Marjorie look foolish in front of her family, he hoped there would be no repetition of such rudeness. He and Marjorie would, in conclusion, be grateful for an assurance from Gideon that they would never have to meet Dominic again. So that went well then.

The unfortunate thing was that I had, naively in retrospect, been quite looking forward to Christmas. The Christmases of my childhood had been rather odd affairs. Aunt Audrey had felt, even more strongly than most, that Christmas was a time for giving. On Christmas morning therefore we would go to the children's ward at the local hospital and give away my meagre stock of presents. Then we would head to a homeless shelter to help serve Christmas dinner before returning home for beans on toast. A full blown, multi-generational family shebang with a huge roast dinner and nary a homeless person or a sick child in sight would make a pleasant change. Not that I have anything against sick children or homeless people, I just got a little tired of seeing them have a better Christmas than me year after year.

Initially it looked as if everything was going to go with one hell of a swing. The three of us, me, Gideon, and Dominic, arrived to find Marjorie's normally tidy house a riot of wrapping paper. Judging by the mountain of presents in the lounge the children had been well served by Santa and there were some very appetising smells coming from the kitchen, so it looked as if Marjorie had upped her game for Christmas dinner. If Helen seemed a bit less friendly than at our previous meeting I put it down to the strain of managing her children under her mother's disapproving eye.

"Do not take that into the lounge," Marjorie shouted at Hector, or possibly Jake, as one or other of them made their way across the hall from the dining room holding a fizzy drink of a particularly vivid red hue.

"Put that down immediately," she told Ruby (I knew it was Ruby because she has short hair while Martha can sit on hers) as the child reached for a chocolate. "We'll be eating in less than an hour and I haven't spent all morning cooking for you to make yourself sick on sweets before you've eaten. Helen," Marjorie, who was standing in the door of the lounge wearing pink rubber gloves with furry tops on them and a reindeer apron, turned her attention to her daughter. "Can you please control your children? One of them has disturbed the fringe on the hall rug, so I'll have to sort that out on top of everything else."

"Is there anything I can do to help?" I asked, hoping to diffuse what was threatening to become a rather tense situation. I made as if to get up from my seat. "I'm happy to help with anything you need in the kitchen," I added.

"No!" Marjorie exclaimed, rather more sharply than was strictly necessary. "You stay just where you are. All of you." She pointed a rubber glove clad finger at us all in a sinister manner that brooked no opposition, but she did manage to muster a thin smile as she did so. But I was left in no doubt that she didn't want anyone in her kitchen.

Marjorie having returned to her labours I turned my attention back to Helen, with whom I had been making desultory conversation. I expected to share a rueful look with her in recognition of Marjorie's overbearing manner, but she just looked at me blankly. Thankfully Celeste came in at that moment and began to talk animatedly with Helen in French. I had been surprised to see Celeste there as I would have assumed, had I given it any thought at all, that she would have gone home to France for the festivities. It was obviously a good thing she was there though, as her presence seemed to cheer Helen enormously. Not long after this Marjorie announced that lunch was ready and we all trooped into the dining room, skirting round the massive (artificial) tree that dominated the hall.

Quite how the conversation that Christmas lunchtime made the leap it did in the few minutes that I was in the loo I have no idea. When I left everyone was discussing the merits of TV Christmas specials and whether or not they add any real value (in my view they don't). When I returned the topic had moved on to the fact that (according to Dominic) pretty much every terrorist outrage or plane crash in recent times has been orchestrated by a global cabal intent on world domination (in my view they haven't).

"So because that's what the media," here Dominic did that really irritating thing of waggling the first two fingers of each hand to indicate quote marks when he said the word media, "says you believe it?" Dominic was most definitely astride one of his favourite hobby horses and not going to be easily unseated. "Only an idiot would believe that a plane could simply go missing. And the train that brought the so called bombers to London, it was cancelled. A few minutes research on the internet and it would be clear to anyone with half a brain that there was far more to all these events than they want you to know."

"And who are 'they'?" asked Malcolm, waggling his fingers in much the same way that Dominic had just done.

"The people that really run this place," my brother replied, waving a roast potato he had just speared on the end of his fork at my future father-in-law. Dominic can become very voluble after a couple of drinks and he had been knocking back some very expensive wine (I know it was expensive not because I am a connoisseur but because Marjorie told everybody it was) with a seemingly unquenchable thirst.

"I can see no reason whatsoever to doubt the official account of events," said Malcolm patiently. "You don't have any evidence to back up any of your so called theories, not that you have shared with us so far anyway."

"So you don't think it's just a little bit suspicious that there were twenty people from the same company on board the so called 'missing' plane?" Dominic had by now taken a big bite out of the potato he had previously been waving around and was now talking with his mouth full, although this was probably the least of his social faux pas at that moment.

"Why would that be in the least bit suspicious?" Malcolm responded. He clearly wasn't about to fold in the face of Dominic's onslaught. "Surely it's far more likely that it just crashed than that it was part of some plot," he continued.

"If that helps you to sleep at night Malc, then believe what you want." Dominic chose this moment to refill his glass, managing to slop red wine onto the pure white table cloth as he did so. Marjorie tutted loudly but Dominic was not about to let a little tutting stop him.

"I just have two words to say to you, young man," said Malcolm. Uh oh, I thought, I can just imagine what those two words will be. Or at least I could imagine which two words I thought Dominic deserved to have said to him at that moment. Malcolm was, however, clearly much more patient, and certainly less potty mouthed, than me. "Occam's razor" were the two words that he chose.

"Occam's what?" replied Dominic.

"Occam's razor," Gideon repeated on his father's behalf. "It's the principle that the simplest solution, the one that requires the fewest assumptions, is the one that is most likely." I was glad of the explanation, having had absolutely no idea why Malcolm had started going on about shaving equipment but, even I have to admit, Gideon did sound a little patronising regardless of the usefulness of his contribution.

"Huh?" said Dominic.

"To put it more simply," Gideon continued, "your suggestion that the plane was somehow spirited away by a shady cabal because of a desire to get hold of, or get rid, of, twenty people, requires a lot more assumptions than the suggestion that the plane simply crashed into the ocean and has yet to be found." If Gideon had been teetering on the edge of patronising before, he had now dived headlong into it. I knew he was right and I was furious with Dominic, but I couldn't help feeling just a little protective towards him. He's an idiot, but he was completely outnumbered and there was no need to make him look anymore foolish than he had already made himself. "And the ocean," Gideon concluded, "is a very big place."

"And surely, mate, there'd be much easier ways to get rid of a few people than to make a whole plane disappear." Joe, who had been listening intently to the, for want of a better word, arguments had decided it was time to wade in. "If I wanted to get rid of a few people I'd take 'em somewhere out of the way and shoot 'em." Having seen Joe armed and in his natural habitat I could believe this. "What I wouldn't do, mate, is get everyone in the world looking my way. Not smart, not smart at all." Joe tapped the side of his forehead with his fork as if to reinforce the idiocy of

Dominic's suggestion. I could see Dominic shaking his head as if in weary resignation at the gullibility of the masses. I desperately wanted the conversation to move on before he made an even greater fool of himself, especially as it was now three against one.

"These parsnips are delicious Marjorie." I piped up. "What did you do to them? You must give me the recipe."

"I cooked them," Marjorie replied, rather sharply I thought, considering I was trying to throw her lifeline out of this conversational morass.

"Yes," I persisted, determined to keep off conspiracy theories long enough for the conversation to take a different, less contentious, turn, "but what did you cook them in?"

"The container they came in," she replied rather sharply, "from the shop I bought them from."

"So that's why it's all so tasty!" Joe let out a roar of laughter. "Marjorie, you sly fox. You didn't make this meal at all did you?" He clearly thought this was hugely funny. Marjorie, equally as clearly, did not. Unfortunately my intervention did nothing to end the conversation (Dominic finally got around to mentioning lizard eyed aliens, another of his favourite subjects, about five minutes later, although it seemed much longer). All I had managed to do was highlight Marjorie's culinary deception. And now, on Boxing Day, I was paying for it.

"I personally don't find anything about this situation funny." Gideon had, somewhat to my surprise, taken his parents side completely and my attempts to diffuse the situation through humour had been as ineffective as my parsnip gambit. "Whether your brother intended to be rude or not," he continued, "he has certainly upset my parents, which was uncalled for after they invited him to lunch. I'd better go around and see how Mum is." Gideon sounded like a complete stuffed shirt and I must admit it got up my nose rather. Having said his piece he got up and headed out of the sitting room, where this conversation was taking place, presumably to get his coat and shoes.

"So if someone feeds you, you have to agree with everything they say, is that what you believe?" I shouted after him, his attitude having got my goat somewhat.

"Of course that's not what I believe." Gideon replied, having returned wearing a coat and some shoes, two to be exact, thus confirming my earlier suspicions.

"What's so wrong with Dominic saying what he thinks anyway?" I was furious with Dominic, but I was also angry with Gideon for taking this all so seriously. Dominic had been an idiot. Couldn't we all just accept that he was an idiot and move one?

"It's not about him saying what he thinks, it's about him being rude." Gideon responded.

"Go round there then," I said. "To your amazing mother. If she's so amazing," I continued, having got the bit between my teeth, "how come she can't even cook parsnips?"

"Don't be childish Eve," Gideon replied, "It doesn't suit you." And with that smugly gittish comment ringing in my ears Gideon swept out of the front door without so much as a goodbye.

The next four hours were not the most pleasant I have ever spent. I couldn't settle to anything. I tried reading. I tried watching TV. I even tried meditating for goodness sake, but nothing seemed to soothe my fevered mind. This was our first real argument. I was very aware that I had known Gideon for not much more than a year and so couldn't really be sure which way this was going play out. It was possible that this could be the end of it all, and I found myself more distressed than I would have imagined, and not just because I would have to find somewhere else to live. The more time I had spent with Gideon the more I had found that I liked him. While I might not have had the purest motives when I moved in to his flat, I was becoming very attached to the great lunk. I didn't want our relationship to come to a shuddering halt, especially not on account of my brother and some parsnips.

Having exhausted every possible way of entertaining myself, having got myself into a state of righteous anger and indignation several times, and having run through all the possible scenarios I could think of for what was going on between Gideon and his parents I decided, possibly foolishly, to self-medicate. Gideon returned home just as I was pouring myself a third, very large, glass of red wine.

"So?" If I had thought that the wine had calmed me down, as soon as I saw Gideon I knew that all was still far from well, and that I was still far from calm.

"So, she's very hurt." Gideon ran his hand through his hair. Anyone would have thought he was talking about something really serious, not his mother getting hysterical because Christmas Day hadn't followed her script to the letter. "She just wanted our first Christmas together to be a memorable one, which is why she bought the food in. But then you and Dominic made a fool of her and ruined the day for everyone." You couldn't say it wasn't memorable then I thought, but decided it would be impolitic to say. "She doesn't know what she's done to make you want to treat her like this," he concluded.

"I asked her," I said through gritted teeth, "how she had cooked some parsnips. How is that treating her like anything?" My speech might, at this point, have been a little slurred.

"That may be true," Gideon countered, "but Dominic was certainly very rude. And you asked him for Christmas even though you know what he can be like."

"Dominic's my brother, my only family and..." I could feel tears welling up. I hate that. I can't understand how men don't cry as it seems to be a reflex action, like getting goosebumps when it's cold, for many women including, unfortunately, me.

"Oh, let's not start with the poor me bit again shall we?" Gideon almost sneered, and for a moment I could see a resemblance between him and his mother I had never noticed before. I couldn't believe he was being so vile. I was infuriated by his attitude, which seemed to be that his mother was wholly right and I was wholly wrong, and I fully intended to let him know how I felt by giving him a cold, hard and (assuming I could do all three at once) withering stare. Instead I found that, totally against my will, my bottom lip was beginning to quiver and tears, damn them, were beginning to roll treacherously down my cheeks.

"I'm not starting anything," I snuffled, "I just wanted to have a nice family Christmas and I couldn't leave my brother all alone..."

"And all my mother wanted was to have a nice family Christmas," Gideon said, with menacing calm, "but your brother had to muscle in on it and be rude to everyone."

"He wasn't rude to everyone," I replied pedantically. "He was perfectly charming to Celeste."

"The blonde, beautiful au pair who's young enough to be his daughter? Yes he was perfectly charming to her." Gideon replied. "Unfortunately he found it harder to be perfectly charming to the people who had invited him for lunch. And who were paying for everything."

"Oh, here we go again." My nose was now running quite profusely and I didn't have a handkerchief so was forced to try to sniff and speak at the same time, which is not conducive to making one's case coherently. "He who ... (sniff) ... pays the ... (sniff) ... piper ... (sniff) ... calls the ... (sniff) ... tune."

"What did you say?"

"You heard!" I bellowed.

"No I didn't," Gideon replied through gritted teeth, "that's why I asked what you said."

"Oh." I said, rather more quietly.

"You're clearly in no state to have a proper discussion so I suggest that we leave things there for now." Gideon said. "I have had an afternoon dealing with one hysterical woman, I don't want an evening dealing with another."

With this Gideon marched off down the hall and disappeared into the kitchen where I could hear him getting himself something to eat. How he could possibly think of food at a time like this was beyond me. It was almost inhuman. I think that was the last straw. I was now beyond angry. Me, hysterical! How bloody dare he? I thought about following him and shouting very loudly at him, but then I thought better of it. I knew enough of Gideon to know that shouting wouldn't get me anywhere. So I went to bed, but not to sleep, as it was only just after eight o'clock.

When he did eventually join me at around midnight, I was still awake. If I couldn't sleep alone I certainly couldn't sleep with him next to me. I therefore pretended to be asleep until I was pretty sure that he actually was (thankfully he goes out like a light as soon as his head hits the pillow so I didn't have to wait long). I slipped out of bed and went into the spare room. The bed was a mess, having been occupied by Dominic the previous night, but I got in anyway and looked forward to a sleepless night. I must have slept eventually because I woke up in the morning, but I felt dreadful and wasn't much looking forward to what the day might bring.

Breakfast was a sullen affair. I bashed and crashed around, slamming things down on the table while huffing and puffing in a fashion designed to elicit questions about my wellbeing but Gideon failed to deliver on that front. He was calm, polite, and totally uninterested in my emotional wellbeing, the bastard. After several minutes of this I could contain myself no longer.

"So," I demanded to know, "are we going to talk about this?"

"Talk about what?" he enquired calmly, which only maddened me further.

"You know very well what about." My voice was in serious danger of going wobbly again, a lack of sleep and a surfeit of emotion not being conducive to reasoned discussion.

"What more is there to say? You seem intent on defending your brother, while I believe my mother to be the wronged party. There's nothing to discuss. I am going out." Gideon got up from his chair and, having delivered a perfunctory "see you later" he left. Just like that. The urge to throw something at his retreating back was almost more than I could resist, but resist it I did.

Having spent the previous afternoon and night in an agonising state of purgatory, unsure of what was going on, it looked as if I was going to have another day of the same. Well sod that, I thought. I decided to get, quite literally, on my bike. When they tell you that exercise is good for improving one's mood (whoever 'they' are) they are right. After two hours of vigorous cycling, accompanied by a good deal of yelling at the few drivers inconsiderate enough to also be on the roads, I was feeling much better. Arriving home I had a bath and then lay down for a couple of hours during which I slept.

At the end of this process I had come to the conclusion that I was completely ambivalent about the outcome of my first major row with Gideon. If he was the kind of man who could treat me with cold disdain while siding with his mother (who was clearly the driving force behind this whole debacle), I was better off without him. I had survived very well before I met him and I would survive very well after he was gone. I didn't need a cold hearted, weak willed mummy's boy in my life. Never had, never would. Any idea that he might actually be the man with whom I wanted to spend the rest of my life was obviously a chimera of my own making. I was relieved to have come to this conclusion. I was almost looking forward to ending it all as quickly as possible. It would be like pulling a plaster off, quick and painful but easily recovered from. It was a much calmer me therefore who welcomed Gideon on his return. It was late afternoon by then, and already dark.

"Been anywhere nice?" I enquired as Gideon, still in his outerwear, entered the sitting room and sat down heavily in an armchair. I was determined to be neutral. If it was going to end, it would end with dignity. But on seeing him I realised that I didn't want it to end, not one little bit.

"Walking, mainly, around London. I went to the South Bank and then walked north. Ended up at Hampstead Heath." He looked less closed off than before. His face had returned, almost, to normal. "And you?"

"Cycling, bath, sleep," I said, before adding emphatically, "and packing."

"Packing?" That had certainly made him take notice.

"I can't go today," I said, "but it won't take long to find somewhere. There's no point in drawing this out any longer than necessary." I picked at the fringe of a cushion I had recently bought as part of my ongoing guerrilla redecoration of the flat. "I'll leave this," I said, indicating the cushion.

"Don't be so ridiculous Eve, we're not splitting up."

"Aren't we?" I asked. Relief flooded through me, but I still replied as haughtily as I could manage.

"No, we're not," he said, decisively. "Quite frankly you can be a complete pain in the arse, and I heartily dislike your brother but, and it is a fairly big but, I've never met anyone quite like you before. And I mean that in a good way. And if we did split up you could have that cushion, it's horrible. So, why don't you go and unpack your stuff and then we can have something to eat?"

"No need. And it's not, it's lovely." I replied, stroking the cushion.

"No it's not," he said, "and I said go and unpack and I meant it, and quickly, I'm starving."

"I meant there's no need for me to unpack. But I would have gone and packed really quickly if you'd been foolish enough to split up with me."

"You know something?" Gideon asked, looking at me appraisingly, "I love you." It was the first time that he'd ever said that to me.

"I can't say I blame you," I replied. "I'm lovable." I should have told him that I loved him too, but I had said it too many times before to too many people and it had always been a lie. I was strangely scared to say it now because this time, for the first time, it actually felt like it might almost be the truth.

Chapter 8

So after all that, the invitation to Marjorie's Burns' Night party seemed to signal a welcome rapprochement, as it would be the first occasion on which I had seen Gideon's parents since Christmas Day. The party was already in full swing when we arrived, if the term 'full swing' can be applied to a group of people standing around in an uncomfortably warm room making small talk. There were four other couples, excluding our hosts, making us twelve in all. I am not sure if there is a recognised scale, like the Beaufort or Richter, for social gatherings but to my mind this constituted less a party and more a large dinner, but perhaps they view things differently in Sheen.

Malcolm greeted us at the front door as if nothing untoward had occurred over Christmas, and as if a kilt (for that was what he was wearing) were his normal party attire. Gideon and I were, it turned out, the only people not dressed in some outlandish tartan rigout that night. All the women had some form of tartan about their person ranging from a little piece worn as a cravat to a skirt entirely comprised of the stuff. The men were all wearing tartan ties, a couple were wearing tartan trousers, and one had gone so far as to add a tartan waistcoat to his ensemble but none, wisely in my opinion, had followed Malcolm's sartorial lead. There was, as yet, no sign of Marjorie.

"And Melissa has just achieved grade eight at piano," a large woman, whose name I hadn't caught, was telling me about her many, highly talented grandchildren. Why I should be interested in the aptitude at the piano of a child I would never meet was beyond me, but the woman whose granddaughter Melissa was seemed to believe that Melissa's accomplishments deserved as wide an audience as possible and right now I was that audience. Clearly labouring under the misapprehension that I knew all about her family, Melissa's grandmother went on to share with me the fact that Hugo could now walk almost completely unaided. It was only after I had expressed the socially appropriate level of delight, adding "Isn't it hilarious to see them tottering around at that age?" that I discovered Hugo was her ninety eight year old father and currently recovering from a knee operation, not another grandchild. The only way out of this conversational quagmire was to exclaim that I simply had to try the delicious looking canapés, plates of which were balanced precariously on side tables around the room. They were surprisingly good and so had probably come from the same place as Christmas dinner. I had just picked up my fourth, or possibly fifth, when my hand was slapped quite hard. So hard, in fact, that I dropped the tiny roast beef and horseradish topped Yorkshire pudding that I had been about to stuff in my mouth, which was a shame as it looked very tasty.

"Don't touch the canapés!" said Marjorie, who was the slapper (for want of a better word). She had taken the tartan theme much further than any of her guests and was dressed in the stuff from head to toe (literally, she was wearing a Tam o'Shanter and had tartan bows on her shoes). "It might," she exclaimed "have oats in it and Eve doesn't eat oats." She broadcast this last piece of information to the entire room just in case, I suppose, anyone should be tempted to force feed me oats. "Everyone, carry on, please. Malcolm, drinks," she barked and then, mission accomplished, disappeared back into the kitchen where she was presumably putting the finishing touches to the Burns' Night supper. Piercing the film, removing the lid, that sort of thing.

A few minutes later she reappeared to call the assembled throng into the dining room where place names indicated where each of us should sit. My heart sank when I saw that Melissa's grandmother was seated directly opposite me, as it meant that I would undoubtedly be hearing about another of her grandchildren, or possibly her most recent holiday. She had grabbed me by the elbow as we walked across the hall and told me, sotto voce, that she simply had to tell me about Devon, so it could have been either.

All conversation was, however, rendered impossible for a few minutes almost as soon as we were seated. That Marjorie made claim to Scottish heritage (royal Scottish heritage no less) had not been unknown to me. That she would make Malcolm carry a haggis aloft into the dining room accompanied by a recording of what I supposed were bagpipes but which sounded more like a pair of foxes mating in an echo chamber did take me somewhat by surprise. It took some time for me to recover the power of speech, although Melissa's grandmother was made of sterner stuff and filled my silence with a very detailed description of her second home, a charming little cottage on the north Devon coast.

Oats being the mainstay of any Burns' Night dinner, Marjorie had, in an act of thoughtfulness I had not been expecting, prepared a small crumble topped meat pie for me.

"I made it myself," she said, as she plopped it in front of me. I wasn't sure how to take this. Was it a shared joke or a snide remark intended to shame me? Either way, the pie was surprisingly tasty. For pudding everyone else had cranachan, which is basically just raspberries and cream to which oats have been unaccountably added. Marjorie did, however, give me a bowl of raspberries and cream sans oats, which was also very thoughtful. Perhaps she was feeling bad about making such a fuss over Dominic's behaviour at Christmas and was trying to make it up to me. Whatever the reason I went home feeling as if I was back on track with my soon to be in-laws, especially Malcolm who despite (or perhaps because of) his ridiculous rig-out had been quite the life and soul of the evening. I had initially taken him for a very dour chap, which he generally was in Marjorie's company, but as soon as the social circle expanded he became quite a different man altogether.

The next morning my kind feelings were, however, sorely tested when I awoke to find a chemistry lab had been installed in my stomach during the night. It bubbled away, causing me to belch noxious gases through every possible orifice and generally feel terrifically unwell. I knew exactly what the symptoms meant. How, I wondered, had any oats sneaked through my usually impenetrable anti oat barrier? Was it possible that Marjorie had deliberately slipped oats into my food? Surely not. I mean, why would she want to do such a thing?

Chapter 9

Whether or not Marjorie had deliberately fed me oats, the events of the next few days conspired to push any thoughts of her right out of my head. I had heard nothing more from Dominic about the court case he was supposedly bringing against Sophie. I had therefore assumed that, like so many things Dominic has absolutely committed to do, it had come to nothing. Turns out I assumed wrong. I suppose I should have realised that something was up when I got a call from Sophie asking me to spend the day with her and Pixie. While this doesn't, on the face of it, sound very suspicious Sophie (like Dominic) generally only calls me when she wants something.

"So I was wondering if you would be, you know, a witness." Sophie, Pixie, and I had spent the entire morning shuffling at a snail's pace through the dinosaur exhibition at the Natural History Museum (not because we simply couldn't get enough of the dinosaurs but because seemingly millions of other adults and children were also doing the same and so progress was very slow). We had, eventually, escaped and made our way to Hyde Park and were now sitting on a bench by the Serpentine, wrapped up warmly against the cold and eating the picnic Sophie had brought with her. I had offered to bring the food but Sophie was in the midst of one of her many health regimens (they are really diet regimens as her acting work tends to rise and fall in inverse proportion to her weight, but for Pixie's sake she always talks about health rather than thinness). I have no idea what the basis of this latest diet was, but the food she proffered was unappetizing in the extreme. I'm quite sure I used up more calories eating it than it could possibly have provided. It really wasn't what one needed on a cold day.

"Be a witness to what?" I asked. I was pretty sure I knew what Sophie meant but I wanted her spell it out. I had learnt to take nothing for granted when Sophie, Pixie, and Dominic were involved.

"Why don't you go and feed the ducks sweetheart?" Sophie directed this last comment at Pixie who, while she clearly couldn't have been less interested, was nonetheless party to our conversation being only a few inches away from her mother.

"Do I have to? Ducks are boring." Pixie was kicking her heels against the legs of the bench and staring listlessly into the middle distance.

"I'm sure they feel very much the same way about you," I said, "but if you take them this," I handed her the plastic box containing the remainder of my lunch (which looked far more suitable for ducks than humans anyway), "I'm sure they'll perk up. But," I added, "don't get drawn in if they start arguing about who gets the biggest portion or you'll never hear the end of it."

"Ducks don't argue," Pixie responded, "they can't even talk!"

"Oh, they do," I said, very earnestly. "And they hold grudges. Look it up if you don't believe me. Of all the aquatic birds native to these islands, the duck, and more specifically the mallard, which is what those ducks over there are," I pointed to some ducks that may have been mallards, "is the bird most likely to hold a grudge for a minimum of one mating season, but often for much longer. Swans are pretty bad, that's why they break people's arms so often, but mallards are the worst."

"Really?" Pixie looked at me in utter wonderment.

"Yes, really," I confirmed before watching as she headed off, rather warily, towards the water.

"A character witness." Sophie wasn't as easily distracted as her daughter unfortunately. "To say I'm a good mother to Pixie. That I would only ever put her interests first."

"I don't really want to ..." I began, but Sophie interrupted before I could finish.

"Dominic can't be allowed to get away with it, he just can't!" She was clearly close to tears.

"Get away with what?" I asked.

"Joint custody, he wants joint custody of Pixie. He says she should live with him one week and with me the next. And he wants her for the whole of each school holiday! The whole of every holiday! That can't be right, can it?" Sophie looked at me imploringly. I had to hand it to her, she did implore very well and for a moment I almost weakened.

"Of course it's not..." I didn't want to say anything that might be used against me later so chose my words carefully, "likely to happen." I concluded weakly.

Dominic no more wanted joint custody of Pixie than I did. He just wanted to get back at Sophie for banning overnight stays, but I couldn't see how his ploy could possibly succeed, so equally I couldn't see why I should get involved. "The thing is Sophie, my relationship with Dominic isn't great at the moment," it's never great so I was on safe ground, "if I were to get involved in this ... well, it would only make things much worse than they already are. And I really don't think you have anything to worry about. He won't go through with it, and even if he does he won't win."

"But how can I not worry? It's not about me, it's about Pixie and her safety." Sophie grabbed both of my hands in hers and looked at me even more imploringly. She really knows how to implore, but I am made of pretty stern stuff.

"Do you actually think Pixie's not safe with him?" I asked. I knew he could be thoughtless but I had never thought Dominic was a danger to Pixie.

"You don't know what he can be like with her." Sophie said, still clutching my hands.

"Tell me then. What can he be like?" I asked, gently removing my hands from her grasp. I always find it awkward when someone impulsively grabs a bit of me as I'm never sure how much time I should let pass before I can retrieve my body part.

"Pixie told me that he used to leave her in the bathroom on her own while she was having a bath." Sophie looked at me, her eyes like saucers.

"She is getting to that age though, isn't she?" I replied. "She might well not want her father, or anyone for that matter, in the room with her."

"It was nearly four years ago! She was five, Eve, five! She could have drowned!" Sophie was clearly very exercised by this incident, although she had never mentioned it before. "My solicitor says that alone could be enough to cut off Dom's access."

"Then you don't need me, do you? I mean you've got enough on him already. What use would it be if…." Again Sophie cut me off, but this time it was to let out an almost inhuman wail. I had never heard anyone make a noise quite like it before. It sounded like something from a wildlife documentary. Painful though the sound was to hear I couldn't help but feel that Sophie was overreacting somewhat. It was, after all, quite some time since Pixie had been left unattended in a bath and no harm had come to her. Sophie, however, was still wailing, and had now leapt up from the bench and begun waving her arms around wildly. It was as I was wondering how she ever got any work (she really was hamming it up terribly) that I realised that she was pointing to something behind me. Turning around I could see nothing that could possibly cause such alarm. Then I realised that I couldn't see Pixie either, but that there was something thrashing around in the water a few feet from the shore.

Before I could think how ironic it was that we had only just been talking about the possibility of Pixie drowning, Sophie had shot off towards where her daughter presumably was (I couldn't see any part of Pixie above the water) and was on the verge of throwing herself into the Serpentine. I don't think of myself as naturally heroic but I am pragmatic and I know, from visits we have made to the pool with Pixie, that Sophie is a very poor swimmer. I, on the other hand, am an extremely strong and proficient swimmer. I therefore ran after Sophie and grabbed her arm before she did something stupid.

"Leave this to me Sophie," I bellowed, stripping off my outer layer of clothes and my shoes with extraordinary speed. I did a quick assessment of where beneath the surface I thought Pixie was likely to be and waded in. The water was every bit as cold as I had feared it would be and my body attempted to defy my will and stop me going any deeper than up to my knees. But I knew Pixie was under there somewhere, and with Sophie's animal howl still ringing in my ears I felt I had no choice but to disappear beneath the surface myself. As soon as my head was under the water I became disoriented. I couldn't see a thing and all I could hear was the sound of the water rushing passed my ears. Nonetheless I waved my arms around in all directions hoping one of them would make contact with my niece. After what seemed an eternity I had to come up for air. I gulped a huge amount of the stuff into my lungs and headed down again. This time, miraculously, I felt a human seeming bundle below me. Using all my strength and determination I grabbed the bundle and pulled it to the surface. God Pixie was heavy. While she isn't the slightest of children I really hadn't expected her to weigh this much. It must be her sodden clothes I thought, that made her so difficult to manoeuvre. Luckily the Serpentine is quite shallow, at the edges at least, and I was, with a superhuman effort, able to heave the bundle to the surface and drag it to the water's edge, where I threw it onto the path in front of Sophie and, as it turned out, Pixie.

"You really shouldn't have done that madam," the paramedic said, as he handed me a cup of hot, sweet tea a few minutes later. Normally I might have been affronted to be referred to as 'madam', which is a word I associate with old ladies. Maybe when I'm ninety I'll be happier about it. Right now though, my teeth were chattering so hard I couldn't say anything, let alone 'please don't call me madam'.

"The thing is madam," give up with the madam already, "the thing is, we put more people in body bags that have gone in after someone, or something, usually a dog, than drown in the first place." While I didn't feel as if I could make any facial expressions, my face being so cold, I must have looked quizzical because the paramedic continued. "The person, or dog, that goes in first usually comes out of their own accord, you see. They're not looking for anyone else so as soon as they surface they make for safety. Now your heroic types, like you madam, you keep bobbing up and down, going back to look again until you're exhausted. And then you get too cold, or swallow too much water and then you die. Lucky you found that sandbag really, or it wouldn't be tea I'd be giving you."

Sophie had not, it transpired, seen her daughter drowning. With thoughts of Pixie's watery demise filling her head she had, instead, misinterpreted the sight of a black dog (Pixie has dark hair) thrashing around in search of a stick, for her daughter. For my part, and following Sophie's lead, I had not taken the time to reflect on the fact that Pixie had actually headed in the opposite direction. It had also not occurred to me that Sophie wouldn't be able to tell the difference between a dog and her own child. The upshot was that I had, according to the paramedic, risked my own life to drag a sandbag from the Serpentine. Brilliant, bloody brilliant.

"Brilliant, bloody brilliant."

"Well thank you Dominic, I was only doing what came naturally, I mean I didn't really even stop to think." I was unused to receiving so much praise for my bravery, never having done anything particularly brave before, but I was rather enjoying it. Gideon had been extraordinarily impressed and said that he was exceedingly proud of me, which was nice. Marjorie also seemed to think I deserved especial treatment. She and Malcolm had treated Gideon and me to a meal at a Michelin starred restaurant. We did go at lunchtime and have to choose from the set menu, but it was a generous thought.

Sophie could hardly speak for gratitude, even though it was only some sand and a bag that had benefitted from my heroics. "But just think," she kept saying, "what if it had been Pixie?"

"I'm just glad," I would reply, "that it wasn't." At this point I would cast my eyes down and look wistful. Little did I know that my brother, far from calling to heap yet more praise on my already swollen head, was about to bring me back down to earth with a bump. As soon as he heard about what had happened he was on the phone, and as soon as I had hung up he was at the front door. Dominic can move very quickly when the mood takes him, and the mood had most definitely taken him, but it was not somewhere I wanted to follow.

"I can definitely use this," he announced, clearly delighted by recent events.

"Use it?" I enquired. "Use it for what?"

"To help my custody case." He sounded very glib considering what a momentous and life changing (and not just for himself) path he was heading down. We were seated at the kitchen table, two cups of coffee (one each) and a plate of homemade muffins, one of which Dominic was scoffing as we talked, between us. I had been practising my baking of late and it was coming on quite well. I didn't eat very much of what I baked, not being a cake fan, but Gideon was lapping it up (not literally, my efforts were better than that).

"Oh come on," I said, "surely you can't really want Pixie every other week. You can barely manage a weekend without calling me in to take her off your hands. Imagine, all those school holidays, you'd hate it."

"That is completely untrue!" It was, in actual fact, completely true. "And I have to, don't you see?" All I could see was that Dominic was being a monumental arse.

"Why? Why do you 'have to'?" I asked, exasperated, and not for the first time, with my brother's behaviour. "As far as I can see no one is making you do this." The prospect of Sophie having to give Pixie up to Dominic's care for so much of the time was too awful to contemplate. Poor kid, he'd have her believing the moon landings were faked before you knew it.

"Sophie is making me do it," Dominic said morosely before taking another huge bite of muffin.

"How the hell do you figure that out?" I replied.

"If I don't stop her Sophie will take Pixie to Canada. How would you like that?" Dominic pointed his muffin at me, presumably for emphasis, before shoving all that remained of it into his mouth.

"I wouldn't," I agreed, "but that would be up to Sophie."

"So you think she's going to do it too!" he exclaimed, his mouth still full.

"No I don't." I replied. "She's never even hinted that she wants to do any such thing."

"Don't you see? That just proves that she does. If she wasn't then she wouldn't be so secretive about her plans." Dominic threw himself forward, his arms thumping on the table between us, causing some of my coffee to leap free of its cup.

"So, the fact that Sophie has never said she wants to take Pixie to Canada is proof that she intends to take Pixie to Canada?" I tried, in vain, to point out the craziness of Dominic's reasoning. This was the same logic, after all, that had led him to some of his most heartfelt beliefs. Being told that something is untrue is, for Dominic, virtually proof positive that it is true.

"See, it makes perfect sense," Dominic announced. Only to a conspiracy theorist who believes that the Queen (the

Queen!) is an alien lizard intent on world domination. "But I'm going to make sure she doesn't," he continued. "And you're going to help me."

"I am not!" I replied.

"Yes you are. I'm going to prove Sophie's an unfit mother who watched as her daughter fell into the Thames. If she thinks that leaving a perfectly capable child in a bath is grounds to stop me seeing my own daughter, let's see what she has to say when I can prove she let my daughter nearly drown."

"Firstly it was the Serpentine and secondly Pixie didn't fall into it. And thirdly Sophie would have died herself to save Pixie." I counted the reasons off on my fingers, but even this didn't convince Dominic.

"Yeah right, and what good would that have done?" he replied fiercely. "The fact Pixie's not dead is no thanks to Sophie. If you, my sister, hadn't been there god knows what might have happened."

"Nothing would have happened, except there'd be one more sandbag in the Serpentine." I tried to tether Dominic to reality, but he wasn't listening.

"It's like this," said Dominic decisively, "either you help me, or that's it."

"That's what?" I asked. I knew perfectly well what he meant as we had played out this scenario any number of times before.

"That'll be it," he replied

"Say it Dominic. You'll never speak to me again, is that it?" On one occasion Dominic stopped speaking to me for several months because I wouldn't agree that it was at least possible that the Moon was an inter-dimensional portal controlled by aliens. Another time we had had a huge argument about whether or not Pixie should have the MMR jab (as it happened she'd already had it). Our most recent falling out had been about money. I had refused to lend Dominic a thousand pounds (which I didn't have anyway) so that he could invest in a new and revolutionary energy source that was going to make everything else obsolete. So, dramatic though his threat might sound it didn't impress me much. And, anyway, I wasn't about to back down in the face of his emotional blackmail. If he seriously thought I would help him to take Pixie from Sophie for so much of the time because it served his ego and paranoia to do so he had another think coming.

"Go on then Dominic," I said, "off you go. I'm not about to help you to do something so despicable and downright spiteful just because..." And that was it. He leapt up from the chair in which he had been slouching (he doesn't ever sit, only slouch) and stopping only to grab another muffin, he left.

"You'll be sorry," he yelled as he headed out the door. "You have no idea, no idea at all, what you've just done!" Maybe I hadn't, but I was sure I could live with the consequences, whatever they might be.

Chapter 10

"That would be the best thing ever!" I replied enthusiastically to Gideon's suggestion. We had been discussing our forthcoming nuptials one morning over breakfast and getting nowhere. I was not very keen on any of the ideas put forward by Gideon. It all seemed so unnecessarily complicated and fraught with possible problems, not to mention the expense. As soon as you append the word 'wedding' to anything the price goes up – wedding dress, wedding reception, wedding cake, wedding favours (I don't even know what these are). I also have a horror of being the centre of attention, which is where you tend to be if you're the bride. I know some women begin planning their weddings at the age of four, but spending an entire day flouncing around in a big dress being gawped at was never one of my girlhood dreams. And even if it had been my dream I had already done it once already (not that I had mentioned this to Gideon, obviously). We had been going over our options for some time and whichever way we looked at it, it seemed impossible to have a small, inexpensive wedding that suited both of us. Until, that is, Gideon came up with the idea of, for want of a better word, eloping.

"We could go to Gretna Green, or Vegas!" I suggested excitedly. "We could be married by Elvis in Vegas!" I'm not a particular fan of Elvis but fired up with enthusiasm for the idea I was, perhaps, getting a little carried away.

"That isn't exactly what I was thinking," Gideon replied, "and going to Vegas wouldn't help keep the costs down. What we could do is go to the local register office, get a couple of strangers to be witnesses, or at least a couple of people we know who will be discreet and not tell anyone ..."

"I could ask Claire," I interrupted, "she is very discreet. She is, in fact, the queen, no, the empress of discreetness."

"Discretion," said Gideon.

"What?" I queried.

"The word is discretion, not discreetness."

"Are you sure? I've always said discreetness." Gideon often corrects what he perceives to be my linguistic errors and I am always eager to learn, so I don't, as one might imagine, find it intensely irritating and want to hit him every time he does it. Or at least that is the impression I give. I am the very soul of discretion, or discreetness, which, personally, I prefer.

"Then you've always been wrong," he said. "And I'm not sure we need imperial levels of discretion, but Claire would be good, and Bob." Bob is an old school friend of Gideon's who, and I have to be honest here, I'm not very keen on. I find him a bit creepy.

"Bob, really?" I asked. I was trying to sound neutral but clearly I wasn't successful.

"He's my friend," said Gideon, "and he's every bit as discreet as Claire, more if anything."

"More? Are you mad? No one is more discreet than Claire, it's not possible." I wasn't about to have Claire out-discreeted by Bob. "The only reason Bob is discreet is that he has no one to tell anything to."

"So we're agreed then?" Gideon continued. "A purely functional wedding, with nothing but a marriage to show for the day."

It was hardly the most romantic of weddings, but it suited me so perfectly that (having decided not to pursue the argument about whose friend was most discreet) I could only nod my head vigorously in agreement. For one thing I wouldn't have to worry about the fact that my side of the room would look a little sparse, guestwise. After his behaviour at Christmas I certainly didn't want Dominic at any wedding of mine, even if he had been speaking to me, and although I do have some very good friends they tend to exist in separate compartments, which is where I would rather they stayed. When I had agreed to marry Gideon the wedding itself was the one element that troubled me. Now, in one fell swoop, all my wedding related concerns were at an end.

"Won't your mother mind though?" I asked. "Surely she'll want to be at your wedding?"

"Don't you worry about that. I'll make sure everything is all right with Mum." Gideon assured me.

"Will you tell her when we're getting married? If it's a secret from everyone then..."

"She knows we're getting married..."he began.

"I know that," I reminded him. "I was there when you told her."

Gideon and I had told his parents about our forthcoming marriage at the Burns' Night party, after everyone else had left. Marjorie's response had been to say that she had been saying only that evening to Brenda (whoever she was) that she thought (hoped?) Gideon would never marry. I wasn't really sure how to take that.

"But will you tell her that we are getting married and she's not invited?" I continued.

"I said I'll make sure everything is all right with Mum, and I will. You don't need to worry about it. She'll be amazing about it whatever we do." Gideon really did overuse the word 'amazing' in relation to his mother. Nothing I had seen of Marjorie made me feel that 'amazing' could be applied to her in a positive way. She clearly cut a very different figure in Gideon's mind than she did in mine, but I had no idea why, other than being his mother, he felt that way he did.

"Just think," I said as I sat in bed moisturising my elbows (I'm not normally a great one for such things, but this was a special occasion), "this time tomorrow we'll be married."

"I know, good isn't it? I'm glad you're moisturising your elbows," Gideon continued, "I wouldn't want to marry a woman with dry elbows."

"Who would, really, if they had the choice?" I concurred.

It's astonishing how quickly and easily a wedding can come together once you drop all the usual nonsense. Here we were, just two weeks after deciding on a no fuss wedding, and the whole thing was pretty much done and dusted. We had only had one disagreement during the whole process, which was about where we should eat afterwards (I don't know why, but we both felt that a wedding should be followed by food, even an unconventional one like ours). Gideon wanted to go to Nando's (because he loves peri peri chicken) while I favoured fish and chips (because I don't) in the comfort of our own home. I had won mainly because Nando's doesn't serve champagne, which was non-negotiable for both of us.

It was as I was moisturising my elbows and reflecting on how very happy I was that my reverie was interrupted by the phone. It was after ten, a time at which no one should call anyone unless they are bringing news of a life or death nature, and the only time I find it impossible to ignore an incoming call.

"Go and answer it," I said, giving Gideon a nudge.

"I'm not getting out of bed to answer the phone at this time of night," he replied, pulling a pillow over his head to block out the sound.

"It might be an emergency." I said.

"It won't be, go to sleep." He clearly wasn't about to get out of bed but at that moment, as if on cue, the phone ceased ringing.

"Told you." Gideon mumbled. Almost as soon as it had ceased to ring however, it began again.

"Oh for god's sake," muttered Gideon as he reluctantly headed down the hall to answer it. A few moments later he was back in the bedroom, the handset clamped to his ear. He didn't say anything beyond a few uninformative 'hmms' and the odd 'oh dear' for the next few minutes. Eventually, however, my suspicions as to the identity of the caller were confirmed. "I'll come over first thing Mum," he said, "No, I'm not coming now... No, I can't... No it's nothing to do with Eve, I just don't see how I could make any difference right now... you could sleep in another room... he could sleep in another room. I'll see you in the morning. Night." He clicked the off button on the phone and then looked to check it had really disconnected.

"What's happened?" I asked

"She thinks Dad's having an affair," he replied wearily.

"What!" I squealed. I know lots of men have affairs, but I really wouldn't have put Malcolm down as one of them, he didn't seem like the type.

"She says," Gideon explained, "that she was uploading some pictures from her digital camera and stumbled across some photos on his computer of some woman in, as she put it, intimate poses." The mind boggled.

"But she always says she hates computers." I pointed out.

"She may hate them, but that doesn't mean she can't use one." Gideon said.

"True, but I had always got the impression she couldn't use one." I had got this impression from hearing Marjorie berating Malcolm for the hours he spent researching his family's ancestry on "that bloody computer". She had gone on to say that she had no idea how to use a computer and no intention of finding out, but perhaps I had misunderstood her meaning.

"So she knows how to use a computer and you thought she didn't, and your point is?" Gideon sounded quite exasperated, although whether with me or with his mother I was unsure. My point, I wanted to say, is that there is more to your mother than meets the eye. I was probably being ridiculous, but for some reason I found Marjorie's sudden computer literacy worrying.

"I don't have a point, it was just an observation." I said. "So she wants you to go over. Right now?"

"Yes." Gideon climbed back into bed.

"And you won't go now? You want to leave it until tomorrow?" I clarified.

"Yes," he confirmed.

"But we're getting married tomorrow."

"I do know that Eve," Gideon said rather impatiently. "I'll be done in plenty of time."

"At eleven. In the morning." I wanted to make sure he was in no doubt about the time.

"It'll have blown over by then."

"Blown over?" I prompted.

"Mum and Dad have these sort of bust ups occasionally."

"Over extra marital affairs?" I queried.

"Well, this is a new one, but about something or other. It always blows over. This will too." Gideon yawned theatrically. "I'm going to sleep, and I suggest you do the same."

"I'll go with you." I said. I didn't want Gideon disappearing on the morning of our wedding not to return for hours on end. I recalled the events of my birthday. Had Gideon told Marjorie when we were getting married? I could hardly ask without sounding suspicious. "Does your mother know we're getting married tomorrow?" I asked. Turns out I couldn't help myself.

"What's that got to do with anything?" he snapped. "Now go to sleep."

"I was just asking," I replied huffily. "Night."

So, Marjorie had not only ruined my birthday and caused (with some help from my brother admittedly) Gideon and I to have a huge row at Christmas, she had now disrupted the happy ambience of my pre wedding night. What was it with that bloody woman?

The next morning found the four of us (me, Marjorie, Gideon, and the man of the moment, Malcolm) in one of Marjorie's many guest bedrooms. A shrine to the nineteen eighties (the room was a riot of pink and white stripes and florals), the setting was rather incongruous given the reason for us being there. But having not been allowed (by Marjorie) to convert any of the guestrooms into a study, it was here that Malcolm's computer lived.

As we all stared at the machine, Marjorie was trying, and conspicuously failing, to hold back great sobs of distress. It was a rather theatrical performance, but Gideon seemed to be very impressed by it.

"How could you do this to me?" she gasped through her sobs, "How could you...?" She stopped, seemingly lost for words, so great was her distress. "What have I done to deserve this?" Marjorie managed to say before another sob shuddered through her body. It was at this point that she grasped my arm and buried her head against my shoulder. With her other arm she groped for Gideon. As she could not see him her arm waved around wildly until it made contact with his sleeve. Her fingers closed over the fabric and she pulled him towards her.

"I just thank God that I have my family around me at this difficult time." She raised her head from my shoulder to make this melodramatic statement. "And you, you Malcolm." She looked accusingly at Malcolm, who had been standing impassively behind us. "How could you risk your family for this... this hussy?"

This seemed an unpleasant way to describe the middle aged woman in the pictures we had been looking at, which comprised some pretty standard issue holiday snaps as far as I could see. They absolutely didn't fall under the heading of 'intimate poses' as described by Marjorie in her phone call of the night before. From the evidence presented so far I couldn't see quite why Marjorie thought that this woman and Malcolm were having an affair. It turned out, however, that the woman (who I learned was called Janet Temple) had been Malcolm's secretary many years before. Marjorie had always disliked her and believed that she was intent on stealing Malcolm away from his family. That Janet had been married herself (as I later learnt from Gideon) had done nothing to dissuade Marjorie from the notion that Janet was a potential home wrecker.

Having exhausted herself with theatrical weeping Marjorie managed, with much help from Gideon, to make it downstairs. Malcolm followed behind silently. Having settled Marjorie at the kitchen table Gideon offered to make some coffee. "I'll do it," I said, leaping up and heading for a cupboard in which I was sure I had once caught a glimpse of a cafetiere. "Where do you keep the mugs?"

Having supplied everyone with a mug of piping hot, very strong coffee I sat down. I had no idea what would happen next. I only hoped whatever it was would happen quickly. It was only half past eight so Gideon and I had plenty of time to get to the Register Office, which was only fifteen minutes' drive away, by eleven. As long as we got away within the next couple of hours we could still be Mr and Mrs Rowe by lunchtime.

"I feel utterly betrayed." Marjorie wailed, clutching one of Gideon's hands with both of hers. "I can't believe you could treat me in such a way. I want a divorce." I had not been expecting that.

"If that's what you want I will call my solicitor." Malcolm responded, equally unexpectedly. "You can stay in this house of course. I will leave as soon as possible." Marjorie was clearly unprepared for Malcolm's acquiescence. She had, I suspect, been expecting him to beg for forgiveness. Having failed to get the required response she tried again.

"If we divorce you will never see your children again!" she announced dramatically. Gideon and I shared a look of disbelief and I had to stifle a laugh.

"I'm sorry you feel that way." Malcolm rose from his seat in a fairly dignified fashion, unmoved by Marjorie's empty threat. "I will begin proceedings right now, if you don't mind." I was disappointed to see that he hadn't even tried my coffee as I had been hoping that it might wean him away from his awful machine. Marjorie, however, was not about to take this lying down and launched a counter attack.

"Is that all our marriage means to you?" Marjorie narrowed her eyes as she hissed the words through gritted teeth. "You're prepared to throw forty years away, just like that. How could you Malcolm?"

"It was you, Marjorie, that asked me for a divorce, not I that initiated this." Malcolm replied.

"No, but it was you that initiated an affair into this house." Even I knew that this wasn't an appropriate use of the word initiate, but I don't suppose Marjorie cared as she proceeded to fling insults, threats, and insinuations at Malcolm. He was a bad father, he was incapable of displaying emotion, he had intimacy issues arising from having been evacuated as a child. Marjorie, calling on years of watching daytime TV and reading women's magazines, chose to diagnose him with attachment disorder (although I'm sure she had no idea what this meant, I certainly didn't), and claimed that he confused sex with affection (which was much more information than I wished to know about the inner workings of their marriage). Malcolm had, she claimed, offered her no support with the children, he didn't include her in his hobbies and activities, and treated her as little better than a cook and housekeeper. At one point she even thrust her diamond ring in his face.

"I even had to buy my own ring," she screeched. "You," she went on, all the while stroking the huge rock lovingly, "didn't even think I was worth a decent diamond. I had to use my own money to get myself a ring I wasn't ashamed of." And all the while Malcolm simply stood stock still, not a flicker of emotion on his face.

There was much more of this kind of stuff, but I will stop there, except to say that what she seemed most put out by was his willingness to be divorced by her. His protestations that he was just trying to give her what she wanted (one of the few things he did say while she ranged far and wide over his faults) had no effect. At one point I actually feared she was going to box his ears.

While I desperately wanted this whole thing wrapped up as quickly as possible, it was an enthralling spectacle. I looked at the clock from time to time and found that it was moving at a preternaturally fast rate. In no time at all it was ten o'clock and I began to get a bit panicky. I tried to catch Gideon's eye but he was focussed on mediating, to no avail, between his parents. Eventually, at around ten thirty, Malcolm announced that, as nothing was being resolved, he was going out to get some fresh air. This, I thought, was our opportunity to get away.

"Perhaps," I said, "this would be a good time for us to make a move as well?" I looked questioningly at Gideon.

"Yes," he said, "perhaps we should go. Give you two some space."

"Noooo!" Marjorie wailed. "You can't leave me, not now!" Impassioned though this request was, I noticed that Marjorie's eyes, like mine a few moments before, were fixed on the kitchen clock. I gave Gideon a hard stare. He shrugged hopelessly in response. We had no option but to stay.

"So she didn't know that you were getting married that day?" Claire and I were having lunch at a French restaurant in Sloane Square. I was paying as an apology for making her wait for over an hour and a half at the Register Office with Bob. I hadn't been able to call her as I'd left my phone at home that day. Bob was also uncontactable as he doesn't have a phone (he thinks they give you cancer). It wouldn't have been so bad if Claire could have just read the book she'd brought with her, but Bob was determined to engage her in conversation. He doesn't have a very wide range of interests but he does know a lot about the few things in which he is interested. An hour and a half on the propagation of orchids would be long enough for even the most committed orchid lover and was about eighty five minutes too long for Claire, so an expensive lunch was the least I could do.

"Not according to Gideon." I replied through a mouthful of the cheapest salad on the menu.

"And you asked him directly?" Claire fixed me with a penetrating look.

"Not exactly. I sort of talked around the issue. He thinks his mother is, and I quote, 'an amazing woman' so it's a bit difficult to come out and accuse her of engineering the whole thing."

"And what exactly makes you think that she engineered it?" Claire asked while cracking a lobster claw with evident relish.

"The first thing" I said, holding up an index finger, "is that at twelve, on the dot, Marjorie stopped crying. She had suddenly remembered that she had a lunch date she didn't want to miss. A lunch date!" I added for emphasis. "The second," I held up a second finger, "is that she then said that she shouldn't have involved us, and that she and Malcolm would sort it out between themselves. And the third is that the whole thing has been forgotten, and she and Malcolm are completely back to normal." I waved my three fingers at Claire, who didn't immediately respond. She was too busy dipping some lobster meat into melted butter before popping the whole delicious buttery mess into her mouth.

"This is very good," she said once she could speak, "you have no idea! And this woman, she was Malcolm's secretary?"

"Yes, but years ago." I explained. "He had just come across her on Facebook. There was no more to it than that."

"So you really don't know if Marjorie knew about your wedding and concocted the whole thing or if it was just an awful coincidence?" Claire asked.

"No I don't. But after what happened on my birthday..."

"But she has been perfectly pleasant to you, hasn't she?" Claire interrupted.

"Well, yes, I suppose so, but she's just not a very easy person to be around, at least I don't think so, and she's certainly not amazing." I stabbed at the last of my salad and looked longingly at Claire's lobster. "And she might have slipped oats into my food on Burns' Night." I muttered, knowing this wouldn't impress Claire one little bit, and I was right.

"Yes," said Claire, "she might have. Or then again, she might not. There must have been oats everywhere, it was Burns' Night for heaven's sake. You," she pointed her fork at me, "have a rather idealised view of what mothers should be like. You lost your mother when you were very young and so she never had the chance to disappoint you."

"Why do you suppose she would have disappointed me?" I replied, somewhat affronted.

"Parents invariably disappoint their children," Claire went on, "if they live long enough. How can anyone hope to live up to the ideal of perfection that society builds around the notion of parenthood? And how can any woman hope to retain the unquestioning love of her children, especially once they reach puberty? I have teenaged children, believe me, I speak from bitter experience."

"So you think I'm suspicious of Marjorie because I have mother issues, not because she's trying to ruin my life?"

"Occam's razor," said Claire. "It means..."

"Yes, yes," I said impatiently. "I know all about Occam and his bloody razor. It's far more likely that there's something wrong with me than that Marjorie is trying to ruin my life. Thanks for that."

"I'm not saying there's anything wrong with you, only that you may be seeing Marjorie's behaviour through your own psychological filter. Gideon seems to think she's a perfectly satisfactory mother. Oh yes please." The last remark was directed to the waitress who had asked if we wanted to see the dessert menu. Claire was clearly determined to extract the maximum pleasure from having had to endure Bob's company for so long, and I can't say I blame her.

"Gideon thinks she's Mother Theresa and the Virgin Mary rolled into one." I said, having rejected dessert on the basis that there was nothing for less than a tenner.

"That does sound a little unrealistic, I must admit. Do you have any idea why Gideon is so enamoured of his mother?" Claire asked.

"None, I'm afraid, none at all." I replied.

"It is odd, I will grant you that. I mean it's not as if she is very good company, from what you say. I wonder if there is something in their shared history that might shed light on the attachment. Ooh," Claire said, eyeing the dessert menu, "it all looks so good!" she cooed before going on to order the most expensive pudding the place had to offer.

"Yes, I suppose it does," I replied, "I suppose it bloody well does."

Chapter 11

"I'm an actress." I said. I'm not, but I have worked as an extra. Sophie was an under housemaid in a couple of episodes of Downton Abbey and got me a gig as one of the villagers you used to see all the time walking briskly in the background as if on a mission of great importance. It was good money but it did get pretty boring so I popped my iPod in my pocket, stuck it on shuffle, and ran some earphones up inside my sleeve. Everything was going swimmingly until someone noticed me clearly indicating that if he liked it he should have put a ring on it. An investigation by the director revealed that I could also be seen walking like an Egyptian and singing and, more importantly, dancing in the rain in the background of some pretty serious drama. They had to reshoot a whole week's exterior shots on account of it, so that was the end of my career in showbusiness.

I was responding to an enquiry from, of all people, Marjorie's identical twin sister Meg. I was sitting in a cafe on the King's Road not far from where I had just paid an arm and leg for Claire's lobster lunch watching Meg tuck into her lunch, for which I was also paying. She had stopped, her fork halfway to her lips, to ask what I did for a living.

It had been as Claire and I were saying our goodbyes that I had seen a familiar figure coming out of the doors of Peter Jones.

"Got to go Claire. Great advice as ever. Bye." I said as I headed off in hot pursuit of the woman I was quite certain was the mysterious Meg. Having heard such differing accounts of her I was intrigued to find out for myself what Marjorie's doppelganger was like. Was she lovely, lively Aunt Meg, or a depressive recluse? Now was my chance to find out.

Not wishing to startle her unnecessarily, I followed Meg from a distance as she headed off briskly down the King's Road. It was a busy day and I had to keep my wits about me. Following people is much harder than one might think, a moment's inattention and one's target is gone. Fortunately I have some experience in this field, having worked for a private detective called (or so he claimed) Phillipe Merlot on and off for a number of years. Mostly it had been very boring stuff, but sometimes there was something juicier that involved following someone. It's not rocket science (although rocket science isn't actually that hard according to Claire, who used to be a nuclear physicist and rather looks down on rocket scientists, or 'one shot jockeys' she calls them) but you do have to be constantly vigilant while ensuring that your target doesn't become aware of your presence. Having kept my eyes firmly fixed on Meg for almost the entire length of the King's Road I decided the best way to approach her was to, quite literally, bump into her. Choosing my moment carefully, I waited until she seemed about to make a left turn and knocked her shoulder with my arm.

"Oh my goodness..." I began to say but got no further as Meg (it couldn't be anyone else so startling was her resemblance to Marjorie) spun around and landed me a pretty heavy punch on my jaw.

"Unhand me young woman," she shouted rather dramatically as I clutched my jaw. I was quite pleased to be addressed as young woman, especially after the paramedic who had made so free with the term 'madam', but I was less pleased to be punched on the jaw.

"I'm not handing you." I was unsure what the opposite of unhand was but I knew as soon as I said 'handing' that this wasn't it.

"I," Meg continued in the same dramatic tone, "have done nothing wrong and yet you, you," she repeated the word 'you' for emphasis while pointing at me accusingly with forefinger of the very hand that had just punched me, "decide to chase an old woman all the way along the King's Road. It's harassment. I could have you arrested." She had gone positively puce with indignation. People were beginning to stare and I could see a couple of them surreptitiously filming us on their phones. That was just what I needed, a video of me having a fight with Meg on the King's Road going viral.

"I don't think you've done anything wrong," I said. I had to raise my voice rather more than I would have liked, but Meg was in such a state of fury that I felt I could only get through to her by shouting. "I thought I recognised you, that's all. You look exactly like someone I know."

"So you're not a store detective?" Meg looked at me through narrowed eyes.

"No!" I exclaimed. "Why would you think I was store detective?"

"Because you said you were." Meg replied.

"I didn't," I replied. "I bumped into you and you socked me on the jaw." I rubbed my jaw at this point to reinforce that I was the injured party, but it really didn't hurt very much. Meg is a lot shorter than me and it may have been an exaggeration to say that she punched me on the jaw, it was more of a glancing blow.

"Who are you then?" Meg asked. "And why did you follow me?"

"I'm Eve and I thought you were ..."

"Thought I was who?" Meg interrupted me, her eyes narrowing again.

"Marjorie." I said, almost in a whisper, hoping to convey apprehension. If, as I suspected, all was not well between the sisters Meg was more likely to look kindly on me if she thought I didn't have a great relationship with Marjorie. "I thought you were Marjorie." I almost whispered while glancing down nervously. The acting establishment didn't know what it was throwing away when it blacklisted me.

"Oh, my dear, I'm not Marjorie!" Meg put a reassuring hand on my arm and let out a hoot of laughter.

"I know that now!" I exclaimed. "I was pretty sure of it the moment you hit me. You do look exactly like her though."

"We are twins so that's hardly surprising. I'm Meg," she said, extending her hand to me. "Nice to meet you Eve."

"And it's nice to meet you too." I shook Meg's hand vigorously. "I have heard so much about you."

"Who from?" Meg asked.

"From Helen," I said, "and from Gideon. I'm Gideon's girlfriend."

"How lovely, how very lovely. And how are they both?" Meg asked.

"They're well. Anyway," I said, "it's lovely to finally meet you but I should let you get on your way, goodbye."

"I'm not going anywhere in particular. I just popped out to do a little shopping." Meg explained. "Couldn't I least buy you a cup of tea?" I had been hoping she'd say that. "I feel I owe you something, having punched you."

"As long as I'm not interrupting you ..." I acquiesced, "that would be lovely."

"And I should like a scone." Meg said to the waitress in the tea shop we had found a little further down the King's Road. "Now," she continued. "I like lots of preserve on my scones, so you must bring at least three, no, four of those tiny little jars. Blackcurrant jelly, if at all possible, but definitely not raspberry jam, I can't stand the pips." Although it was after three Meg must have missed lunch as she was clearly very hungry. The table at which we were sitting was very small and I wasn't at all sure that it would hold all the food she had ordered which, in addition to the scone, included a slice of asparagus quiche, a bottle of orange juice ("I don't want any of that freshly squeezed stuff, it gives me terrible wind, and don't open the bottle, I'll see to that.") and a pot of tea. She had also asked that everything should come at once, hence my concern about the ability of the table to hold it all.

"This is very kind of you," she said, "I can't imagine how I managed to mislay my purse." Rather than being treated to tea by Meg as promised, it seemed that I was going to have to pay as, having rummaged through her bag, Meg had announced that her purse was missing. She seemed remarkably unperturbed by this, simply saying that she was sure it would turn up.

"So, you are my nephew's lady friend?" she said, her lunch order finally complete.

"Yes, yes I am." I confirmed.

"So you know my sister?" A flicker of disgust passed across Meg's face for the minutest of moments. According to Claire we give our true feelings away all the time through tiny micro expressions over which we have no control. Meg's micro expression told me that she really didn't like her sister at all.

"Yes, yes I do." I replied.

"And how is she?" Meg demanded to know.

"Well, she's..."

"Isn't she?" Meg pursed her lips in disdain. You didn't need to be an expert in micro expressions to read that one. "And Malcolm, how is Malcolm?" Meg's face lit up as she asked about Gideon's father. There was nothing in my acquaintance with Malcolm to indicate that he could cause anyone's face to light up, but there it was nonetheless. "Is he well?" Meg leaned in, clearly warming to her subject now that all talk of Marjorie was out of the way. "I do hope he's well," she added.

"He's..." I began.

"And Helen and Ian?" Meg's questions were coming so thick and fast I barely had time to answer one before she was on to the next. "Are they well? Are they happy?"

"He's Gideon now. Ian that is. He uses his full name." I explained.

"Yes, I'm sure he does." Nothing about Meg matched Marjorie's description to Helen. She didn't seem in the least gaga to me, and I didn't think depressive recluses went out to tea. "I don't blame him, you know," Meg continued. "He couldn't help it."

"Gideon? To blame? What for?" What was she talking about?

"I wasn't talking about Gideon!"

This was intriguing, but I wasn't destined to find out who Meg was talking about as she stopped her stream of questions to pop a forkful of quiche into her mouth. "I adore asparagus," she said, having finished the quiche in no time flat. "I would eat it all the time if I could afford to. Don't you love asparagus?" I had honestly never given asparagus much thought.

"Mmm, yes, it is delicious." I replied.

"Do you have any secrets?" Meg suddenly asked out of nowhere.

"I'm sorry?"

"Oh, ignore me. I'm just a silly old loon." She laughed as she rotated her right index finger next to her temple. I had been observing Meg quite closely as she tucked into her meal. She was a little thinner than Marjorie, although only very marginally, they were both a little overstuffed. Not that Marjorie had always been plump. "When I was young I had trouble keeping my weight up," she had once told me, "I had to eat and eat and eat just to maintain a normal weight. You can have no idea!" she had concluded while looking me up and down appraisingly.

Apart from this very slight discrepancy in their weights, the similarity between the two women really was remarkable. Their hair was styled in a similar manner, and they wore similar clothes, although it was clear that Meg's were rather more bargain basement than Marjorie's. Meg's mannerisms were also disconcertingly familiar, to the point where I had to keep reminding myself that it wasn't Marjorie sitting opposite me.

"When did you last see Marjorie?" I asked, as Meg piled butter and blackcurrant jelly onto her scone.

"Oh, sometime ago," she replied evasively.

"A long time ago?" I asked, wary of appearing pushy.

"Just a normal amount of time." This was proving a very unproductive meeting. "Well, this has been lovely, I must say," Meg suddenly announced, having eaten everything on the table, "but I really must go."

I don't know what I had expected from a meeting with Meg. I had hoped, I suppose, for a bit more than simply being out of pocket for a second lunch that I didn't eat in the same day. As it was, it seemed that meeting Meg was to be a dead end.

"Well, this has been lovely," Meg repeated, gathering up her things, and slipping a bowl containing little paper tubes of sugar into her bag in the process. And when I say bowl, I mean literally the bowl and all its contents. It jostled for space with the little jars of blackcurrant jelly she hadn't consumed and the orange juice she hadn't opened. "So if you'll just give me your phone number I will call you anon." Meg tapped the side of her nose as she spoke.

"I'm sorry?" I replied. "My number?"

"We have more to talk about, don't we? We are potential allies. So I must have your number." She stopped fussing with her bag to look me in the eye.

"Why don't I take your number?" I countered, glad that this wasn't a dead end, but also hoping to retain some control over the situation.

"Oh, I don't have a phone!" she exclaimed.

"You mean you don't have a mobile phone?" I queried.

"I mean I don't have a phone, any phone, they are so terribly expensive, don't you think?" Meg removed a pen from her bag and, grabbing a napkin from the table, thrust them both towards me. I dutifully wrote my number on the napkin and handed it back, wondering where this strange alliance might lead.

"Thank you," said Meg, putting it in her already bulging bag. "And now I really must be going." And with that she swept off dramatically. Rather too dramatically as it happened, as she managed to bump into a woman at another table causing her to spill her tea and knock a chair to the floor on her way out. I wasn't sure whether or not I would hear from her, or even if I really wanted to, but there was nothing more I could do, so having paid the bill, I headed off home myself.

Chapter 12

The weeks went past and winter gradually gave way to spring. I heard nothing from my brother or from Meg so I consigned them both to the very furthest reaches of my mind and simply got on with my life. Marjorie had also been put on something of a backburner, as she and Malcolm had gone on a very long, very expensive cruise to the Antarctic that lasted from the beginning of March right up until Easter.

Marjorie, so she told me, had a passion for penguins and had, for many years, harboured a longing to see them in their natural habitat. While it was unsurprising that I knew nothing of Marjorie's love for these flightless sea birds, that neither Malcolm nor Gideon had had the slightest inkling either was odder. The reason behind this never before mentioned mania did become a little clearer, however, when I discovered that the woman next door (Meryl Bloody Streep) had been on just such a cruise the year before and had rammed it down Marjorie's throat ever since.

"She seems to think she's the only one that can afford to cruise to the Antarctic, the stuck up madam," Marjorie had told me as we sat waiting for Malcolm's coffee machine to do its worst following another spectacularly awful Sunday lunch. "Well, I shall go and I shall see a polar bear as well. See how she likes that!"

"That's unlikely," said Malcolm, entering the lounge bearing a tray.

"I don't see why." Marjorie snapped.

"Because polar bears live at the North Pole," he explained, tenderly placing the tray on a side table.

"But that's where we're going!" Marjorie exclaimed, clearly exasperated with Malcolm.

"No, we are going to the South Pole, or rather the Antarctic." Malcolm explained.

"Well, the tour operators promised polar bears and penguins so that's what I shall demand." Marjorie continued. "If there aren't any polar bears, I for one shall want to know the reason why."

"Because they don't live there," Malcolm muttered under his breath as he handed me my coffee cup. "And I am paying for it, not you," he added before, I'm pretty sure, also winking at me. But polar bears or no, with Marjorie thousands of miles away Gideon and I were free to do as we pleased with our time, and with no need for me to find ways to avoid spending any of it with his mother.

Everything in my garden was therefore pretty rosy and it was with real pleasure that I accepted an invitation from Helen to accompany her and her children on a day out. What could be more fun, I thought, than the chance to spend some time with my future sister-in-law and her children, so soon to become my nieces and nephews? I was, I thought, about to become part of a real family, and what said 'real family' more than a family day out? Nothing, that's what.

"I'm sorry it's such short notice," Helen said when she phoned. "Celeste was supposed to be coming but she's got one of those twenty four hour bugs and doesn't think she'll be up to it. So, anyway," Helen continued, "there's a spare ticket and I could do with some adult company so if you fancy it ...?"

"It sounds lovely," I replied. How I would come to rue those words. "Let me know which train you're on from Clapham Junction and I'll hop on at Chiswick and away we go!"

The first intimation I had that my day was going to be far from lovely was when I attempted to get on the train. I did manage to board, but it was touch and go. The thing that hit me first was the noise. It was ear splitting. It sounded very much as I imagine hell (which someone did once say was other people) might. The carriage was packed to the rafters with humanity. Each and every one of them, adults and children alike, seemed to be shouting at the top of their voices.

"Stop that! Put that down! Sit still! No! Because I say so!" The chorus of adult voices was pitched at a very slightly lower tone than that of the children, who were like a squawking back drop out of which no specific words were identifiable. It sounded, when all put together, like a raging torrent and I couldn't imagine how it could get any louder until, once we reached our final destination, it did.

"I suppose I thought it was an actual park," I yelled to Helen as we surged forward on a tidal wave of humanity towards the entrance to the theme park.

"I'm so sorry," she yelled back, "I thought you knew."

"No," I replied, "but it's fine. And anyway, it's all about the kids, and I'm sure they'll have a great time." I said, although I wasn't convinced that anyone could have a great time here. It looked very much like the kind of place slave labourers are forced to build to prove what fun the inhabitants of totalitarian states are having.

Having finally negotiated the entrance I naively thought that queuing would be over for the day. Turns out that the main thing one does in theme parks is queue, for hours and for everything. Helen and I decided that the best way to negotiate the differing wishes of four children (best being a relative term as there is no good way to do such a thing) was to split up, taking two each. We would then meet up at a prearranged time and place for lunch. I headed off with Martha and Ruby in tow while Jake and Hector went with their mother. If I thought that taking the two younger ones would mean I was spared the more terrifying rides I was mistaken.

"I want to go on this one," said Martha, dragging me towards a heart-stoppingly huge roller coaster. It rose vertically into the air for several miles, before plummeting an equal distance back down. I felt sick just looking at it. I have never understood the appeal of roller coasters. Why, when life holds so many physical and mental challenges, are so many people prepared to pay good money to be terrified? Civilisation has, I would suggest, gone a bit far when it starts making machines whose sole purpose is to scare the user witless. What, after all, are planes are for? And least, for the price of a near death experience, planes take you from one place to another. Roller coasters simply land you back exactly where you started. Pointless, utterly pointless.

"All right," I agreed reluctantly, "we can go on it, but you should appreciate the risk you're running." I had noticed, as we made our way through the park, that several of the more outrageously awful looking rides had cut outs of children next to them, sometimes several. I assumed that they were a record of the number of child deaths that had occurred, much like the cut outs one sees by the roadside in France at accident black spots. I was relieved, therefore, when Martha explained that they were there to denote the minimum size of child allowed on the ride.

"So no one has actually died on any of these rides?" I confirmed.

"Of course not," Martha scoffed, "do you think they'd let children on if they could kill you?"

"I suppose not," I said, but that didn't make the vertiginous ascent look any less potentially fatal. We duly joined the queue next to a sign that had "One Hour" written on it. "Is that how long the ride lasts?" I asked, horrified at the thought.

"No," said Martha, who was the more talkative of the two, "that's how long we have to queue."

"You are kidding me?" I exclaimed. "Seriously? We have to wait an hour before we even get on the da... the thing?"

"Yup," said Ruby, not one to waste words. As it happens the hour passed quite quickly. We wended our way through the endless switchback queue watching the other families, some of whom put on quite a show. It was as I was doing a rough calculation of the calories one woman had given her already podgy child (every time we passed them the child was stuffing something different into its mouth with its fat little paws) that I noticed the other queue. While we were shuffling along like tourists on Westminster Bridge, this queue was belting along at a cracking pace. No sooner had someone joined it than they were being hustled into the next available roller coaster carriage and swooshed out of sight.

"That's not fair!" I huffed. "Why the hell do they get to jump the queue?"

"Because they paid more," said Martha, seemingly unmoved by the awful inequity of such a system. "They're being fast tracked."

"That is outrageous," I said, ready to launch into an attack on theme park owners who thought it was morally acceptable to have a two tier queuing system based purely on the ability to pay. I was planning to expand my argument to include fee paying schools and private health care, but I never got that far as we had, finally, reached the head of the slow track queue and were about to be loaded into the next available carriage. It was then that Ruby found her voice.

"I don't want to do this," she said.

"Oh come on," I coaxed, "it'll be fine. It's perfectly safe." I didn't believe for a moment that it was perfectly safe, but felt I ought to at least pay lip service to this notion.

"You thought that children had died on it," Martha pointed out unhelpfully "Four children," she added.

"Yes," I said, "but I was wrong, wasn't I? I doubt more than one or two have actually failed to come out alive." My joke was, unfortunately, spectacularly misjudged and in no time flat both girls were in floods of tears and we were all being led away by an attendant through a door with a sign on it saying Emergency Exit. It should have said "Free at last, free at last, thank God almighty, free at last" but it didn't.

The three of us spent the rest of the morning twirling around and around sedately in a huge teacup, which was much more to my taste and for which there was, miraculously, no queue.

"Thank you so much for agreeing to come," said Helen as we stood in the queue (naturally) to buy the high calorie, low nutrition lunch that was the only food available. Having chosen the least disgusting thing on display (I don't know what it was but at least there wasn't much of it) Helen and I settled ourselves at a table a few feet from the children and left them to it. The boys were showing off about the death defying rides they had been on and the girls were trying to make the teacup ride sound far more exciting than anything based on tea could ever be, so they were better off without adult supervision.

"I just wanted to say," Helen began, "that I'm so happy for you and Gideon. You're great together. I think you'll have a great marriage. You make him happy."

"Well that's very kind of you to say," I replied. "He makes me happy too."

"The thing is ... Celeste ... she isn't ..." Helen seemed to be having trouble getting her words out. "She isn't ill." Helen finally managed to say. "I'm sorry that I lied, but I thought we should, you know, get to know each other better. And this seemed like the perfect opportunity."

After the morning I had had, the suggestion that there was anything perfect about this experience amused me. But it was an opportunity to speak more with Helen, even if we did have to speak very loudly to hear each other over the cacophony.

"It's nice for me too," I said. "I hope that we'll get to see more of each other, become friends." Helen was very different from me, but I liked her. She was honest, and kind, and also quite funny when she wanted to be

"But you mustn't let Mum ... you know, interfere." Helen said, looking about nervously as if her mother might overhear from her ship in the Antarctic.

"Why should she interfere with us being friends?" I asked.

"Not with us, with you and Gideon."

"Oh," I replied.

"She does, I'm afraid, have rather a lot of influence over Gideon, and I ..." Helen came to an abrupt stop. "Oh do shut up Helen," she said, after a pause, "You're being ridiculous." She let out an unconvincing little laugh.

"Helen," I said resolutely, "you have to tell me what this is all about. You hinted at something when I came to your house and it's not fair, not really. Either say what you want to say or..." I was going to say shut up, but I thought she might take me at my word. "I would really like to know what I am dealing with. I really care for Gideon and..."

"And I love Gideon too," she said decisively, even though I hadn't used the word love, "he's a great brother, mostly, but he gets on so well with Mum... he doesn't understand that it's not as easy for... other people. To get on with Mum that is. I don't understand it, really I don't." Neither do I, my dear, neither do I.

"You just need to be very careful about coming between them," Helen continued. "The thing is," she dropped her voice even though the sound levels in the cafeteria were so off the scale someone only inches away from us couldn't have overheard a thing. "The thing is," she stopped to look around the room as if fearful of being observed, "there's more to their relationship than meets the eye. There's always more to my mother than meets the eye." Helen looked at me knowingly. "He doesn't... he can't see what... he always takes her side, or rather he always gives her the benefit of the doubt however badly she behaves."

"And you really don't know why Gideon is so close to your mother?" I asked, very much hoping for a straight answer.

"No idea, I'm afraid." Helen replied. "But," she went on, "they've been thick as thieves ever since he was a teenager. Just when most people start to question everything about their parents, Gideon seemed to decide that Mum could do no wrong. If I can give you one bit of advice Eve," she leant across the table and grabbed my hands in hers, pulling me quite sharply towards her, "it's to be very careful what you say around my mother, very careful indeed." She practically hissed these last words.

"What do you mean?" I asked.

"Oh nothing really." She released my hands and leant back. "Ignore me, I'm just being silly. That's what Mum would say. But," she leant in and grabbed my hands again, "if my mother were to learn anything about you that you didn't want Gideon to know, then ... well let's just say it would be best if she didn't know anything about you at all. Poor Sasha," she suddenly said. Thankfully she equally suddenly let go of my hands. The table was quite wide and she had pulled me quite far over it, jamming my ribs up against its edge in the process, which was pretty uncomfortable.

"Why poor Sasha?" I asked. "What's she got to do with this?"

"You know that she and Gideon were engaged and she broke it off?"

"Yes," I replied, "you told me about it before. You said she got cold feet."

"Yes, I did, didn't I?" Helen looked uncomfortable. She clearly hated lying. "That wasn't entirely true," she continued. "Just before Gideon and Sasha split up she, Sasha that is, came to see me. She was furious. You know I told you that she and Mum were close?"

"Yes." Gideon had had a lucky escape from Sasha as far as I could see. Any woman that could be close to his mother should, I felt, be treated with some caution.

"Sasha," Helen resumed, "she said, well ... she said that Mum ... well that Mum was making things very difficult for her, Sasha that is, and Gideon. I got the impression that Mum had found out something, I have no idea what, but something Sasha didn't want Gideon to know. Oh," Helen sighed deeply, "but it was a long time ago and Sasha was very angry."

"And you have no idea what it was that had made her so angry, just that it was something to do with your mother?" I asked.

"I don't know, she didn't say, but what she did say was that she wasn't prepared to put up with Mum, not even for Gideon's sake." Helen replied.

"Put up with her?" I prompted.

"Mum likes to... well she knows her own mind, and so did Sasha. She was some really high up government type," Helen continued, "she was involved in all sorts of important stuff, all very top secret and, to use her exact words she 'wasn't prepared to be held to ransom by a bourgeois little housewife.' "

"What on earth do you think that meant?" I asked. "How could your mother possibly hold a woman like that to ransom?"

"I have no idea, no idea at all. They had got on famously at first, but then, not long before she dumped Gideon something changed and she and Mum could hardly bear to be in the same room."

"Do you think your mother made Sasha leave Gideon?" I asked.

"Not in so many words, but there was more to it than either of them let on, I'm sure of that." Helen explained.

"That's awful!" I exclaimed.

"I know, but whatever the reason she dumped Gideon rather than have Mum on her back. He was a bit of wreck for a while after, but he got over it."

"Why didn't you tell Gideon what Sasha told you?" I asked.

"Because first of all she didn't really tell me anything and second of all Gideon would have thought I was just trying to get at Mum."

"Has your mother interfered in any of Gideon's other relationships?" I knew from what Joe had told me that she had, but it didn't hurt to get a bit of corroboration.

"She's always had an opinion, but I really don't know. My guess however would be yes. But as long as you've got nothing to hide you've got nothing to worry about have you?" She gave a little laugh, but her heart clearly wasn't in it. "Aleksandra Arnesen." Helen suddenly said.

"Sorry?" I looked at her blankly.

"Sasha. She was called Aleksandra Arnesen. I was quite intimidated by her at first. She was always very nice, but also…I don't know, powerful I suppose." Helen went all dreamy at the memory of Aleksandra Arnesen. "She had quite exotic ancestry, Russian and Finnish I think." Helen explained. "She was very tall, very blonde, very…"

"Have you any idea what happened to her?" I interrupted, not really wanting to hear any more about how very whatever Aleksandra Arnesen had been.

"She moved to Cheltenham when she and Gideon split up. Although I haven't heard from her in years so she may not be there any longer." Helen replied. I suddenly had the strangest feeling. It was as if I could see something out of the corner of my eye but when I turned to look there was nothing there. But however hard I tried, I couldn't rid myself of the feeling that there was something that if I could only look quickly enough I would be able to see.

"Mum, Mum, Mum!" Martha came bounding over. "Can we go on the log flume? Please, please, please!"

I have tried my hardest to blank the rest of that afternoon from my memory. I can, from this distance, only recall a few hazy details so successful have I been. What I do know for certain is that when I got home several hours later I was soaked to the skin (bloody log flume), and feeling as if I had truly been to the heart of darkness. When Gideon came home from work he found me lying prone on the sofa muttering “the horror, the horror,” over and over again and swearing that I would never go on another family fun day as long as I lived.

Chapter 13

Looking up at the gold Buddha in Battersea Park I couldn't help but reflect on the huge figure. Not that I was planning on becoming a Buddhist. Dominic had been a Buddhist for a short while and it had made him quite furious. Buddhism, at least according to Dominic, virtually guaranteed that if people did bad things (to Dominic) they would suffer for it, but as far as he could see the world was full of people getting away with all sorts of awful things while he got no reward at all for being what he referred to as 'the good guy'. He also gave up eating beef but it turned out that that was a different religion altogether, so what with one thing and another he gave up on the whole malarkey after a couple of months. My reflections on the Buddha were, I'm afraid, much more prosaic. All that the statue made me think was how uncomfortable his crossed leg position looked and how if I were to pursue enlightenment I would choose a more comfortable position to pursue it from. But I wasn't there for the purposes of enlightenment, at least not the sort offered by the Buddha. The reason for my being in Battersea Park was that Meg had finally called me and demanded that we meet.

"I can't come today," I had said, "I'm on my way to work."

"How odd, acting in the morning." Meg had replied. I had forgotten that I had told her I was an actress so was quite glad of the reminder.

"I'm not acting at the moment," I explained. "I have to temp to make ends meet. You know what the theatrical world's like."

"Oh, I thought you might be going to a rehearsal." Meg replied. "I've always been fascinated by the theatre. I go whenever I can. Have you ever done a Pinter?" I had no idea what doing a 'Pinter' might entail, so I thought it best to say I hadn't.

"I can meet you tomorrow," I added, "if that's any good."

"I suppose I could do that," Meg said, "and it will give me time to think of lots more questions for you. Have you ever performed in the round?" In the what?

"I'm not really that kind of actress." I said, hoping this would suffice as an answer.

I wasn't at all sure that meeting Meg was a good idea as my reflections, both while standing by the Buddha and over the previous few weeks, had made me realise that I was very probably making a massive mountain of a teeny molehill where Marjorie was concerned. Claire was almost certainly right (she was right about most things) when she said that the issues I had with Marjorie were more about me and my unrealistic expectations of mothers than about the woman herself.

What Joe had told me about Helen's relationship with her mother was troubling it's true, but mother and daughter still saw each other, so how bad could it really be? Helen herself had told me nothing substantive about Marjorie. It was all rumour and innuendo and, as Claire told me, all families had their issues. As for Gideon, why shouldn't he think his mother was amazing, and why shouldn't I accept his assessment? Marjorie loved her son and no woman would ever be good enough for him, but she was hardly alone in feeling like this. I would just have to deal with it. And Marjorie had, as it happens, been rather pleasant in the weeks since she and Malcolm had returned from their cruise. She had even thrown herself with gusto into the preparations for our upcoming wedding.

Our secret wedding having been such a wash out, Gideon had had second thoughts about excluding his parents, or more specifically his mother. We had therefore gone back to Plan A, which comprised a very small Register Office wedding followed by a meal at a local restaurant for about twenty people. As all my favourite weddings (including one of my own) had been small affairs, this was fine by me, not that I shared this observation with Gideon.

Marjorie had also, in her own way, been charm itself since her holiday in the Antarctic. Maybe it was the sea air, but a few days after her return she had invited us to dinner and been quite jolly (although the food was as horrid as ever, so not everything had changed for the better). After an extensive penguin based slide show (no polar bears I noticed, and no mention of them either) she had announced that it was time for what she called 'pressies'. For Gideon there was a strangely shaped parcel which contained quite the most horrid cowboy hat I had ever seen. Made from very stiff tan coloured leather it had what I assume were indigenous South American designs tooled into the surface (they had incorporated a tour of South America on the way back from visiting the penguins). Had my one and only been a llama farmer (which as I mentioned earlier was never likely to happen) it would have been the ideal choice, but for a psychology professor from Chiswick, not so much.

"And for darling Eve." Marjorie said, handing me an equally large package. "I saw this and I thought of you!" She almost squealed with delight as I took the present from her. Quite why Marjorie had thought of me on seeing an enormous, brightly coloured, stripy poncho I don't know, but I murmured my thanks nonetheless and swore to wear it on the next chilly day, or, to be more precise, when hell froze over.

I therefore wasn't at all sure that there was any purpose in meeting Meg, but she had been quite insistent. So here I was, waiting next to a great gold Buddha and hoping that he was wrong about reincarnation, as I wasn't too sure how well I would come out of it next time around.

"Now," said Meg, when she finally joined me some fifteen minutes later than agreed. "I'm going to tell you the same thing that I told the other one."

"The other one?" I asked.

"The other one that came to see me!" Meg sounded rather annoyed as if I should have known what she was talking about.

"But who was this other one?" I replied, still none the wiser.

"Gideon's girlfriend of course!" Meg exclaimed as if I was being terrifically thick. "Tall, blonde, beautiful," she added, unnecessarily I thought. "She seemed to have some idea that she and I might join forces to take her on." Meg continued.

"Take who on?" I queried.

"Marjorie of course." Meg exclaimed. "But when it came to it she didn't have the stomach for it."

"Marjorie didn't have the stomach for it?" I tried to clarify. Talking to Meg was like wading through glue.

"No!" Meg almost shouted. "She didn't. Sasha didn't."

"OK," I said, feeling as if I had finally got a handle on what Meg was trying to tell me. "Gideon's ex-fiancée Sasha was having difficulties in her relationship with him that were caused by Marjorie and she, Sasha, thought that you might join forces with her to try to outwit Marjorie. Is that right?" I summarised.

"That's what I said isn't it?" said Meg.

"Yes," I concurred for the sake of amity, "that is exactly what you said. I was simply clarifying things for my own sake. So what did you tell Sasha?"

"That I was in!" Meg punched the fist of one hand into the palm of the other. "Marjorie, you see, was interfering, like she always does, and making life very difficult for Sasha. But then she, Sasha," Meg said this slowly, presumably to make sure I was keeping up, "decided that she wasn't up for it, which was a shame. She really was a gorgeous looking creature. She and Gideon would have had the most beautiful children."

"That's hardly relevant," I replied, somewhat tetchily.

"I suppose not, but they would have been very lovely." Meg sighed while looking wistfully into the middle distance.

"The thing is," I said, determined to move the conversation on, "everything is fine with me and Marjorie. I have no need of an accomplice to help me outwit her."

"So why did you follow me all the way down the King's Road?" Meg responded. "And I could you know, help you to outwit her that is."

"I was interested to meet you." I replied. "And now I have. But I don't need your help, thank you very much for offering."

"So you think you can outwit her on your own?" Meg looked at me through narrowed eyes.

"Who said she needs outwitting?" I said airily, as if the matter was of no importance at all to me.

"You did," said Meg.

"I said I didn't need help outwitting her, not that she needed outwitting." I clarified. We were beginning to sound like a couple of owls, what with all the outwitting.

"You obviously don't realise what sort of a monster my sister is," Meg muttered darkly.

"Tell me then," I was intrigued I must admit, despite my recent molehill/mountain reflections. "What sort of a monster is she?"

Meg proceeded to tell me about some of Marjorie's more, in her mind at least, nefarious crimes. As children Marjorie had dropped Meg's copy of The Wind in The Willows in the bath and not replaced it, she had stolen a lavender mohair cardigan that it had taken Meg months to save up for and only returned it once it had shrunk in the wash, and she had copied Meg's homework on a regular basis and then handed it in first, making it appear that Meg was the plagiarist (although how anyone could fall for this more than once was beyond me).

"Is that it?" I asked.

"It! It!" she shrieked. "I have loads more where that came from." An affronted Meg pursed her lips at me in frustration. Her resemblance to Marjorie when annoyed almost knocked me sideways.

"I'm sorry Meg," I said as gently as I could, "but lovely though it's been to meet you, I think I'd better be going."

"You'll change your mind, you'll see. Take this," Meg thrust a piece of paper into my hand. "It's my address. Send me a card when you do and we'll talk."

"Thank you," I said, "you will definitely be the first person I turn to if," I emphasised the 'if' quite strongly, "I ever decide I need an accomplice to plot against my boyfriend's mother."

And with that I stalked off, quite certain I would never see the mad old bird again. I did keep her address though, as you never can be completely certain how things will work out.

Chapter 14

"Does it really matter if they don't come?" I asked Gideon, on hearing the latest news from his family. It was a few days before wedding two point zero and Marjorie had phoned that morning to say that she wouldn't be coming. It wasn't that she didn't want to come, she had explained, it was that she simply couldn't. She was, she professed, delighted to be welcoming me into the family, but she and Helen had had some major falling out which she couldn't bring herself to talk about, but which precluded her from being in the same room as her daughter, even for Gideon's sake. I honestly couldn't have cared less if neither of them came, I just wanted to get married but Gideon didn't, it seemed, share my feelings. He had therefore invited Marjorie around for coffee in an attempt to get to the bottom of the problem, but we were none the wiser following her visit.

"I simply cannot bear to see your sister, not now, not under any circumstances," Marjorie had declared when she arrived. "I'm only sorry that you have been caught in the middle of our family's problems," she had said turning her attention to me while patting my hand and looking with what I supposed was meant to be infinite regret into my eyes. Looked more like she was about to sneeze from where I was sitting.

"But you won't have to talk to her Mum." Gideon pleaded. "You can sit at different ends of the table. Please, for my sake, can't you put this aside, just for one day?"

"I can't Gideon, not even for you, and you know that I'd do anything in my power for you," Marjorie paused to look deeply into Gideon's eyes. "I'd do anything for you," she repeated. "But I can't do that." I wouldn't have had Marjorie down as a Meatloaf fan, but she had just quoted the refrain from one of his most famous songs almost word for word, so perhaps she had a hinterland I could never have guessed at.

"I know you would Mum," Gideon replied. How he could fall for this guff was beyond me. If someone says they would do anything in their power for you and then refuses to sit down for a very few hours in the same room as their own daughter I think you have reason to doubt their sincerity.

"I don't want to stop your sister coming to your wedding." Marjorie continued, dabbing at her nose with her ever present tiny hankie. "I know the children are very excited about it, and I wouldn't want them to miss it on my account." Her concern for the happiness of her grandchildren was touching, if a little out of character. She had always seemed supremely uninterested in them as far as I could tell. She literally never mentioned them and had barely spoken to them on the one occasion I had seen them together (although that had been at the Christmas dinner when Dominic had rather dominated the conversation). "I hate to do this to you Ian, and you dear Evie," Marjorie turned to me, a quite ghastly smile contorting her face. Evie? Where had that come from? No one calls me Evie, not more than once anyway. "But you know that I wouldn't do this unless I felt I really had no choice," she concluded, her eyes cast down to denote the great sadness this caused her.

Gideon was clearly falling for this charade hook, line, and sinker. I, on the other hand, was rather less impressed by Marjorie's act. Never, they say, bullshit a bullshitter and my finely tuned bullshit detector told me that the whole thing stank to high heaven of bullshit. So, having left the details of the falling out between mother and daughter sufficiently vague Marjorie departed, wafted away on a cloud of what I was convinced was faux regret.

"It'll be interesting to see what Helen has to say about all this." I observed as we stood at the sitting room window watching Marjorie drive away, the roof of her very expensive sports car open to the elements and Meatloaf very possibly pumping out of the stereo.

"There's no point in asking Helen anything." Gideon replied, rather sharply.

"What do you mean?" I asked.

"It'll be something and nothing," he replied, not very helpfully.

"What does that even mean? It's something or it's nothing. It can't be both." I reasoned.

"Oh yes it can," Gideon responded vehemently. "Helen," he continued, "gets stupidly upset with Mum over silly things. She always thinks Mum's having a pop at her, when all Mum's trying to do is help. Helen will have got upset over something she thinks Mum has said or done, and which Mum is too kind to mention." Gideon, supposedly, knew his mother and sister far better than I, but this sounded nothing like the behaviour I would have expected from the pair of them. If anything, what Gideon suggested was the exact opposite of what I would have supposed to be the case. And a few days later I learnt that I was right and he was wrong.

"I am so sorry Eve," Helen said, having phoned me on my mobile. "I wouldn't have done this to you for the world, but I had no choice."

"What do you mean, no choice?" I asked. I was whispering very quietly as Gideon was in his study, which is next to the sitting room where I was taking Helen's call.

"Mum told me that either she or I could go to your wedding, but not both." Helen explained.

"I know that much," I replied. "What I don't know is why. What did you argue about?"

"We didn't," said Helen, "she just rang and told me what she was going to do and that I had to back her up. I'm sorry. Don't tell Gideon though because he won't believe you. I just wanted you to know. I feel really bad, but there's nothing I can do about it."

"Who was that?" asked Gideon a few minutes later.

"No one," I said, "or rather a wrong number. Coffee?"

So, I thought, I am lying to Gideon about talking to his sister on the phone. May be Marjorie was a mountain of a problem rather than a molehill after all. I had no real idea what was going on, but the time had come, I felt, to neutralise Marjorie's influence. If only I knew someone who knew a lot about Marjorie and who would be willing to help me ... hang on just a god damn minute!

Chapter 15

"We are going to have to find a way to neutralise Marjorie," I explained to Meg.

"Neutralise her? What good would that do?" She looked mystified. "She's already well past child bearing age."

"Neutralise," I explained, "not neuter. She's not a cat." While Meg was hopefully going to be very useful to me she might also, I sensed, test my patience.

"Oh yes, I see, of course, silly of me." Meg said. "So how will we neutralise her?"

Meg and I were sitting in the cafe of a favourite haunt of mine. Having sent her a postcard asking her to call me we had arranged a day out. London, big though it is, has far too many people in it for comfort. You can, in London, go for literally years without seeing anyone you know but as soon as you are either somewhere you shouldn't be, or with someone you shouldn't be with, it is guaranteed that friends and acquaintances will start to rain down on you like confetti. I was once on the Northern Line (the Northern Line!) when I should have been in school (in Norwich) when Mrs Litton, my Chemistry teacher, got into my carriage. She shouldn't have been there either, and she shouldn't have been with Mr Lawrence, my History teacher, so I didn't get into trouble for playing hooky. As a matter of fact I did much better in both my Chemistry and History mocks than had been expected, but my point still stands.

I had already had reason, however, to regret going out in my car with Meg as she had nearly caused a major accident even before we left Chiswick. I had picked her up from a bus stop near Chiswick roundabout, but as I couldn't stop for any length of time in case I got a ticket she hadn't had time to put the huge bag she always seemed to have with her in the back of the car. She had therefore shoved it into the footwell in front of her where, I presumed, it would stay. As I pulled back into the traffic my eye was caught by a strange movement from within the bag. I thought I was imagining it and turned my attention back to the road, but as I extended my left hand to slip the car into second gear (while looking over my right shoulder to make sure it was safe to pull out), instead of my hand coming into contact with the cold hard plastic of the gear stick, I felt something warm and furry. I screamed in alarm and, having instinctively moved as far as I could to the right of my seat, I also managed to turn the steering wheel to the right as well. The upshot of this was that I only just missed having a head on collision with a bus that was coming the other way.

"What the f... !" I screamed.

"Silly Pookie," said Meg, interrupting my expletive.

"Who are you calling Pookie?" I yelled, having managed to swing the car back to the left in the nick of time and pull in again at the curb.

"This little fellow, the silly ickle wickle lickle Pooker." Still muttering this gibberish Meg shoved the smallest dog I have ever seen into my face.

"What the f..." I began to say again, only to be interrupted again by Meg.

"We go everywhere together, don't we my ickle pickle ..."

"That's enough of that," I snapped. "Put Poo ... whatever back in the bag and keep it out of my way while I'm driving."

"He's a he." She said before beginning to mutter gibberish again. "Aunty Waunty Evie Wevie doesn't like lickle Mr ..." I've no idea how long this went on as I stopped listening at this point, but I do know it was over by the time we reached the M40 when I tuned back in. It's not that I don't like dogs, I've just never had time for them, or for cats for that matter, except Mr Perkins of sacred memory. It was all I could do for much of my life, particularly when I first returned to London at that age of sixteen, to look after myself, without taking on the responsibility for hangers on.

The dog safely stowed back in its bag we did, thankfully, manage to make it to our destination without any further life threatening incidents.

"Ooh," said Meg, when she saw where I had brought her, "this is absolutely heavenly!"

The Old Barn Vintage and Antiques Centre (or OBVAC as it's known to regulars like me) is one of my very favourite places in the whole world. It is housed, as the name suggests, in an old barn (or several old barns to be precise) and is chock full of the kind of bits and bobs that I adore. It has everything from vintage (old) clothing, to reclaimed (junk) furniture as well as china, glass, old jewellery, table linen, old kitchen equipment, I could go on. I was thrilled by Meg's response and could almost forgive her having smuggled a mutt into my car and nearly killing us both as a consequence. It was the kind of place I just knew Marjorie would hate. She only ever wanted shiny new things, the more expensive the better, while I adore old stuff, worn out stuff, stuff that has a history. I suppose I feel an affinity for it, having a bit of a history myself.

Meg and I spent a happy, companionable hour wandering around the barns looking at the vast array of things on offer, and finding that we shared a lot of the same tastes. Meg would pick something up, maybe a champagne coupe, or a decrepit cheese grater and say "isn't this gorgeous?" and I would agree. If only Marjorie were more like Meg, I thought, how much easier my life might be. I did notice however, that one or two of the items that Meg picked up didn't make it back on display. Luckily she needed the loo just as this idyll came to an end, so I retrieved everything from her bag, which she had asked me to hold along with Pookie, and shoved the bits and bobs back on to the nearest shelf.

"So," I said, once we were settled in the OBVAC cafe. "Let's begin shall we?" I took out a notepad that I had brought with me, ready to get down to business.

"What's that?" Meg looked horrified, a forkful of carrot cake halfway to her mouth.

"It's a notepad." I explained.

"I can see that," she said. "What's it for?"

"For taking notes." I replied.

"Do you have to take notes?" Meg looked aghast.

"Of course I do!" I exclaimed. "I can't possibly remember everything we might talk about, and I might only realise the importance of something when I look back over my notes." Phillipe Merlot had drilled me constantly on the importance of good note taking and I had on many occasions been grateful to him for inculcating me into this practice.

"All right then," said Meg. "In for a penny in for a pound I suppose."

We spent some time discussing the past, what Marjorie had been like as a girl (pretty much the same unpleasant so and so she was as a woman it seemed), and Meg regaled me with numerous incidents of Marjorie's unkindness and manipulation, but there was very little of substance. Nothing in fact that gave me any idea where to start looking for something that might neutralise her.

"What exactly do you mean by neutralise?" Meg asked, having just finished telling me a story about how Marjorie had encouraged her to cut off all her hair only for it to provoke the fury of their father who hated short hair on girls.

"There must be something that Marjorie has done," I explained, "something that she wouldn't want anyone to know about. She must have some secret that, if revealed, would reduce her influence on Gideon, and," I added hurriedly, "everyone else, obviously."

"Hmm," said Meg rubbing her chin with one hand while stroking Pookie, who was on her lap, with the other. "I've always thought there was something funny about the time when Gideon was ill."

"What do you mean, ill?" I asked.

"Unwell, sick, in need of medical treatment." Meg explained.

"I know what ill means," I replied, "What sort of ill was he?"

"I'm not sure exactly, but it was quite serious." Meg explained. "He was in and out of hospital for months."

"So you don't know what was wrong with him?" Gideon had never mentioned any childhood illnesses so this was news to me.

"No idea, I'm afraid." Meg was stroking and nuzzling Pookie, who was clearly loving all the attention and displaying his pleasure by farting like a dairy cow. "But there was definitely something funny going on."

"What do you mean by funny?" I asked.

"Odd, unusual, out of the ordinary," Meg explained. I wasn't about to tell her that I knew what funny meant just as I had known what ill meant.

"In what way funny," I asked, as patiently as I could manage.

"It was funny that it was only when Gideon was actually getting better that she told me that I was to have nothing more to do with her or her children," said Meg.

"She told you what?" This sounded more like it.

"She forbad me to see her children ever again." Meg spoke as if this was perfectly normal sibling behaviour. Perhaps it was in her family, but then again perhaps it was in mine too, it was just the kind of thing Dominic might say.

"And you agreed to this? Why?" I asked.

"Because I have a little..." Meg paused. "Hobby," she finally said. "And Marjorie knows about it and has always used it to get me to do what she wants."

"And that hobby is... Oh!" Of course, Meg was a kleptomaniac. Meg and I looked at each other. She knew that I knew and we left it there.

"So," I began, determined to dig deeper into the reason for Meg's banishment from Marjorie's life. But that was as far as I got when I was interrupted by a voice coming from behind me.

"Why, hello Marjorie," said the voice, "I didn't imagine I'd see you in a place like this!"

I whipped around to look at the owner of the voice. It was Melissa's grandmother, the woman who had spent so much time telling me about her grandchildren at Marjorie's Burns' Night dinner. What the hell was she doing at OBVAC? I'd have had her down as more of a John Lewis sort, but I would obviously have been wrong. I flicked my eyes back to

Meg, fully expecting to see her looking as dumbstruck as I, but I had clearly underestimated her.

"Why shouldn't I be here?" Meg demanded to know, suddenly the very living embodiment of her twin. "I'm free to go where I please, you know."

"Well, yes, of course you are," Melissa's grandmother replied nervously. "I ... I ... I just meant I was surprised to see you ... here."

"We're leaving," said Meg imperiously, "so you won't need to be bothered by my presence any longer." Why on earth was she being so rude?

"I'm not ... you can ... I'm ..." Clearly lost for words at the extreme reaction she was receiving Melissa's grandmother simply stood aside as Meg, closely followed by me, swept past her out of the cafe. "And you can take this thing," said Meg, thrusting Pookie into my arms. "It belongs to your friend after all."

"What the hell was that all about?" I demanded to know as soon as we were safely out of earshot.

"Good, wasn't I?" Meg giggled, relieving me of a wriggling, and very smelly, Pookie. Meg really was welcome to the odd little creature. "I was Marjorie to a T, don't you think?"

"Well, yes," I agreed. "You were very convincing, but why be so rude to her? I mean what if ... ?" I didn't get to finish my question as Meg interrupted me.

"Think about it my dear," she said, tapping the side of her head, "how likely is that woman to mention to Marjorie that she bumped into her? Would you," she continued, "bring up an encounter with someone who had been so rude to you?"

"Wow, I must say I'm impressed. I didn't think ..." I began.

"You didn't think I had it in me?" Meg said, a look of immense satisfaction on her face. "You're not the only one who knows how to use her noggin when she's in a tight spot, you know."

While the encounter had unnerved me, it had also given me a new found admiration for Meg. Perhaps she was, after all, just the accomplice that I needed.

Chapter 16

"So you don't have any long term conditions? Nothing you're on medication for?" Wedding two point zero having been no more successful than its predecessor I had done the only thing I could and thrown myself back into my detective work. Marjorie wasn't going to get away with manipulating events to suit herself anymore, not if I had anything to do with it. So, with nothing else to go on for the moment, I had decided to make it my business to find out more about Gideon's mysterious childhood illness.

"Nope." Gideon replied to my question.

"Have you ever had a condition so serious that it necessitated spending a night in hospital?" I was sitting at the kitchen table hunched over a piece of paper, a pen clutched in my hand as I ticked boxes and apparently wrote down the answers he was giving me.

"Wouldn't it just be easier if I filled the questionnaire in myself later?" Gideon was in the middle of preparing our supper. He doesn't have a wide range of dishes in his repertoire but he does make a delicious Thai chicken curry. He prepares it completely from scratch, making the curry paste and everything, which was particularly useful right now as it meant that he couldn't see that the paper I was hunched over was an application form for an additional parking permit.

"You don't honestly think that Claire would be able to decipher your handwriting, do you?" I observed. "It looks like a drunken spider with inky feet has wandered across the page. I couldn't do that to her." I had told Gideon that Claire needed data for a paper she was writing so, as a fellow academic, he had been only too happy to help.

"And your writing is so much better?" he replied.

"Err, yes!" I exclaimed. "I won a calligraphy prize at school, I'll have you know." I hadn't. There wasn't a calligraphy prize at my school, half the pupils could barely even write, but my handwriting is, nonetheless, a lot neater than Gideon's. "Just answer the question."

"Yes." Gideon said.

"Go on then." I replied.

"Yes is the answer to your question," he clarified. "I have had a condition so serious that I had to stay in hospital."

"Oh, I thought you were saying yes, you would answer the question."

"Glad we cleared that up."

"So am I! So which part of your body was the cause of the condition?"

"That's a really odd way to ask about an illness." Gideon was chopping and bashing away over the other side of the kitchen.

"I know!" I exclaimed. "You wait until you hear some of the other questions." I laughed ruefully while shaking my head in apparent disbelief at the idiocy of Claire's questions. She would have killed me if she had known that I was destroying her reputation for academic rigour in pursuit of my own aims, but needs must. And she didn't know. "So, which part was it?"

"I had kidney problems when I was a teenager." Gideon explained.

"I did not know that." I was genuinely surprised.

"And why should you?" Gideon turned away from his pan for a moment to look at me. "You don't know everything about me. It's good to have a few secrets from each other isn't it? Keeps the mystery alive."

"Absolutely." If only you knew my darling, if only you knew. "So were you very ill?"

"Is that the next question?"

"No," I said, "I was just asking. Out of, you know, interest, but if you'd rather keep it a mystery..."

"I was quite ill. They thought I was going to need a kidney transplant at one point."

"Oh my, that is ill." I said.

"Oh my indeed, but I didn't and I got completely better."

"Well done you! So," I continued, "did your illness have any negative effects on your family?"

"No, they were delighted to see me laid low by a life threatening condition." Gideon replied.

"Really?" I asked. "How odd."

"Of course they weren't. It was a stupid question so I gave a stupid answer." Gideon had started to fry stuff by now, which was even noisier than his chopping. He had to shout to make himself heard over the racket. "How many more questions are there in this thing? I thought Claire was very bright but this seems like a load of nonsense to me. I can't imagine," he blathered on over the sound of frying, "what she will be able to do with the data she collects. It's not even clear," having got the bit between his teeth he wasn't about to let up on this one, "whether this is a quantitative or a qualitative study." He was by now so infuriated that he had all but abandoned his pan.

"That'll burn if you're not careful," I said, not wanting him to come over and snatch the parking permit application from me. “Nearly finished,” I said brightly. I felt that I had pushed this almost as far as I could but I just wanted to squeeze a tiny bit more information out of the exercise. “So, stupid though the question is, what were the effects of this illness on your familial relationships?”

“Let me look at that,” he said, coming over to where I sat and reaching over as if to grab the paper from under my hand.

“Oh no you don’t,” I cried, pulling it sharply away, “you’ll get curry paste all over it. Just answer the bloody question and then it’s all over.”

“It just infuriates me when research is done so badly. There’s so much rubbish out there that gets media attention while real research is ignored, and then people do this kind of worthless nonsense.” This is one of Gideon’s hobby horses. I had wracked my brain for days about how to bring up the illness that Meg had mentioned and this was the best I could come up with, so if Claire was collateral damage, so be it. They barely knew each other so Gideon would, I was sure, be far too polite to draw attention to her rubbish research.

“How about I add your thoughts in the ‘any other comments’ section?” I offered. “But in the meantime please, please just answer the question. I promised Claire, and you know how hard it is to get participants for research studies.” I knew this would appeal to his sense of academic camaraderie even if he thought that the research was, in his words, worthless nonsense.

“OK. I suppose, or rather I know that it was through being ill that I found out what a truly amazing woman my mother is.” There was that word again, amazing. Why, I longed to ask, do you think that that difficult, manipulative woman is amazing?

"In what way, amazing?" I asked, rather more diplomatically.

"Is that the next question?" Gideon looked at me incredulously.

"No, obviously not. That was my question. I just wondered what it was that your mother did, specifically, to make you think, I mean realise she was amazing?"

"Doesn't everyone think their mother is amazing?" Gideon asked. Many people may well feel that their own mother is very special, but very few people I had met seemed to share Gideon's assessment of his particular mother.

"I was only asking because it sounded as if something specific had happened to make you see her differently after you were ill." I replied.

"Oh, well, yes, maybe." Gideon turned back to his pan. "I know she can be quite demanding, Mum that is, but she only wants what's best for us." He took that pan off the heat and turned his full attention to me. "Helen still has quite a childish relationship with Mum and I think that when I was ill I grew out of that. I was quite a rebellious early teen. I knew she hated the name Gideon but I started using it anyway, mainly because it annoyed her." He came and sat at the table next to me, but I was able to get the paper out of sight in the nick of time on the pretext of saving it from damage.

"Mum wasn't very demonstrative when we were young," Gideon went on. "She could seem cold, and I suppose I compared her unfavourably with Aunt Meg. But then when I was ill she was amaz… ." He grinned at me. "She was supportive and practical and I saw there was much more to her than I had thought. And Meg disappeared off the scene around that time anyway, so she obviously didn't care about me as much as I thought she did, so there was only Mum, and we became much closer.

"She and Dad have never had a brilliant marriage," he continued in the longest speech had had ever made about his family, "and Helen was a difficult teenager. Mum had to send her away to France to save her from getting into real trouble. So I became Mum's confidante and ... well that's just how it is. Is that enough for your survey?"

"It'll do." I said. "Now when's dinner going to be ready? I'm starving."

What Gideon had said all sounded very plausible, but I just sensed that there must be more that he hadn't told me, or perhaps didn't know. He didn't know, for example, that Marjorie had blackmailed Meg into disappearing, or that she had engineered the cancelling of our wedding on two different occasions (I was by now quite sure that the whole adultery business was a concoction designed for her own ends). I was clearly going to have to work a bit harder to find out what was behind Gideon's relationship with his mother.

Chapter 17

"Please Meg," I said, "just put it down and get off the table. This won't solve anything." I had just shared some intriguing information with Meg and her reaction had been rather more extreme than I had anticipated. I didn't really know what to do now as I'd never had to dissuade anyone from self-harming before. If only, I thought, I'd lasted longer as a Samaritan, but I didn't even make it through the training. I'd volunteered on the advice of Claire, who thought that it might help me to understand what I would be up against if I became a counsellor. It turned out that my approach to helping those in a fragile mental state was, according to my supervisor, more robust than he felt comfortable with. I didn't agree and argued my case quite strongly, which only seemed to make matters worse, I'm afraid. And now the consequence of Derek's lack of imagination was that I was ill equipped to manage the difficult situation in which I now found myself. Thanks a bunch Derek.

It had all started when, in a moment of clarity, I realised that I had been wasting my time digging around trying to find the cause of Gideon's attachment to his mother. What did it matter why he was so attached? What I had to do was break that attachment. It is really frustrating when one looks back over events and realises that one (and by one I mean me) has been extremely stupid. The key to neutralising Marjorie had been staring me in the face for ages. All the clues had been there if I only I had been able to see them.

Marjorie, in her own twisted way, loved Gideon, but there was something else that she loved just as much, and that was money. Or to be more precise, the superiority over others that money gave her. Take her recent cruise for example. She hadn't been motivated by a love of penguins, she had simply wanted to show Meryl 'bloody' Streep next door that she could afford to go. She was obsessed by the status that expensive things (in her mind at least) conferred on her. Her car, her ring, her house, all these things meant a huge amount to Marjorie, and in order to have them she also had to have money. Malcolm had, I assumed, bought the house and he had certainly paid for the cruise. But Marjorie had made much of the fact that she had bought the car and the ring with what she had referred to as her money. Where, I wondered (eventually) had that money come from? As she hadn't worked since having her children, it seemed unlikely she had earned it. She might have saved it from her housekeeping but the sums involved made that unlikely. She could have won the Lottery but, as anyone who regularly buys a ticket will know, that was the most unlikely source of all. So, presuming she hadn't robbed a bank, the most probable source was an inheritance, and the most likely source of that was her father.

The idea of following the money hadn't, I admit, come to me unprompted. It was as I was returning from sending Meg a postcard one day that I realised someone was trying to send me a message. I had, however, been too caught up with my own plans and schemes to see what was right in front of me. I had been sending Meg a postcard because, as she had neither a phone nor a computer, it was the only way that I could communicate with her. I would send her the details of a proposed meeting, and she would only need to call me if my suggestion was inconvenient. It was a simple yet effective technique that I had picked up (amongst many other things) from working with Phillipe Merlot. And, as it turned out, it was this postcard malarkey that had alerted me to the possibility that someone, also versed in subterfuge, had been trying to guide my actions. The thing I had imagined I couldn't quite see when I was at the theme park with Helen suddenly came into view.

Once home I headed straight for the book shelf by my side of the bed. I always have several books on the go and am always in need of bookmarks as I absolutely hate it when people turn down the corners of pages to mark their place. I have broken off friendships, and even dumped a boyfriend (although, to be fair, it was just the last of many straws) as a result of getting back dog eared books that I had leant out in good faith.

Sure enough, having shaken out five or six books I found what I was looking for. Three postcards, all from Cheltenham. I had assumed that they were part of an advertising campaign, although I had no idea what for as they were extremely cryptic. The first one had caught my interest because it had arrived only a few days after I had moved in to Gideon's flat, and I didn't know how anyone could have known at that point that this was my new address. It pictured an enormous ring doughnut shaped building which was, according to the back of the card, GCHQ in Cheltenham, and read Careless talk costs wives. The second, which arrived about two months later, showed the entrance to the Gloucestershire Royal Hospital, in Cheltenham again, and read Patients will out. The third, which was of Cheltenham

Racecourse, had arrived only a few days before and simply read Follow the money.

Looking at them again I realised that they must be, could only be, from Gideon's ex-girlfriend Sasha. She had, Helen had told me, moved to Cheltenham after she and Gideon split up, and she was something to do with the government and so could (if Dominic was even a tiny bit right) find out pretty much anything she wanted to about anyone.

The first postcard was, I now saw, telling me to be wary of someone, presumably Marjorie, who would try to cost me my role as a wife. She'd certainly done that so far, having halted two wedding attempts. The second was not misspelled but was telling me to look into Gideon's illness, but having done this it didn't seem to be a very useful line of inquiry. The third though, well that was the reason why I was trying to persuade Meg to get off her dining table and put down the large wooden cat she seemed intent on throwing across the room.

"The bitch," she bellowed, "how could she?" I have no idea what good Meg thought would come from hurling large wooden cats around, and from quite a height, in a small space. We were currently in her home, a bedsit which comprised the former drawing room of a once grand but now rather dilapidated house just off the King's Road. After the run in with Melissa's grandmother we had decided it was altogether the safest place to meet. All Meg would achieve by chucking stuff around in here was to damage her own home, and possibly herself. I think she was just so overwhelmed by rage that she didn't really know what she was doing.

On hearing my news she had jumped up and down on the spot several times, picked up a china shire horse and made as if to throw it but, presumably deciding it wasn't heavy enough, had put it down and picked up the cat instead. She had then climbed on to the dining table clutching the cat and was now threatening to chuck it across the room.

"Meg, please," I said. "You'll pull a muscle if you're not careful. Or twist your ankle."

"Aaaaarrrghh," she roared, leaning back ever further in order to give the cat the best possible chance of doing the most possible damage.

"How is this helping?" I pleaded. "Do you want to get even with Marjorie or do you want to sprain your back?"

"I can do both!" Meg shouted in reply.

"Yes, you can, but why not just settle for getting even? After all, if you sprain your back it'll only make getting your revenge that much harder. It's so much easier to wreak revenge when one is fit and healthy, you know that."

The reason for Meg's anger was that, having done some research, I had discovered the probable source of Marjorie's money and it turned out that a portion of it should have been Meg's. I had found out, to be precise, that the main beneficiaries of Meg's father's will were Gideon and Helen. With a little judicious questioning I had also discovered that Gideon, and therefore I assumed also Helen, knew nothing about the will and had not received a penny. The will had also specified that Meg should get a small bequest, which she had also not received. Marjorie had been left nothing.

"The thing is," I had explained, "Gideon and Helen should have received cheques from the executor of your father's will."

"But there was nothing left after the debts had been paid." Meg replied. "That was what Marjorie told me." Meg had taken the news that her sister had defrauded her remarkably well up to this point.

"She lied," I continued, "there was quite a lot of money actually. But," I paused to heighten the dramatic effect of what I was about to say, "do you know who the executor was?"

"What's an executor?" Meg asked.

"It's the person who's supposed to make sure the money goes to the right people." I explained. "And do you know who it was?" I asked again.

"Was it the fellow that lived next door to Dad? Oh no," Meg went on, answering her own question, "it couldn't have been him because he was albino."

"Why couldn't an albino person execute a will?" I found myself asking, goodness knows why.

"Did I say albino? I meant Albanian. He went back to Albania, that's why it couldn't have been him."

"Anyway it was..." I readied myself, again, for my big reveal.

"Oh, I know," Meg squealed, "it was Dad's friend Bernie, wasn't it? Bernie... Bernie... Winters?"

"I doubt it," I replied. "He was a comedian. He had an act with his brother, Mike. Mike and Bernie Winters." God only knows why I decided to volunteer this information, it was hardly relevant.

"They had a dog didn't they, as part of their act?" Meg reminisced. "I seem to remember that they were dreadfully unfunny, but I had no idea that Dad even knew Bernie Winters let alone asked him to execute... is that the right word?... to execute his will."

"He didn't. It was Malcolm." I said through gritted teeth, my big reveal having been rather ruined by all the interruptions.

"I thought you said it was Mike," said Meg, clearly bemused.

"Malcolm," I said very slowly, "it was Malcolm who was the executor of your father's last will and testament."

And that was when all the screaming, throwing, and leaping on tables had started. Having taken the loss of her inheritance pretty well, Meg was driven to fury, it seemed, by her brother-in-law's role in all this.

"She lied, and Malcolm was in on it." I reiterated. "Can you believe that?"

"The … the …" Meg had, much to my relief, put the cat down and was climbing rather inelegantly off the table. But she was still clearly furious. "She must have made him do it. I can't believe he'd have done such a thing if …" I wasn't really interested in whether or not Malcolm had been coerced into taking part. The only thing that concerned me was that Marjorie had defrauded Meg, Gideon, and Helen out of their inheritance. Now, that really did make her amazing, although clearly not in the way Gideon meant.

"And that," I said with a flourish, "is how we will neutralise Marjorie!"

"I'll do more than neutralise her, I'll …" Meg had both fists clenched and a look of utter fury on her face. "I can't wait to see the look on her face when we confront her with this. I'd like to see her …"

"We're not going to confront her." I interrupted just as Meg began to wring her hands as if throttling a chicken.

"Why ever not?" Meg exclaimed, clearly outraged to be denied a showdown with her sister.

"Because," I said, "it wouldn't work." I then went on to explain why we had to take a less direct approach to unmasking Marjorie as a fraudster.

The way I saw it, if I were to reveal to Marjorie what I knew I would also be revealing to her that I had been investigating her. I would, in addition, run the risk that she would call my bluff and tell me to do my worst. She would know that I couldn't go to Gideon with my incendiary information without revealing my role in uncovering it. The most likely outcome of this encounter would be that, however angry Gideon was with his mother, he would be equally angry with me. It would undermine his trust in me, and ultimately could (in a risk I wasn't prepared to take) bring our relationship to an end, which was the exact opposite of what I was hoping to achieve. I therefore proposed a different plan which would, I hoped, lead to a satisfactory conclusion for me rather than for Marjorie.

I needed to act quickly however, as I was fearful that Marjorie was closing in on my past. The cause of my unease was an incident the week before when I had stupidly answered the phone in Gideon's flat without checking the caller ID first.

"Oh, hello," said Marjorie, clearly less than pleased to hear me on the end of the line. "I wish to speak to my son." I was no happier to hear her. Her voice had an unpleasant nasal quality which I had grown to heartily dislike.

"He's not here," I replied, inwardly cursing myself for my moment of inattention. 'Check the caller ID' has been my mantra for many a long year and this was no time to start getting sloppy. I also noticed that Marjorie was markedly less pleasant to me when Gideon wasn't about to witness events. The pleasantries, such as they were, over Marjorie launched into the reason for her call. She was inviting us, yet again, for Sunday lunch, a week hence. I had eaten far more of these meals than I cared to remember, the most recent having occurred only two weeks before, and I was therefore not about to accept yet another invitation.

"I'm really sorry Marjorie, but I don't think we can, we're..." What could we plausibly be doing that we couldn't get out of? "We're going to my cousin's graduation." I said.

"You don't have any cousins," Marjorie countered, rather sharply. I don't have any cousins, but I was pretty sure I had never shared this information with Marjorie.

"Well, she's not actually my cousin," I dissembled (which is just a fancy word for lying), "I just call her that." Stupid, I know. No one calls someone a cousin if they're not a cousin. Aunt or uncle, either of those would have done, but cousin? My only excuse is that I was caught off guard. Given more time I could have done much better, but that won't butter any parsnips, or whatever it is one says in these circumstances.

"And on a Sunday?" Marjorie clearly wasn't going to be fobbed off easily. "This person who you call your cousin, she's graduating on a Sunday. Is that normal?"

"Oh, sorry Marjorie but that's the door buzzer, I'll have to go." That was marginally better, perhaps I hadn't lost my touch altogether.

"I didn't hear anything." Marjorie whined.

"It is very faint at the moment, but it's being fixed next week." I replied. "Oh, there it goes again, I really must go. Bye."

In retrospect I realised that I had behaved stupidly. Now that I was actually on to Marjorie the last thing I wanted was to annoy her. I should have just said we'd go but it was too late for that now. And what else, I was concerned to know, had Marjorie found out about my past? Nothing she was ready to reveal, that much was clear, but enough to send the odd flare up. Things were moving on and I couldn't have come across her part in the great inheritance swindle at a more fortunate time.

What Meg and I were going to do, therefore, was to devise a way to inform Gideon and Helen that they should have received an inheritance on the death of their grandfather without revealing our involvement. We then had to hope very much that one or other of them would take the matter up with their parents.

"Oh, I have an idea!" said Meg. "I could call Gideon using one of my voices…" Meg, I had learnt in our short acquaintance, was under the misapprehension that she was a good mimic. Whenever she told a story she was in the habit of impersonating all the characters in it. Unfortunately her impersonation skills extended only so far as being able to mimic her twin perfectly, and that was hardly a stretch.

"Or, alternatively I could write a letter and…" I countered.

"…I could pretend to be Scottish and…" Meg wasn't giving up that easily.

"…I could put it on official looking letter headed paper and…" I continued.

"…say that I was rrringing frorm a fearm of…" Meg said, giving it her best shot at what I assumed was a Scottish accent, but then again it might have been Welsh.

"So we'll go with the letter then." I concluded.

"Oh, well, if you think that's for the best." Meg clearly didn't, but this was my plan and so we were going to do it my way.

"And we'll send one to Helen too, just in case Gideon doesn't bite, and because it will add verisimilitude." It was almost worth all I'd had to put up with from Marjorie just to be able to slip the word verisimilitude into conversation.

"They'll bite, you can be sure of that." Meg said, only just stopping short of rubbing her hands with glee and letting out an evil cackle.

"OK, so we fake a letter from some made up solicitors explaining that there were some irregularities surrounding your father's will. We'll put in a form for them to return so they won't need to call anyone." I explained. "We say that they have been reviewing some old paperwork and discovered a discrepancy..."

"But what if Helen or Gideon call anyway?" Meg asked.

"Good point," I replied. "OK," I said having given the situation a little more thought. "I will get you a mobile phone and you will simply tell them the person they need to speak to is out and will get back to them. We'll worry about what to do next only if that happens."

"Och," said Meg, "thart's grrreeeet!"

Chapter 18

Gideon and I were each standing on a piece of newspaper by the back door in Marjorie's kitchen as we were, she had deemed, far too dirty to be allowed any further into the house. We had been cycling in Richmond Park and as it had been raining overnight and much of the park was now attached to us there was some justification for her actions. When we entered the kitchen Malcolm had been sitting at the kitchen table, his Sunday newspaper laid out neatly in front of him, waiting to be read. He was not allowed, I had learned, to take newspapers into the lounge for fear they would leave black marks on the furniture. He was not destined to read this newspaper at all, however, as it had been whipped from the table by Marjorie, hastily pulled apart to make two mats and was now fast being made illegible under our soggy feet.

"I got a letter the other day Mum." Gideon began.

"Oh, did you?" Marjorie was now busying herself wiping the worktop. She wiped her worktop incessantly. I don't think I was ever in that kitchen without seeing her wiping the worktop at some point.

"It was from the solicitors who handled Granddad's will. They seem to think that I should have received some money when he died," Gideon went on, "well me and Helen, we should both have received some money, but neither of us can remember getting anything." Gideon paused for a moment, perhaps expecting a response. He didn't get one. "It seems," he continued, "that they think there may have been something odd going on. Do either of you know what they are talking about?"

I once worked as a paralegal and despite having left under something of a cloud (for the record, I still believe that if you don't know that something is illegal you should be given the benefit of the doubt, for a first offence at least), I do know how to put together a very legal sounding letter. My letter had therefore been so convincing and comprehensive that neither Helen nor Gideon had felt the need to call the fictitious solicitors, and so were spared Meg's execrable accent.

"I have no idea what you are talking about." Marjorie said sharply, but she did look rather discombobulated. Having made her pronouncement she returned to wiping her worktop with renewed vigour. Behind us Malcolm made a coughing sound as though readying himself to speak. Marjorie stopped wiping long enough to glare at him. If anyone has ever been turned to stone by a look, which I doubt, it would certainly have been a look very like the one Marjorie gave Malcolm that morning.

"The letter says that they," Gideon continued, "the solicitors that is, raised a cheque each for Helen and me but, and this is the funny thing, we never received them." The funny thing, I had to stop myself from saying, is that your 'amazing' mother pocketed the cheques. "I know it was a long time ago ... maybe you don't remember." Gideon was being a bit hopeless. I had to, quite literally, clamp my mouth shut to stop myself from speaking up. I really didn't want to draw attention to myself, but I had a horrible feeling Gideon was going to accept being brushed off, which would not suit my purposes at all.

It had taken quite some effort and all my extraordinary powers of persuasion to get him this far. He had been almost ready to ignore the whole thing. I had, in the end, appealed to his sense of the greater good. What if, I suggested, his mother had been defrauded too? What if there were lots of other people who had also gone without their inheritance? Could he, I asked, stand idly by and let evil triumph? I might not have used those exact words, but that was the gist of my argument.

"Do you remember anything Malcolm?" I asked, having released the clamp from my mouth. In my defence I really couldn't help myself. "The thing is that you were the executor of the will. I thought the executor was responsible for making sure everyone got their money, although I could be wrong. I'm not a lawyer."

"Marjorie and I decided that the money should go to her." Malcolm rather unexpectedly dived right in with a confession. I had thought it might be harder to extract the truth, but perhaps he had been waiting to get this off his chest for years. I once read about a man who confessed to having murdered his wife thirty years previously. A skeleton had been found near his home and when he read about it in the local paper he handed himself in at the earliest opportunity (not the absolute earliest, obviously, as that would have been right after he'd killed her) to the local wooden tops. As it happens the skeleton was a couple of thousand years old and male, but the poor fellow (if one can call a murderer a poor fellow) had been weighed down by guilt all that time and found it, so he said, a relief to come clean. Not that this did his dead wife much good. Perhaps Malcolm felt the same. Whatever Malcolm's reason, he had clearly decided to go ahead despite, or perhaps because of, that look from Marjorie.

"Shut up Malcolm!" shrieked the woman herself, her furious wiping of the worktop finally ceasing.

"Sorry, I don't understand." Gideon looked genuinely befuddled, but then he didn't yet know the truth, but when he did...

Malcolm cleared his throat again and continued. "Your mother gave up her career to raise you and your sister. As a result she was forced to be financially dependent on me, which was very difficult for her." He sounded very much as if he were reading from a prepared statement. Perhaps he was, he'd had long enough to come up with one. What utter nonsense it was though. Had Marjorie been desperate for a career of her own? I don't think so. Marjorie had told me many times how wrong she believed it was for mothers to work, and had even gone so far as to suggest that women working at all was only acceptable if there was no suitable man for the job. She had, as far as I was aware, never shown the slightest inclination to do anything other than ensure her house was a shrine to cleanliness, go shopping, bitch about the neighbours, and plot to stop me from marrying her son.

"So," Malcolm continued, ignoring Marjorie's ever more penetrating glare. "Your mother, we, I," he was clearly not quite on message, "decided that the money should go to her in lieu of the salary she had been forced to give up. The money would, she, we, I thought, give her a small measure of independence."

"It was mine anyway," Marjorie added shrilly, "he only cut me out of his will to teach me lesson." Quite what lesson this might be wasn't clear.

"So, let me get this straight," Gideon began, "Granddad left money to me and Helen, but you two decided that Mum should have it?" I was rather worried as Gideon looked bemused rather than furious, but perhaps he was just having trouble comprehending the awfulness of what his mother had done. She had kept her children's inheritance (and her sister's but Gideon didn't know that and I could hardly tell him). How could she? I started to feel a sense of righteous anger and I had known about her perfidy for a while. I had only really seen the incident as a way to cut Marjorie down to size, but now I realised that she had behaved in a quite appalling manner. I'm no saint, but this really was beyond the pale.

"It was my decision, as executor." Malcolm announced. "Your mother took a lot of persuading." I'll bet she did.

"Right, well I need to think about this," said Gideon, rubbing his temples as if he had a headache. "It's all come as a bit of a shock." He looked genuinely dazed. His mother, on the other hand, was clearly clicking through her options. She took the one she always took – play the victim, go on the attack, and finally shift the blame to someone else.

"I gave up everything for you and your sister," she almost whispered, her voice apparently betraying a deep sense of hurt. She really was a piece of work. "My father," her voice rose slightly as if she was gathering her strength, "was simply being vindictive. He made my life a misery and then he tried to hurt me from beyond the grave." Her hand flew to cover her mouth as if stemming a sob. It was far more likely that she was trying to hide the look of satisfaction she felt on having come up with a usable defence. "Your father felt that I had suffered enough." This was dramatic stuff, but it came across, to me at least, as a little too pat. It sounded, much like Malcolm's earlier statement, too well rehearsed.

"What exactly did you give up, Mum?" Gideon asked. "Were we such a burden to you?" This was more like it. Go get 'em Gideon.

"Now, Gideon, I don't think you should talk to your mother like that." Malcolm intervened. "She's had a great deal to put up with over the years, and I can only try in whatever way I can to make up for all the distress she has suffered."

"Ian, Gideon, my darling," Marjorie had a slight catch in her voice that could have been an incipient sob but I think was more likely to have been a stifled laugh as she saw that the tide was turning in her favour, "you know I'd do anything for you, risk anything for you." Even the director of a South American soap opera might have asked Marjorie to take it down a notch, so impassioned was her performance. "Haven't I proved that to you, in every way possible? What more do you want from me?" Marjorie buried her head in her hands and began to weep (or possibly laugh) into them.

"And where is the money now? I mean, is there any left?" Gideon was clearly having trouble processing what had happened and was not taking much notice of his mother's quite terrific performance.

"Well, not that specific money. That's been spent but..." Malcolm was clearly not as accomplished a liar as Marjorie. He may have been going to say more, but his words were drowned out by a shriek from Marjorie. Going for maximum drama she had fallen forward clutching her head with one hand and her stomach with the other. It looked to me as if she had been struck down by appendicitis, but I think she was going for guilt ridden repentance.

"What's the matter Mum?" Gideon asked. Marjorie had sunk to the floor and was slumped, dramatically if inelegantly, against the dishwasher, one hand grasping at the worktop above her head. Watching Marjorie emote in her kitchen was becoming rather repetitive. Malcolm, Gideon, and I had already been treated to an entire morning of this stuff on account of Malcolm's supposed infidelity. Now it looked as if we were to get another chance to marvel at Marjorie giving it her all. I only hoped she would add some variety to her performance as, for this audience member at least, it ran the risk of becoming a bit samey.

"I'm so sorry." She gasped out the words as if they caused her physical pain. She began to sob copiously but I was quite sure I saw her take a sideways glance at me in which she looked anything but tearful. I have never had any time for Dominic's theory that the world is ruled by a secret cabal of lizard people but as Marjorie looked up from where she had collapsed in a supposed paroxysm of emotion, I swear that just for a moment I saw an inner eyelid flick back to reveal her true lizard self.

Gideon, clearly more impressed than I by his mother's dramatics at this point, had rushed to her side and was attempting to comfort an apparently distraught Marjorie. You had to give it to the woman, she knew how to play him. From her position on the floor she reached up a claw like, bejewelled hand and clutched Gideon's wrist.

"I'm sorry, I knew it was wrong, but your father..." Marjorie paused to dab at her nose with the tiny handkerchief she always had, along with many other things as I was discovering, up her sleeve. Malcolm looked on awkwardly as if, despite being technically part of the family, he would rather be anywhere than where he found himself. You made your bed, I wanted to tell him, I hope you're finding it comfortable.

"That was... interesting." I said once we were home and ensconced in the sitting room with a mug of coffee each.

"Yes, it was." Gideon replied, non-committally. He had, so far, said nothing to indicate which way the wind was likely to blow.

"I wonder what Helen will make of all this." I pondered.

"Oh, I expect she'll be pissed off with Mum. She'll want to blame her rather than Dad."

"I thought mothers and daughters were meant to be close." I said. "How come she doesn't see your mother in the same way that you do?"

"Because she has no idea what Mum did for me when I was a teenager." Gideon said.

"Neither do I." I replied. Just bloody tell me I wanted to yell. As if he could read my mind (which thankfully he can't) that was exactly what he did.

"Well, you know that I had kidney problems when I was a teenager." he began.

"I do." I replied.

"For a while it looked as if I might need a kidney transplant."

"Yes, but you said it didn't come to that." I wanted to do that thing producers do on live TV and wind my arm furiously to indicate that he should get to the point as quickly as possible, but I was just going to have to let him crawl along at his own pace.

"No it didn't," he continued, "but if I had needed a transplant I would have needed a donor." Get on with it man. "So Mum offered herself as a living donor." Was that it? I was a little disappointed in Gideon if I'm honest. It really didn't sound to me like that was worth a lifetime of devotion. I mean, anyone can offer an internal organ. I once seriously thought about becoming a bone marrow donor after seeing a documentary claiming that they were just crying out for the stuff. I didn't get around to it in the end, I can't remember why, but my point is valid. Offering body parts to others is a doddle, and Marjorie didn't have to go through with it as Gideon hadn't needed a transplant anyway. I waited silently to see if there was any more to come, because I was distinctly unimpressed so far. Turned out there was.

"When they realised that I didn't need a new kidney," Gideon resumed after a quite unnervingly long pause, during which I had wisely, and with not a little effort, managed to keep quiet, "Mum donated one of hers to another family anyway."

"Oh!" Now, that was a surprise.

"She said," Gideon stared dreamily into the middle distance as if he were repeating the words of some mystical eastern guru, "she said that having been through what she had she couldn't bear the thought of another mother suffering in the same way."

"Oh, did she?" It sounded like utter tosh to me. From what I'd seen of Marjorie I very much doubted she would have given a stranger her toenail clippings let alone a major internal organ. But I had no evidence, only intuition, to contradict this stomach churningly heart-warming story.

"And Helen doesn't know about this?" I asked.

"No one does, except Dad. She really doesn't want anyone to know." I'll bet she doesn't. "So you see why I can't share my sister's view of our mother. Helen seems to only see the bad side of Mum."

"The bad side?" I asked, hoping to have found the chink through which I could make him see how awful his mother truly was.

"I don't mean that Mum has a bad side." OK, so no chink then. "I mean that Helen only sees bad things in Mum, she interprets everything Mum does negatively." While you, my handsome dupe, interpret everything she does in a ridiculously positive light.

"So what do you think Helen will make of your mother having..." I searched for a non-judgemental description of what Marjorie had done following her father's death. "Appropriated your inheritance?"

"But it wasn't Mum, was it? It was Dad. He gave it to her, she probably didn't even realise what she was doing was wrong." If there had been a handy wall against which to bang my head I would have done so.

If I was frustrated by Gideon's inability to see his mother for what she really was, this frustration was as nothing to my sense of impotent fury the following day when Marjorie played a blinder. I was getting ready to bellow to Gideon that dinner was ready when there was an unexpected buzz at the door.

"It's Mum," Gideon said, coming onto the kitchen, "she's on her way up."

A simple "oh," was all I vouchsafed.

"Gideon, my darling boy," I had never heard Marjorie use such florid language before. I was even more surprised when she threw herself into his arms, declaring "I am so, so sorry. I didn't realise, I didn't know, I was a fool!" She clasped Gideon to her well-padded torso (she had no bosom to speak of) before continuing. "I believed your father when he said it was the right thing to do. He convinced me that I was safeguarding the money for you both. And I was!" She must have been up all night working on that one. And it had been time well spent. She had, in one fell swoop, exonerated herself and made Malcolm the fall guy. I actually felt a sense of relief. After the kidney related revelations of the day before I had wavered for a while. What if she was a good person and I, like Helen, was reading her wrong? But I wasn't, any fool (but not Gideon unfortunately) could see that she was the most transparent fraud. And there he was, the fall guy, Malcolm. He stood a few feet behind Marjorie in the hallway, head bent in contrition taking whatever Marjorie dished out, just like he always did.

"So," Marjorie said with a flourish, "here it is." And with that she waved an envelope under Gideon's nose.

"Here what is?" asked Gideon, taking the proffered envelope.

"The money of course, plus interest. Your sister's is in the post."

"But Mum," he exclaimed, "you didn't need to do this!" Oh yes she bloody did. Even I had to admit a sneaking admiration for her at that moment. From absolute zero to almighty hero in one easy payment.

"I only hope you can forgive me." Marjorie simpered, clearly loving her role as Lady Bountiful. "I was led astray, I should have been stronger, stuck to what I knew was right. And a little extra won't hurt right now will it? You and Eve can put it towards your wedding!" She clapped her hands together in glee as she said this. The look she shot me, though, told a quite different story. It was gleeful all right, but it was also triumphant. She had, it seemed outwitted me. Where next, I wondered dismally, where next?

We all made our way through to the sitting room while dinner spoiled in the kitchen. "I was so sorry that Helen's behaviour caused you to put off your lovely wedding," Marjorie continued in the same flowery vein, "so if this can in any way, in any way at all, make your day, whenever you decide to go ahead with it, even better, then nothing would make me happier." Nothing would have made Marjorie happier than to see me fall under a bus, of that I was quite certain, but Gideon was lapping it up.

"Oh, Mum, you really, really didn't need to do this." Gideon gushed. Oh she did, she really, really did.

Chapter 19

"I'm a retherearcher for the National Thtatithtical Offith." I explained.

"I thought it was the Office of National Statistics," my interviewee, in whose living room I was sitting, queried.

"We often get confuthed," I continued. I had never had cause previously to consider how many sibilant sounds there are in everyday speech. Even if I had, I couldn't have anticipated that the false teeth I was wearing would have caused me to have quite such a problem with them. I suppose that I should have tried the teeth out beforehand, but it was too late now as I sat opposite Malcolm's sister in her home in Basildon.

I had learnt of Cynthia's existence during one of Marjorie's many execrable Sunday lunches. On this particular occasion Marjorie had been even frostier than usual, and uncharacteristically silent. It had crossed my mind that I might have been the cause of her selective muteness, but it turned out not to be the case.

"Who would want to live in Basildon anyway?" she had snapped, about halfway through lunch. Up to that point Basildon hadn't made an appearance of any sort in the conversation, so I was rather bemused. Malcolm's response shed a little light on the matter though, and just enough for me to surmise the cause of Marjorie's ill humour.

"She is my sister and I am very fond of her," he had said. "I am quite happy to visit her on my own, you know."

"But Basildon, I ask you," Marjorie had sneered, ignoring Malcolm's offer to go alone. She spoke as if Malcolm's sister lived in Basildon solely in order to upset her. "And that daughter of hers. Dreadful creature. But I suppose she can't help who her mother is, poor girl." Marjorie gritted her teeth, she may even have gnashed them a little. "But if she was my daughter I'd..." what she would have done I wasn't to find out because at that moment Malcolm had some sort of coughing fit and, once he had recovered, Marjorie dropped the subject.

So here I was, sitting chatting with Malcolm's sister Cynthia, in Basildon, which didn't seem that bad from what little I had seen of it. As I couldn't be sure I would never come across her again at a family event, as well as the ill-fitting teeth I was wearing a wig that made me look a little like Richard III, and a pair of pebble glasses. As well as this I had smeared a huge amount of peacock blue eye shadow on my eyelids, I swear they were actually heavier than usual I'd used so much. I had also bought myself an outfit from a charity shop. It would have been perfect for someone three sizes bigger than me and it crackled whenever I moved, but other than that it was perfect. I was here on a fact finding trip having decided that I needed to prove that Claire was wrong and I was right.

Having told Claire about Gideon and Helen's stolen inheritance, or as much as I could without revealing my role in the events, she still refused to see things in exactly the same light as me.

"The truth is that you don't have any evidence that things are anything other than they appear to be." Claire had said. I had, I will admit, been hoping for a more supportive response. Claire was, at the time of this conversation, weeding her vegetable garden while I sat on a bench a few feet away drinking tea. Claire loves growing fruit and vegetables, but the attraction is lost on me. To spend so many hours tending plants which yield so little produce, most of which is eaten by bugs and rabbits anyway, seems to me the definition of futility. Claire on the other hand, thinks gardening is life affirming, so each to their own. "Are you sure that you're not guilty of ..." she continued.

"If you're going to say the final contrition error I'll punch you." I interrupted.

"Fundamental attribution error actually, and I wasn't going to say that. I was going to say that you may have your own reasons for believing the worst of Marjorie." Claire got up, took off her dirt caked gloves and came to sit by me. It was a warmish autumn day, and her garden was looking quite lovely. She lives just beyond Kingston on Thames in an Arts and Crafts style house that has seen better days. It would be spectacular if it was only tidied up a bit and redecorated, but Claire's mind is always fixed on higher things, like vegetables and God, so interior design doesn't really figure in her world.

"Why on earth would I want to see the worst in Marjorie? That makes no sense at all." I responded.

"It does, if you would just think about it for a moment," Claire replied. I paused for a moment and thought about it.

"I've thought about it and it's nonsense." I said conclusively.

"You could," Claire suggested, "be self-sabotaging." She wasn't easily going to give up on the idea that it was me and not Marjorie who was the problem.

"Oh, could I?" I responded. "First of all, why would I do that? And second of all what does that mean?"

"You have a long history of failed relationships." Claire replied, getting straight to the point. Claire doesn't beat about the bush. She tells it like it is, or at least as she sees it. I like her for it and it annoys me intensely at the same time.

"It's not that long!" I exclaimed, although the list was, if anything, longer than even Claire knew.

"And you very much believe that this might be it, with Gideon. I have never known you to become so attached to anyone. I do believe you actually care for Gideon, I mean really care for him, and you are afraid it won't work out. Now, this is where the sabotage comes in. If your relationship with Gideon were to fail..."

"That's a mighty big if..." I scoffed.

"Yes, well..." Claire swatted my 'big if' away as if it were nothing. "It's possible that you don't, unconsciously, believe that this relationship will work out, but you have convinced yourself that you want it to."

"I do want it to!" I exclaimed.

"It's possible that, having fallen for Gideon, you don't, deep down, believe you are worthy of him. He's a really good man, which is not a characteristic widely shared by your exes." Claire had a point. I have, it's true, been out with some real stinkers. "And you have done some bad things in your life." True again, although Claire didn't know the half of it. "And some bad things have happened to you. It's perfectly possible that you don't feel good enough for Gideon."

"Not good enough! Me, not good enough!" I spluttered.

"I've known you for a long time Eve, and I'm a clinical psychologist, or at least I'm training to be one. Do you really think you can fool me?" I had, on several occasions, fooled Claire that is, but it wouldn't help our friendship to acknowledge this.

"So how am I self-sabotaging?" I demanded to know.

"You may be making a monster of Marjorie so that she can take the blame if your relationship with Gideon fails."

"What crap." Of course it was crap. But what if it wasn't crap? I thought back over everything that had happened since I had met Gideon. Categorically that was not true. It was definitely Marjorie and not me. Definitely.

"I would normally charge an hourly rate for my services," Claire slung a muddy arm around my shoulder and pulled me towards her. I like it when Claire hugs me as she is not an effusive person so it feels as if she actually means it. "But as you seem to need more than the average amount of help I can give you a bulk rate."

"I'll give you a bulk rate if you're not careful." I nudged Claire in the ribs with my elbow, quite hard but with affection.

"Well thank you," she said, removing her arm. "I hope you have found this time together useful, and I shall see you the same time next week."

"Whatever." I grunted, doing my best impersonation of her sixteen year old son.

The upshot of this conversation was that I felt I needed to broaden my knowledge of Marjorie in order to utterly disprove (or possibly refute, I'm never sure which it should be) Claire's ludicrous suggestion. Helen might, as Gideon believed, have a distorted view of their mother and Meg might be as mad as her twin. I reasoned, therefore, that I needed an unbiased third party to corroborate my wholly correct intuitions about the evil old hag. The only person I could think of who might be able to shed some relatively unbiased light on the matter was Malcolm's Basildon based sister, Cynthia. So here I was, dressed in my ill-fitting nylon ensemble with my ill-fitting teeth and awful wig, in Cynthia's little nineteen sixties bungalow, sitting in a black leather

Parker Knoll recliner trying to find out... well I wasn't entirely sure what I was trying to find out but I would know it when I saw it.

"It'th very good of you to agree to thith interview." I said. "We are conducting a..." survey, study, why did everything suddenly have an s in it? "... we're trying to find out about how famleeth have changed over time."

"Famleeth?" Cynthia queried.

"You know, famleeth. Mother, father, children."

I had called Cynthia, whose address and phone number I had, with only a little subterfuge, obtained from Gideon, and arranged to visit her for an interview. I did once work for the Office for National Statistics as a researcher, although I left quite soon by mutual consent (let's just say the figures that I supplied might not have been as accurate as the ONS would have liked them to be, but once you've interviewed half a dozen people you can pretty much make the rest up) so I knew the drill. I had my computer perched on my lap and was tapping away as I recorded Cynthia's answers to my questions. I was actually, as it happens, filling out a personality quiz Claire had thought would be instructive for me, but Cynthia couldn't see my screen so it didn't matter.

Malcolm and Cynthia's father had, Cynthia told me, been a bus driver and their mother a housewife. The family had been in Basildon since around the time of the Norman invasion and not a single Rowe apart from Malcolm had ever left. They didn't seem to be the kind of family in which Gideon would have been a much used name, as Malcolm had claimed at that never to be forgotten first Sunday lunch in Sheen, but then I might just be a crashing snob.

Brother and sister had been quite close until he met, in Cynthia's words, 'that stuck up cow' Marjorie. It's amazing what people will tell you if you only ask. By the time we got to this revelation we had shared two pots of tea and a packet of pink wafers, not my favourite biscuit but Cynthia seemed to think they were a sign of the high esteem in which she held me by this point. I therefore scoffed my way through as many as my teeth would allow.

Following his marriage to 'that bitch' Marjorie (Cynthia had many descriptors for Marjorie, none of them particularly complimentary) Malcolm's career had taken off. Having been a lowly bank teller he was, in no time flat, working in the legal department of the multinational business in which he went on to build his successful and lucrative career.

"The thing I never understood was how it took off so fast," Cynthia confided to me. Having bonded over the fact that we both had feckless husbands and disappointing children we were by now the very best of friends. We both had daughters who were bringing up their children single-handedly. We had both suffered greatly on account of these daughters, and had to take much of the burden for raising their children ourselves, but what grandchildren! If our own offspring had been somewhat below par we were both blessed with stellar grandchildren. What a lot we had in common.

"Did Michael ..." I began.

"Malcolm." Cynthia corrected me.

"Oh yeth, of courth. Did Malcolm have any higher qualificationth, in the law for eggthample?" The pink wafers had, happily, made speaking much easier as they had formed a paste between my real and my false teeth, holding them more securely in place. I would never sneer at pink wafers again.

"Not as far as I know. I do think, though, that there's something odd there. I mean it's as if he made a pact with the devil. I thought," Cynthia leaned in conspiratorially, "and so did Mum and Dad, that he'd have been so much better off with other one."

"The other one?" I asked.

"Meg. Marjorie's sister. Identical! She was a lovely girl. When he told us he was married we thought he meant to Meg, seeing as they were engaged. That was a bit embarrassing, I can tell you. But it seemed as if Marjorie had a hold over Malcolm. I've no idea what it might have been, but there you go, it was just something I thought. Daft really, but I just couldn't work out why he would have married... her," Cynthia was out of venomous epithets it seemed, "when he would have been much happier with Meg. Funny, isn't it, what people do?"

"Yeth, it ith, indeed it ith."

"You never told me you were engaged to Malcolm!" I said accusingly.

"You never asked." Meg replied. "It was a long time ago and I'd rather not talk about it," she said, clearly intent on bringing the subject to a close.

"Yes, but you could have..." I began, but Meg held up her palm in front of my face while saying, emphatically, "enough," so I had to let it go.

We were licking our wounds over a cup of coffee in Meg's bedsit. We had been comprehensively outwitted by Marjorie over the misappropriated inheritance. The only positive thing that had come out of the whole sorry affair from my perspective was that Helen and Marjorie were talking again, which meant that my wedding was back on. I wasn't really in the mood for seeing the Rowes playing happy families but I did want to marry Gideon so I was just going to have to suck it up. If, that is, the wedding were to go ahead.

I had recently received some information that had confirmed my suspicions that there was very little chance that Marjorie, having twice put a stop to my prospective nuptials, would simply think to herself 'oh well, I gave it my best shot, but I can tell when I'm beaten'. I wasn't about to reveal the source of my new intelligence to Meg. I had been sworn to secrecy and the person to whom I had sworn was not someone I would cross without very good reason.

"It's hopeless," Meg continued, "there is nothing else we can do, nothing at all." That was how I'd felt until two days before, but armed with my new information I was filled with renewed energy for the fight.

"We may be down, Meg, but we are not out. We," I announced, "are going to search Marjorie's house."

"Oh my!" Meg looked deeply shocked. "Are you quite sure that's a good idea? I don't know anything about housebreaking."

"We aren't going to break in," I explained. "I know where the spare keys are and I know the alarm code. We just need to wait until we can be sure that both Marjorie and Malcolm will be away for a few hours, preferably after dark, and then we simply pop round and have a rummage."

"What do you think we'll find?" Meg was clearly far from convinced by my brilliant plan.

"Secrets. Marjorie's secrets. That's what we'll find." Or at least that was what my informant assured me I would find. But I couldn't tell Meg why I was so sure, so she would just have to trust me. I looked at her intently. "Are you with me?" I asked.

"I suppose I am, but don't you think that ransacking Marjorie's home might be taking it a bit far dear?" Meg replied.

"We're not going to ransack anything," I assured her. "We're just going to slip in," I wiggled my hand to indicate a snake slithering silently in one direction, "take anything that may prove useful and then slip out again." I wiggled my hand back the other way. "She'll never know we've been there."

"Yes, but... breaking into her house, who would do such a thing?" Meg looked perplexed.

"A psychopath, that's who." I replied.

"A what?" Meg asked.

"The kind of person that would do what I'm proposing would be a psychopath," I explained, "and it just so happens that I am one."

"One what dear?" she asked.

"A psychopath." I replied.

"You can read people's minds?" Meg looked deeply shocked.

"Not a psychic," I said, "a psychopath. They don't read people's minds, they murder people."

"Well that's a relief," said Meg let out a little sigh, "that you're a murderer not a mind reader."

"I'm not a murderer." I said. "Only extreme psychopaths murder people, and not all of them even do that."

I'd been doing a little research on psychopaths recently, ever since I had done the personality test suggested by Claire. As far as I could work out it simply meant that I have a healthy disregard for laws and social codes, that I'm not that bothered about the rights of others, and that I'm less likely to feel remorse or guilt than non-psychopaths. I can't see what's so wrong with any of that, as long as I don't take it too far. Which I don't believe I do, but then I'm a psychopath so I suppose I would think that.

"I only have psychopathic tendencies." I continued, "I'm not a full blown psycho, but maybe that's why I'll do something like this and why I'll beat Marjorie. I will not," I said emphatically, "be outwitted by her."

"She's outwitted everyone else," Meg observed.

"Yes, but I don't suppose she's ever come up against a psychopath before, do you?" I replied.

"I doubt that she has, my dear," said Meg, "I very much doubt that she has."

Chapter 20

My new found confidence and determination to beat Marjorie had come as the result of a meeting I had had a few days previously. A fourth postcard had arrived which had completely baffled me. On the front was a picture of a four poster bed while on the back it said N O R W Y C H. I hadn't the faintest idea what it meant and I didn't feel inclined to waste my time trying to figure it out. The previous postcards had ultimately led me precisely nowhere, and I had about hit rock bottom in my quest to stop Marjorie from interfering in my life. I couldn't see a way out that didn't involve leaving Gideon, and that wasn't something I was prepared to do.

I decided, therefore, that enough was enough. I would make contact with Sasha, who I was quite certain was the source of the cards, and ask her what I should do, seeing as how she seemed to know everything. As she was clearly already trying to help me I couldn't see why she should refuse.

Finding her phone number was child's play. I sometimes think that I should have taken Phillipe Merlot up on his offer of a partnership in his private detecting business. Considering where he ended up though, or at least the bits of him that have been found, I probably made the right decision to leave when I did. So that is how I found myself standing in a poorly lit car park under an office block in Chiswick while Storm Brenda raged outside. I had cycled over and so was dressed, due to the severity of the storm and the darkness of the night, in my fluorescent waterproof cycling gear. I looked rather like a PCSO, which is not my best look or one I would have chosen to wear to a meeting with Gideon's supposedly stunning ex, but it was ideal for the prevailing weather conditions. I had arrived early and was just finishing off a packet of Frazzles (I had missed dinner and was starving) when I heard the distinctive click clack of a pair of high heels approaching me from behind. I was taken by surprise as I hadn't heard a car pull up, but maybe the storm had masked the noise.

Spinning around (although spinning isn't really possible when wearing wet weather cycling gear) the first thing I noticed was the red glowing tip of a cigarette. Sasha stopped about ten feet away from me and, despite the poor light, I could see that she was every bit as stunning as I had feared. She looked like a mash up of Gwyneth Paltrow and Cate Blanchett, being tall, slender, blonde, immaculately dressed, and ineffably cool. She had on an exquisitely tailored dark coat beneath which she was wearing a pale silk blouse tucked into a pair of straight legged trousers that skimmed her slender ankles and stopped just above a pair of almost unworkably high, slender heeled shoes. Chic didn't even come close.

"Hello Eve." Her voice had just the tiniest hint of a foreign accent. I honestly don't think I'd have got a look in with Gideon if Sasha had been the competition rather than 'Dirty Nicole'. Thank goodness she hadn't thought he was worth what I was now going through with Marjorie. "You wished to see me?" she almost purred.

"Ye... Yes," I managed to squeak.

"How can I help you?" She leaned elegantly against the wall by which she was standing, and took a long draw on what I could now see was an electronic cigarette.

"The thing is," I stammered, "well, what I wanted to ask was..."

"Yes," she said encouragingly, a faint but kindly smile playing across her perfect features.

"This postcard," I pulled the now rather soggy postcard from my pocket and held it towards her. As the distance between us was longer than that of our combined arms I had to walk towards her, rustling very loudly with each step and leaving a trail of water in my wake. "I don't really understand what you're...what I'm meant to...the thing is..." I seemed to have lost the power of coherent speech. Once I was close enough Sasha reached a languorous, cashmere clad arm towards me and took the soggy offering.

"I'm terribly sorry," she said, having looked at the card. "I seem to have made a mistake, although it does explain..." Her voice trailed off.

"Explain what?" I asked.

"This," she waved the disintegrating card at me, "was meant for my husband. He's overseas, on a tour of duty."

"He's a soldier?" I asked.

"In a manner of speaking," she replied. "This was a message meant for him."

"Knickers Off Ready When..." I began.

"You Come Home. Yes," she concluded, smiling more broadly than before, "I adapted it from the old wartime soldiers' message. Silly I know, but it makes us laugh." So, Sasha loved her husband and she made mistakes. I warmed to her on learning this. She couldn't help it if she was enormously glamorous. I am not by nature glamorous. I am the kind of woman who can't be bothered to reapply her lipstick at a party. Sasha probably wouldn't need to reapply hers as it would never dare to get rubbed off in the first place.

"So," Sasha said, "you didn't get my fourth message?"

"No, I didn't." I confirmed. "What did it say?"

"It was so cryptic I'm afraid I can't remember," she began, "but the point of it was to tell you to search Marjorie's house. She has secrets. If you want to marry Gideon you must find her secrets." She gave me a penetrating stare while pointing her electronic cigarette in my direction.

"How," I asked, "do you know all this?"

"Secrets, as you have probably guessed, are my business."

"You're a sp..." I began, but Sasha interrupted me.

"We prefer operative," she whispered.

"If you're an operative," I asked, "and you know all this stuff about... my partner's mother, why did you let her beat you?" I felt like an idiot asking this in the face of Sasha's almost superhuman competence, but I wanted to know the answer.

"She didn't beat me," Sasha replied, a look of annoyance flashing briefly across her face. "I made a strategic withdrawal." She took another drag on her electronic cigarette. "Gideon is a very lovely man, but he and I weren't well suited enough for me to want to deal with his mother." Quite what she meant by 'dealing with' Marjorie I wasn't sure, but I sensed she didn't mean 'manage to rub along with'.

"I spend all my working life trying to find out things people don't want me to find out. I also frequently have to stop people finding out things I don't want them to know." She looked at me sardonically. "I really couldn't face my personal life being filled with the same."

"I see." I said.

"The efforts you have put into exposing the target so far prove that you are more committed to the prize than I was," she went on. By target I assumed she meant Marjorie, so the prize must be Gideon.

"How do you know how committed I am ... to the prize?" I asked.

"I know all sorts of things," Sasha said. "Your brother is an idiot, but he's not wrong about absolutely everything."

"Even the lizards?" I asked.

"No, he's completely wrong about the lizards."

"Thank goodness for that!" I gave a sigh of relief. "But these secrets, where should I look?"

"They will be close to the target, of that you can be sure. The target is clever, but not as clever as it would like to think. You are clever too. Cleverer perhaps than the target gives you credit for. I have to go now," Sasha blew a perfect smoke ring that rose and gradually dissipated into the air above her head. If you could bottle sophistication and sell it she'd have been the richest person alive. "You know what you have to do. And you are the woman to do it, I know that much."

"Thanks!" I was ridiculously chuffed at Sasha's faith in me.

"But," she said, fixing me with a steely glare, "this meeting never happened."

"No, absolutely, I swear." And I meant it. Sasha struck me as a woman not to be messed with. "Could I just ask one thing?"

"Yes, although I don't promise to answer," she replied.

"Why?" I asked. "Why are you helping me like this?"

"Because," said Sasha, "Marjorie's a monster and Gideon's a nice man. He deserves to marry whoever he wants, and she won't let that happen."

"It's as simple as that?" I asked.

"Yes," Sasha confirmed, "it's as simple as that." And with that she was gone. Again, I didn't hear a car, but there must have been one as she was dry as a bone and so hadn't been outside. I, on the other hand, had to cycle home through the wind and rain and was only glad that I had bought myself a second packet of Frazzles. They would, I hoped, give me the energy I needed to face what lay ahead.

Chapter 21

With my rescheduled wedding fast approaching Marjorie made a great show of throwing herself, and the money she had misappropriated from Gideon, into the affair wholeheartedly. She had even suggested that we go on a shopping trip together to choose my wedding outfit. I had been going to wear a dress I had owned for several years but Marjorie was appalled by this suggestion, and she didn't even know that I had been married in it once already.

"You must have something new. I'll help you choose!" Marjorie had declared enthusiastically as she, Gideon and I discussed the forthcoming nuptials while sitting around her kitchen table. Gideon was delighted at the idea of his mother and me going on a shopping trip together. I was just as enthusiastic but for rather different reasons. Under normal circumstances I would have been horrified at the suggestion, combining as it did two of my least favourite things, clothes shopping and Marjorie. But it did offer an opportunity for me to discover when her house might be empty, and so I slapped on my best smile and acted as if nothing would please me more.

We began our shopping trip in Harrods. I have never bought anything in Harrods, it's not really my kind of shop. I was once there with a friend and thought that I might as well buy some teabags. I needed them and it sells them so it seemed a feasible idea. A few moments later and I was standing open mouthed and speechless with shock as an assistant picked out a box of fifteen teabags that cost thirty pounds. That's two pounds a bag! Sensing that she was on the verge of losing the sale, the assistant tried to justify the price on the basis that the bags themselves were made of cotton. I was still unable to speak, so she went on to tell me the thread count of the cotton out of which the bags were made. It was higher than that of my bed sheets. So, as I say, not my kind of shop.

Marjorie, on the other hand, liked to behave as if she rarely shopped anywhere else, but as I had no intention of buying anything that day it didn't really matter where we went. If I don't like clothes shopping on my own, I absolutely loathe clothes shopping in company. I know what suits me and I don't need someone else muddying the waters. In addition, Marjorie and I had very different ideas about what I should wear. The only thing we agreed on was that I must wear something.

"Oh," Marjorie exclaimed, holding an execrable floral rag against me, "this is beautiful. It brings out your eyes." I would almost rather have had my eyes put out than wear her choice of dress. One might have thought that she wanted me to look ridiculous given some of the monstrosities she threw in my path that day. I, however, simply smiled and murmured my displeasure very quietly under my breath. After an hour or so of this, and having been forced to try on a couple of things in order not to appear deliberately difficult, we made our way to the ground floor via the lifts.

"They get everywhere," Marjorie hissed as we stepped out on the ground floor.

"What do?" I asked, bemused.

"Russians," she replied. "They're everywhere." She spoke so loudly that it was impossible that the very well dressed Russian couple who had shared the lift with us could have failed to hear her.

"But at least they're not Arabs," Marjorie continued, without lowering her voice. "Or Jews. Jews are the worst." I shouldn't have been surprised, but I was. Marjorie had made some vaguely racist comments before in my hearing, but Gideon had always gently admonished her, and she had always asked his forgiveness. "It's how I was brought up, I'm afraid," she had said, smiling obsequiously at him as if that made it all right. She had, however, overstepped the mark by some considerable margin with this comment. But although it felt terribly craven, there was nothing I could do about it. I was sure that she was testing me, trying to get me to react, so I simply had to suck it up while smiling ingratiatingly at the couple and hoping that they realised that I didn't share Marjorie's views.

Once outside Marjorie hailed a cab (she was paying, so what the hell?) and ordered the driver to take us to Peter Jones. I would have preferred not to run the risk of bumping into Meg, for whom the store was almost a second home, and therefore spent an anxious hour running around corners ahead of Marjorie and scanning the crowds in the style of a close protection officer.

"Lunch time I think," Marjorie finally announced. "My treat," she said as she grabbed my arm and practically frog-marched me down the King's Road. "I want us to be the very best of friends," she went on, "now that you're finally going to become one of us." I assumed she meant a Rowe not a complete bitch or a lizard eyed alien, but I wasn't entirely sure.

"That would be…" I searched for an appropriate word, "amazing." I tried not to pull away from her too obviously as she leaned into me as if we were on the most intimate of terms. It was as our lunch arrived that I had the strongest sense of deja vu. Looking at the quiche that had just been placed before her, Marjorie clapped her hands together while exclaiming excitedly "I adore asparagus, I always cook it when we have someone special for dinner." She had never cooked it for me, but I let that pass.

"Oh," I said, involuntarily.

"Oh what?" Marjorie enquired.

"Oh, how delicious it all looks." I extemporised (another of those fancy words for lying). What I had suddenly realised was that we were in the same cafe that Meg and I had eaten in on our first meeting, and Marjorie had ordered the same meal as her twin. Well, not the exactly same, but the sisters clearly shared a love of asparagus.

"Oh," enthused Marjorie, "this is to die for." I have always loathed this phrase, and hearing it issue from Marjorie's lips did nothing to change my opinion. People die for all sorts of reasons, but asparagus quiche, however delicious, has never been one of them. "You must try some," Marjorie continued, using her fork to carve out a piece for me and lifting it towards my mouth. The fork had a smear of Marjorie's shell pink lipstick at the bottom of the tines and was topped with a quivering piece of custardy quiche. As I am not overly fond of being touched without having given my express permission it's possible to imagine how I might feel about sharing other people's food from their lipstick smeared forks. It was all I could do not to retch.

"No," I said, rather too brusquely, "I can't."

"Why ever not? It's divine." Marjorie was being very effusive in her praise of what looked to me like a very ordinary piece of quiche.

"I'm allergic." I said. It was, if not the first untruth, at least the first outright lie of the day.

"Allergic to quiche, I've never heard of such a thing," said Marjorie. Neither had I.

"Asparagus," I almost shouted, "I'm allergic to asparagus. Terribly allergic. It could kill me." I was worried I might have overdone it, but at least the quiche that had been hovering dangerously close to my lips had been withdrawn.

"How unusual." Marjorie looked at me, appraisingly.

"Yes, I suppose it is." I concurred.

After this we carried on making desultory conversation of a most tedious kind, but I did manage to establish that Marjorie and Malcolm were going to be absent from home attending a dinner at the golf club the following Friday evening. So mission accomplished and at the cost of only a few hours in Marjorie's company.

CHAPTER 22

"You have got to be the worst sidekick ever." I snarled at Meg. "If Robin had lead Batman such a merry dance goodness only knows what would have happened to Gotham."

"I'm trying my best, and why am I the sidekick?" Meg muttered in reply. We had successfully entered Rowe HQ but it had not been without incident. Meg had, so far, turned on all the security lights, tripped over the rug in the hallway, almost broken a vase, and made enough noise on the stairs to wake the dead.

"You really have to ask?" I enquired. She and I were both dressed from head to toe in black. I was rather pleased with my outfit. I felt, and looked if I do say so myself, rather like Catwoman, to continue the Batman theme. Meg, on the other hand, looked like a badly stuffed soft toy, but at least she couldn't be seen in the dark.

"I'll start in here." I said, pointing to the bedroom where Malcolm kept his computer, and which also housed a shelf of box files. I was far from sure Marjorie would keep her secrets in such plain site, but I had to start somewhere. I had been methodically going through each file, a small flash-light clenched between my teeth so that I could see without putting the lights on, for several minutes when Meg called to me.

"Oy!" she bellowed, in clear contravention of my instructions to keep quiet. I'll bet Sasha didn't have to put up with this from her operatives. "Come in here."

"I'm not deaf, there's really no need to shout." I hissed as I joined her in the master bedroom.

"Look what I've found!" Meg ignored my comment, looking pleased as punch and holding up a buff folder. "It was under the mattress. It's where she always hid her secret things when we were children," she continued as she handed me the folder, which was about three inches thick. Marjorie was clearly no princess if she could sleep comfortably with this beneath her mattress every night.

Opening it I saw it contained various papers and a selection of photos. Nestling at the bottom of the folder there was also a memory stick. A quick leaf through confirmed that it contained exactly what I was looking for. I didn't want to spend any longer in the house than necessary, but I did notice that there were some documents written in French in amongst the stash. Luckily I am fluent in French. I hadn't lied when I had told Celeste that I had been a complete dunce at languages at school. I had, but a couple of years later I had found myself with a lot of spare time on my hands and nothing much to do with it, so I had used the time to learn French. It all stemmed from a misunderstanding really.

I had been working as a personal assistant for a wealthy couple who spent much of their time out of the country. I loved my job, which mainly involved living in their house and spending their money, or more precisely paying their bills as and when they turned up. With their full knowledge and approval, I became very adept at forging their signatures in order to ensure that everything was paid on time. It was, in truth, a disaster waiting to happen. The problem came when I used my new found skill to make a few unauthorised payments of my own. In my defence the couple really were very rich and very generous so I didn't think they'd mind. If they'd been in the country I would have asked them. But they weren't so I didn't. The unauthorised payments included three months back rent for friend who was about to be made homeless, an MOT for another friend's car without which she would lose her job, and vet bills for Aunt Audrey's horrendous cat (this was the most ill-advised of all as I ended up having to look after it following Audrey's death). Finally I treated myself to a very inexpensive holiday (I spent it in a tent for goodness sake). The upshot was that I was invited to spend a few months banged up (as I believe it is called) at Her Majesty's Pleasure. The couple were really very sorry about what happened, and even offered to give me a reference when I got out, but I felt that I'd best steer clear of that line of work in future so I never took them up on it. I did, however, use my time in chokey productively. I not only learnt French, but also Italian and even a little German, which I have mostly forgotten as it is a horribly ugly and complicated language. It turned out I wasn't a dunce at languages at all, I had just been badly taught, so it's an ill wind that doesn't have a silver lining, although that makes no sense at all in any language. A quick scan of the French documents clarified a lot of things. It was as I was leafing through these that Meg hissed at me.

"I think they may be..." she said, but this was as far as she got because at that moment the little torch I had been reading by was rendered redundant. The bedroom was suddenly brilliantly illuminated and there, in the doorway, stood Malcolm his hand still hovering over the light switch.

"What the..." he said in an ominously quiet voice as he took in the scene, me, the folder in my hands, but mostly

Meg. He simply couldn't take his eyes off Meg. I am not easily spooked but this was not good. I didn't want the opportunity to learn any more languages. "I think that you two better come downstairs, and bring that," he pointed at the folder in my hands, "with you."

Shit, shit shit, shit. And then some more shit. "And be quiet," Malcolm muttered through gritted teeth. Huh? We followed him down the stairs as quietly as we possibly could.

"What are you doing up there?" Marjorie's shrill voice called from the lounge.

"I'll be in with the coffee in a minute." Malcolm called to her before turning to us and putting his finger to his lips, as if we needed to be told that talking was verboten (bit of German there, so I clearly haven't forgotten all of it). Malcolm tiptoed across the hall. We tiptoed along behind him. Meg was, this time at least, watching where she was going and so didn't trip over the rug although I did notice Malcolm quite deliberately disarrange its tassels with his foot. Silently opening the front door Malcolm pointed emphatically to indicate that we should exit through it. We didn't need telling twice. The last we heard was his feigning a coughing fit, presumably to cover the sound of the door closing behind us.

Creeping past the lounge window I could see Marjorie perched uncomfortably on the edge of one of the sofas. Even when alone in her own home she looked uncomfortable. A moment later I saw Malcolm enter the room at which point Marjorie began to berate him, what for I didn't know but I wasn't about to stay to find out. A few minutes later and Meg and I were sitting in my car, which I had parked a few streets away.

"Oh no!" Meg exclaimed. "You didn't put the keys back in the shed."

"Really the last thing in my mind right now," I replied. "Malcolm! Who'd have thought it? Malcolm. And he let us take the folder! He wanted us to take the folder! She is going to be livid when she finds it's gone."

"She might be angry about the folder, but it'll be nothing compared to how angry she'll be when she can't find this!" Meg had a huge grin on her face as she uncurled her palm to reveal Marjorie's diamond ring.

"What the ....?" Why on earth had Meg taken that? The whole point of the exercise had been to get the folder. It was, until Meg stole the ring, a pretty much foolproof plan. Marjorie could hardly call the police to report the loss of a folder of information that she routinely used to blackmail people, my short perusal having assured me that this was its purpose. She could, however, quite legitimately report the theft of a very expensive ring. "Why did you take that?" I asked, appalled at Meg's stupidity.

"You wanted the folder, I wanted this. We both got what we wanted, didn't we?" Meg looked at me, the grin on her face even wider than before. I clenched my fists tightly. OK, I thought, it's done, but it could easily be undone, and hopefully before Marjorie noticed the ring's absence.

"Why don't you let me have that, I can make sure it's safe." I reached for the ring, gently so as not to alarm Meg, but she was too quick for me. Her fist snapped closed around it.

"Oh no you don't," she said. "This is mine." She didn't go so far as to call it her precious, but there was more than a whiff of Gollum about Meg as she clutched the ring to her chest.

"Yes," I muttered through gritted teeth, "I suppose it is."

Chapter 23

I was settling myself down with a glass of wine one evening a few days later, the contents of Marjorie's folder laid out on the table in front of me (Gideon had gone for a drink with Creepy Bob, who had got the idea that he was going to be Gideon's best man – newsflash – he wasn't), when my phone rang. Preoccupied as I was with Gideon's family, I had put what was going on in my own small and dysfunctional one to the back of my mind, but hearing a hysterical Sophie on the line brought it very much front and centre again.

"Slow down, Sophie," I said, "I can't understand a word you're saying."

"He ... he wants ... he wants full ... he wants full custody," Sophie finally managed to say, in amongst the sobs.

"But why Sophie?" I asked. "What's changed?"

"I don't know, why does he do anything?" Her sobbing almost under control, Sophie had become rather more coherent. "It's probably," she said, "because I've got a new boyfriend."

"But you've seen people before." I pointed out. "Why is Dominic so upset this time?"

"Because he saw David with Pixie. She adores David." Sophie explained. "He's so lovely with her. He talks to her and plays with her and everything."

"And Dominic has a problem with that?"

"He's jealous because Pixie doesn't like spending time with him, Dom that is. It's his own stupid fault though. Do you know where he took her last weekend?" Sophie asked.

"No," I replied, "where?"

"Con Con, that's where."

"Con Con? What the hell is that?" I asked.

"The Conspiracy Conference." Sophie explained. "It is, and I'm reading from the website here, 'a conference for those willing to explore the things they don't want you to know'. It claims to be," she went on, her voice dripping with sarcasm, "fun for all the family."

"He takes her to conferences on conspiracy theories, for fun?" I confirmed. "And he's surprised she doesn't want to see him?"

"He claims that I'm poisoning her mind against him." Sophie went on. "Conspiring, you might say." At least Sophie could see the irony in the situation.

"This is awful Sophie," I said, "but I really don't know what I can do about it, I really can't get involved." Appalled as I was by Dominic's behaviour I didn't want to play piggy in the middle.

"But you have to Eve. You have to help me, or Dominic will take Pixie away from me." Sophie begged, clearly on the verge of hysteria again.

"I don't want that any more than you do, but I don't know what I can do to help." I really didn't.

"But you must Eve, you're the only one that can make things all right." I couldn't quite see where Sophie got that idea, but it was flattering nonetheless. "You always get what you want Eve. If you want Pixie to stay with me you can make it happen, I know you can." Touched though I was by Sophie's faith in me, I couldn't see how I could help.

"But I can't Sophie. I'm sorry. I really am, but there's nothing I can do." With one final sob Sophie said goodbye and that was that. Unless ... unless. I did have an idea, but right now I was keen to get back to Marjorie's folder, so that's what I did.

I began by flicking through the photos, but they weren't very instructive. There were several pictures, obviously from many years ago, of a man I didn't recognise in the company of various other men, none of whom I recognised either. Putting these pictures aside, I moved onto the French documents. Unlike the mysterious photos these were crystal clear, and confirmed my suspicions about the nature of Marjorie's hold over Helen.

Finally I turned to the papers that related to me. After wading through four or five pages of print outs about my ancestors (presumably researched using Malcolm's ancestry programs), I thought that perhaps Marjorie was clutching at straws. That I was descended from a long line inconsequential people (although one many times great grandmother did, according to Malcolm's research, supply hat pins to Queen Victoria) would hardly be enough to derail my relationship with Gideon, although one many times great uncle was hung for stealing a sheep, which might hint to criminal proclivities in my genes I supposed.

I was almost disappointed that my foe had proved to be so pathetic when I came to the spidery handwritten notes by the woman herself, of which there several pages. One was headed 'Husbands', another 'Employment', a third 'Timeline', and a fourth, rather ominously, 'Criminal Activities'. While all the information was very sketchy and didn't really amount to much, it was worrying. Where, I wondered, had she got this information? If she'd found out this much might she find out more?

Suffice it to say it did not make pleasant reading. One saving grace was that the only thing on the memory stick was the ancestry stuff, so I felt fairly confident that Marjorie had no backup. I don't suppose it had occurred to her that anyone would steal the folder from under her mattress, more fool her.

What, I wondered, would she do now? It was a month until my next attempt to marry Gideon and I was confident that she would try to do something in that time to prevent it going ahead. So confident, in fact, that I had cancelled everything, without telling Gideon of course, so as not to waste any more money on non-refundable deposits. Now all I had to do was decide how to proceed armed with my new knowledge while waiting to see what Marjorie would do once she realised her folder was missing. That, I must say, made me rather nervous. I don't like situations I can't control, and I was far from in control of this one.

CHAPTER 24

"I'm a translator," I said in response to Malcolm's enquiry.

"No you're not," he replied.

"No," I agreed, "I'm not. But I have done some translation work. I had a friend with a B&B in Croydon who thought she might have more luck with the French than she had with the English."

"I don't suppose Croydon is a major holiday destination for the English." Malcolm concurred.

"Exactly," I went on, "so I translated her website for her but unfortunately I thought that the French for mattress was matelot, which actually means sailor. Claiming that there was a big, clean, comfortable sailor on every bed didn't, as she told me via her solicitor, get her the kind of clientele she was looking for."

"I don't suppose it did," said Malcolm, nodding sagely. "You and Gideon are very fortunate," he went on, clearly done with me and my employment history. "All I ever wanted was a happy marriage, but I made some very poor decisions which precluded that possibility. I trust that you won't do the same." We were sitting in a cafe on the outskirts of Slough. I had not been surprised when Malcolm called asking to meet me, or that he had insisted on a venue where there was not the least chance Marjorie, or anyone that knew any of us, would see us. Which is why we were in a very horrid cafe in Slough.

"What do you mean? Are you suggesting I'm a poor decision maker?" I enquired. I tried to lift my arm to brush some hair out my eyes and was alarmed to find that my sleeve had stuck to the table. Nice.

"Not at all," Malcolm replied. "But Marjorie does not take kindly to having her plans thwarted. It is not part of her plans," he continued, "that you should marry Gideon."

"Me specifically, or anyone?" I asked.

"Either, or both. Whichever." Malcolm replied. "The point is that Marjorie has, so far, ensured that my son has never had a satisfactory relationship. Or that is the construction she has put on events. Whether that is the correct construction or not I couldn't say." Malcolm took a sip of his coffee and shuddered. It was horrible, but no worse than the muck he produced from his abominable machine, and it was ambrosia compared to the bacon sandwich out of which I had just taken a bite.

"I know, I know," he said, seeing that I had noted his reaction to the coffee. "I've been making awful coffee for years. Marjorie," he almost spat out her name, "Marjorie believes herself to be a coffee connoisseur. She's not." Malcolm smiled at me ruefully. "I make the most abhorrent coffee I can manage," he continued, "but nothing I produce can undermine her belief that coffee made in an extravagantly overpriced machine must be good." It was very strange talking to Malcolm. This was partly because I had barely exchanged more than a few words with him up until now, and partly because I had never heard him speak in such an unguarded way before.

"So why did you marry her?" I asked, while surreptitiously trying to remove bacon gristle from between my teeth with my tongue. "Were you happy to begin with?"

"No, we were not. I married her because I was given no choice," Malcolm replied. "Marjorie had obtained information about her sister Meg, with whom I was on very good terms, and threatened to use that information to harm Meg. This makes me sound very heroic and self-sacrificing, but that is not the entire story."

"Isn't it?" I prompted as Malcolm had paused at the end of this sentence for such a very long time I was worried he'd never resume.

"No," he said, responding to my prompt, "it's not. I was ensnared by my own ambition, I'm ashamed to say." He paused again, but I kept my mouth shut this time. He seemed ready to break what I presumed was a silence of many years standing on the subject of his marriage and I didn't think he either needed or wanted me to interject unnecessarily. "I have never spoken of this to anyone," he finally said. "I'm not entirely sure why I have chosen you as my confidante, as you are clearly not an entirely truthful person. Just as you are not, for example, a translator, nor is there any such thing as the National Statistical Office." He looked at me through narrowed eyes, but he was smiling.

"Isn't there?" I asked disingenuously.

"You fooled my sister, but she told me about the encounter, we are quite close despite my wife's strenuous efforts to sow discord. But I already knew you were up to something even before I spoke to Cynthia."

"What do you mean?" I asked, attempting to sound shocked.

"You can drop the act with me, Eve," he said, but kindly. "When you and Gideon came to discuss his misappropriated inheritance, you knew that I had been an executor of the will. Marjorie didn't notice your slip, luckily for you. She was too busy trying to save her own skin."

"Oh," I said, "that was a bit careless of me."

"When you tell as many lies as you do Eve, you're bound to make the odd mistake." This was true, but I still felt annoyed with myself. It had been a stupid mistake and I was lucky that it was Malcolm and not Marjorie who had noticed it.

"It was only when I saw you with Marjorie's folder," Malcolm continued, "that I realised that you were someone to be reckoned with, but back to my pitiful story. I am the author of my own unhappiness. Marjorie, you see, told me that she could help advance my career if I were to marry her."

"Why," I felt emboldened to ask (Malcolm had acknowledged that I was to be his confidante), "did she want to marry you?"

"Not a very flattering question," he actually laughed as he replied, "but a valid one. I believe there were two principal reasons. The first was that I was very fond of Meg and she of me and Marjorie wanted anything that was Meg's. She always had to prove she was superior to Meg, and taking me away from Meg proved Marjorie's superiority beyond doubt. The second was that she had the means to control me, bend me to her will. Had I had the slightest idea what a devious, unpleasant..." He seemed lost for words with which to describe Marjorie. I knew how he felt and I hadn't endured nearly half a century of her company.

"How did she help your career?" I asked. "Cynthia said that it took off when you married Marjorie."

"Marjorie used the same tactics she has always used, blackmail." Malcolm continued. "She had obtained information... had gone to some considerable trouble to obtain information about her superior that, at the time, and remember this was over forty years ago, would have been immensely damaging to him."

"Oh!" I exclaimed. "He was gay, wasn't he?" All those photos of men I didn't recognise in the folder suddenly made sense.

"Yes, yes he was." Malcolm confirmed. "And I profited from Marjorie's actions, although in my defence I didn't know until much later the nature of her hold over him."

"Would it have made a difference if you had?" I asked.

"I wish I could say definitively that it would have, but I was a very ambitious young man. And I was probably as prejudiced as many others were in those days. I might have convinced myself that he shouldn't have been behaving in such a way and therefore deserved all he got. It is amazing what we can convince ourselves is right if it suits our purposes." Malcolm looked at me meaningfully.

"Yes, it is." I concurred, avoiding his gaze. "I have to ask," I continued, "why tell me, and why now?"

"Because I believe my son truly loves you, and I believe that, rather to your surprise, you feel the same way. I would like my son to have a happy marriage, and the pair of you have as good a chance as any two people of making each other happy, so long as you can stick to the truth from now." Malcolm smiled at me and for the first time I realised that he was actually a nice man. A nice man who'd made a very big mistake and had paid dearly for it. "Do you think you can do that?" Malcolm looked at me intently.

"No!" I yelped.

"What!" exclaimed Malcolm, dropping the bacon sandwich he had been about to bite into.

"I just meant don't eat the sandwich, it's awful. Full of gristle. As for the other thing, I can try." I said. "I only lie when I have to, I don't do it for fun." I added. This wasn't entirely true. I do sometimes lie for fun, but not about anything important, or at least I don't lie about important things just for fun.

"That may be true, but you don't dislike doing it. Gideon," Malcolm continued, "is a good man and he sees only the best in you, so that's what he must have, the best possible version of you. And, in my opinion, the best of you would be much better than most men could hope for. You, Eve," he said, fixing me with a steely gaze, "are funny, clever, kind, and extremely beautiful." This was possibly the nicest thing anyone had ever said to me. I must confess that it made me throat constrict a little, and my bottom lip might have quivered ever so slightly. I didn't agree about the beautiful bit, but I'd happily take the funny, clever and kind.

"It's true," Malcolm looked me directly in the eyes as he spoke, "and if only you believed it you might not feel that you had so much reason to be untruthful. So," he said, clapping his hands together as if to dispel the emotions swirling around the table, "I am going to make a suggestion to you about how to remove his mother's malignant influence from the situation. You may choose to do as I suggest, or you may not."

"OK. What should I do?" I waited with baited breath to hear Malcolm's brilliant plan.

"You need to tell Marjorie that it would be mad for you to be at loggerheads." I must confess I had been hoping for something a little better than this.

"Oh, well, that is one idea." I said. "I suppose it is a bit crazy that..."

"Not mad, M A D, it's an acronym." Malcolm interrupted me. "It stands for Mutually Assured Destruction. Marjorie has obtained some information regarding your past that you would rather Gideon did not know, but you are in possession of a folder that, if shown to Gideon, would most certainly make him see his mother in a rather different light."

"Interesting," I mused. "So you're saying that I just need to let Marjorie know that I know what she's done, and she'll back off. And you think this would stop her from holding the sword of Dan O'Cleese over my head?" Malcolm let out a snort of laughter.

"Dan O'Cleese," he repeated, still laughing. I have often heard people use this phrase and I'm pretty sure I was using it correctly. I really couldn't see what was so funny.

"Yes," Malcolm confirmed, suppressing his laughter. "It would remove Dan's sword from over your head." He really did have an odd sense of humour.

"One last thing," I said, as we prepared to leave, "this kidney business. Is it true?"

"Is what true?" Malcolm asked.

"That Marjorie donated one of her kidneys to another family's child."

"I was there, I'm afraid." Malcolm said sadly.

"While her kidney was being taken out?" I was aghast.

"Not literally," Malcolm explained. "I know that you want to believe that Marjorie is second only to Madame Mao in the league of the world's most evil women, but I find it hard to believe that even she would be able to pull off a deception on that scale."

"Really?" This was disappointing. I had hoped that this would be the final nail in Marjorie's coffin when I enacted what I had decided to call Operation Sword.

"I think I might have noticed if she hadn't genuinely had an operation, don't you?"

"I suppose so." I reluctantly agreed.

"Eve, you've got an enormous amount to work with here, there's really no need to overcook anything."

"OK, I guess not." I concurred.

"And one last thing from me," said Malcolm. "Neither you nor I will betray by the slightest look or comment that anything has passed between us. Do you understand?"

"Are you really that scared of her?" I asked. Malcolm looked momentarily annoyed.

"Just watch yourself Eve," he said. "Marjorie really isn't a woman to be trifled with."

No she isn't, I thought, but then again, neither am I.

Chapter 25

The phone rang very early, at around seven. I was so deeply asleep that it was only when Gideon and I woke up over an hour later and listened to the message left on the answer machine that I realised that it had really rung at all. The caller had been Malcolm. "I have to talk to you urgently about your mother's health," said his message.

"Your mother has cancer," Malcolm said with no preamble when we phoned back. While it was possible that Marjorie had cancer, I was immediately suspicious.

"She wants to talk to you," Malcolm continued. He meant that she wanted to talk to Gideon as he didn't know the phone was on loudspeaker. "I will pass you over." I had been mulling over the best way to implement Operation Sword and had not yet decided how to proceed. Marjorie, it would seem, was about to add another element into the mix that would have to be factored into my planning.

"Hello," Marjorie murmured in a teary little voice. "Why didn't you answer when your father called earlier?"

"I was asleep." Gideon responded.

"Asleep?" Marjorie enquired, as if there was something suspicious about being asleep at seven o'clock on a Saturday morning.

"Yes, Mum, asleep. I'm awake now though." Gideon raised his eyebrows at me. Even he found her a little hard to take sometimes.

"It's just that I really wanted to talk to you as soon as possible," Marjorie simpered. Surely, I thought, she must have known that she had cancer the evening before (I couldn't imagine that she'd been given the news that morning, before seven). If she had wanted to speak to Gideon as soon as possible, why wait until now to make the call? My suspicions that she was up to something grew.

"Well, you're talking to me now, aren't you?" Gideon had the patience of a saint (if saints are particularly patient, I can see no reason why they should be) where his mother was concerned. "So," he continued, "what can you tell me?" Gideon is a man who likes facts, unadorned by unnecessary emotion, from which solutions can be worked out.

"I have cancer," Marjorie spoke more quietly than I had ever heard her speak before. I had to lean in to hear her.

"Yes, I got that," said Gideon.

"Don't hurry me Ian," Marjorie said, clearly preparing to milk this for all it was worth. "The doctor said I may..." Her voice cracked and she started to sob before she had to commit to any specifics.

"Said you may what?" Gideon prompted.

"I don't want you to worry," Marjorie ignored Gideon's question, and continued in the same barely audible tone. Her usual harsh nasal quality could cut through pretty much any soundscape so this was something of a departure. "I'm going to get a second opinion," she continued. "Next Thursday."

And there it was, my suspicions were confirmed. How convenient that her appointment should fall on the very day of our wedding. "I'm going to see the top man in the country for this kind of..." Marjorie's words were lost in more sobbing, undoubtedly to obscure having to say anything more specific about what was wrong. "I shall be going privately, of course. I'm not going to let those butchers in the NHS get hold of me."

"I think it's the same doctors Mum." Gideon said.

"Not where I'm going it's not, I can assure you." Marjorie's voice had regained much of its normal strength.

"Where are you going?" Gideon enquired.

"I told you," Marjorie almost snapped, "to see the top man. But let's not talk anymore about this. You don't need to worry, I will deal with whatever hand I am dealt." This little speech was accompanied by some stoical sniffing. "There is, however, something I have to say, now that I..." her voice trailed off to allow Gideon to fill in the blanks.

"What do you have to say Mum?" Gideon asked.

"I have something I have to get off my chest." Marjorie replied.

"Yes?" Gideon coaxed.

"I am not happy about your marrying Eve," she said, the words coming out in a great rush, as if she had had to pluck up her courage to say them. "It would be very bad for my health if any major changes occurred while I was ill, I'm sure you understand. Wendy said you would." And there it was, the pay off, the real reason for her early morning call.

"Wendy? Who's Wendy?" Gideon glanced across at me, a look of puzzlement on his face.

"Wendy is my psychologist," Marjorie announced. "She has been helping me through some issues I have been struggling with."

"What issues Mum?" Gideon asked. "You mean coming to terms with your diagnosis?"

"My what? Oh yes, my diagnosis. No, it's not that," she murmured, her voice apparently cracking with emotion. "I have unresolved feelings about Eve, I'm sorry, but that's just how I feel." Marjorie spoke as if she had been holding back a great torrent and could no longer take the strain. The dam had burst. I was almost relieved to have Marjorie's real intent laid bare. This time she was planning to do far more than simply postpone our wedding. This time she was determined to wheel out the big guns and blow the whole enterprise out of the water once and for all.

Gideon looked at me nervously. I knew he was wishing that he hadn't included me in the call, but he could hardly shoo me away now, and I wasn't about to go anywhere. This was dynamite.

"I'm not at all sure that she's the right woman for you," Marjorie continued. "She can be..." Marjorie paused as if searching for the mot juste, "...charming, very charming indeed. And she's certainly attractive, in an obvious sort of way, but something's not quite right. I can't quite put my finger on it," she paused as if puzzling over an intractable crossword clue. "Something about her," she resumed, "makes me uneasy, very uneasy indeed. You must have wondered..." Gideon interrupted her before she could go any further.

"No Mum, I haven't wondered," he said firmly before reaching for my hand. Gideon is not usually given to affectionate gestures, so I took it as a good sign that he wasn't being swayed by Marjorie and her suspicions. "And this hasn't got anything to do with your cancer Mum." Gideon tried, fruitlessly as it turned out, to get his mother back to the subject in hand. "Let's focus on that shall we?"

"Do you remember my birthday?" Marjorie continued as if Gideon hadn't spoken. "We invited her to join us at that lovely restaurant, the one in town, and she was late. No one is ever really late, not according to Wendy. It always means something," Marjorie paused again, as if all this had only just occurred to her and she was working it through as she spoke. "The intention is to send a message. That's what Wendy says, and she should know." There had been a burst water main on the Cromwell Road which meant that my bus was delayed. The message that my lateness was sending was that buses can't float.

"And whenever we go for a walk," Marjorie wasn't done yet, "she always races ahead. She never wants to walk with me. I see you running to keep up with her. What do you think that means?" What it means is that I am trying to keep up with Gideon who has very long legs and hurtles along at a terrific pace.

"This is all very trivial Mum," Gideon said firmly. "I really don't see what it has got to do with the current situation."

"I'm afraid it has got a great deal to do with the current situation." Marjorie said very forcefully. It was clear she was having trouble getting Gideon to come with her on this one so she decided to up the ante. "If I'm going to die..." Die? Who'd said anything about dying? We didn't even know what sort of cancer she (supposedly) had.

Having quelled a new bout of sobbing Marjorie resumed. "If I should...well, I would need to do so with a clear conscience. I would be failing in my duty as a mother if I didn't try to warn you against making a quite catastrophic mistake. Quite catastrophic," she repeated emphatically. "I'm only saying this because Wendy advised me to. If it was up to me I'd have kept quiet. I would have kept my worries to myself Ian. But Wendy told me that would be selfish. And I can't be selfish, not where you're concerned, I just can't." Marjorie was throwing her all at this. The whole speech had been delivered as a rising crescendo and had ended on a quite theatrically impassioned note.

"So what's the prognosis?" Gideon was still focused on the cancer, or 'so called' cancer as I had already dubbed it. Marjorie no more had cancer than she had a soul.

"The prog what?" Marjorie had obviously not come across this word before.

"What has the doctor said the outcome of your condition is likely to be?" Gideon clarified.

"I don't know!" Marjorie replied brusquely.

"How can you not know Mum?" Gideon asked, almost impatiently. "Surely you asked him?"

"Don't badger me Ian," she snapped, "I have enough to worry about. He's the doctor, why should I ask him all sorts of questions? He knows what he's doing." If she was so sure her doctor knew what he was doing, I wondered, why the need for a second opinion.

"The point is that you must listen to me," Marjorie persisted. "I may not be around for much longer so..." She let the threat of her imminent demise hang in the air.

"Surely the point is that you have cancer and you want to get better." Gideon said tersely. I was glad to see she was finally testing his patience.

"The point is I want you to be happy and I'm far from sure Eve is the woman to make you happy." Marjorie wasn't going to give up easily. "I'm your mother, Ian, I only have your best interests at heart. If I should..." She was rather over doing the death angle, but she didn't have much else to work with I suppose. "I'm sure," she continued, "that Eve might be the perfect wife for any number of other men," nice one, Marjorie, "but you, you should be with someone that you can be sure of. I'm not sure, I'm not sure she can be trusted. There I've said. I'm sorry, but it's how I feel. I mean," Marjorie was on a roll now, "what do you really know about her? Her name isn't really Evangeline, did you know that Ian?"

"That's hardly a reason not to marry someone is it Mother?" Gideon was certainly coming up trumps in the face of his mother's assault.

"And that story about winning a pony in a competition? I've never heard anything so ridiculous!" Marjorie's voice had regained its fingernails down a blackboard quality, all whisperiness vanquished by her annoyance at my pony winning exploits. And while we're at it, where the hell had she got that from? The funny thing was that it was actually true, I had won a pony in a competition. As a child all my favourite television programmes featured horses – Black Beauty, White Horses, Follyfoot – and all the children in these programmes seemed to be having a much better time of it than I was. The common theme seemed to be that they all had horses. I reasoned, therefore, that if I could get hold of a horse my life would be better too. That I had never seen a horse in real life didn't dampen my enthusiasm one bit. Luckily WH Smith ran a Win a Pony competition every year. The competition questions were ridiculously easy, but then you had to write a few words detailing why you should be entrusted with the care of an actual pony. I let my imagination get the better of me one year and detailed at some length the wonderful life I would give Beauty (I had already named the pony so it was practically mine already), on the small holding I shared with my parents and three equally pony mad siblings. All of us would share in the care of Beauty, with the possible exception of my little brother, River (we were that kind of family), who was too small and more interested in tractors anyway. I was obviously very persuasive because on this, my fourth attempt, I finally won. I was then horrified to find myself ignominiously stripped of my prize when it became clear that I had lied and had nowhere to keep a pony and no idea how to look after one even if I had. So heinous was my deception considered to be that I didn't even get the premium bonds given in lieu to winners unable to care for that year's pony. I have, ever since, felt an enormous sense of gratitude to WH Smith's and frequent their shops whenever possible, as they taught me a very valuable lesson. Lies, I learned, are only as good as your ability to see them through successfully to their conclusion, whatever that conclusion may be. How, I wondered, was Marjorie going to get away with not dying of cancer? I would be interested to find out.

"So you go to see the consultant on Thursday?" Gideon said, ignoring the pony story and making a 'but what can I do about it?' face at me. You could, I thought, tell her that you were sorry she wouldn't be able to be there but the wedding was going to go ahead as planned. But I knew he wouldn't, hence my pre-emptive cancellation. One bloody kidney she donated. It was years ago, and she's got another one, get over it already I wanted to scream.

"Yes," Marjorie confirmed. "Thursday."

"What time and where?" asked Gideon.

"I'm suddenly very tired," Marjorie said, weakly, "I think I'd better lie down. I'll call again if we have any further news."

"Where did all that stuff about me come from?" I said once we were off the phone, and doing my best to look astounded by Marjorie's comments. I shook my head gently from side to side while raising my eyebrows and letting a glum little smile play around my lips. We were in the sitting room, still in our pyjamas and drinking tea. In high summer all the east facing rooms in Gideon's flat are filled with sunshine, but it was winter and the sun had barely managed to make it above the roofs of the buses parked outside.

Would I see another summer here I wondered? I would do my very best to make sure that I did, and not just because I loved the view. I also loved the man who was sharing it with me, even if he did have the most awful mother imaginable.

"I wouldn't worry about it," said Gideon, "she's in shock. One thing I would like to know though."

"Mmm?" I said non-committally.

"What is your real name?"

"It's Evelyn," I replied.

"Well, that's nice too. Anything else I should know about?" Gideon asked, a wry smile on his face.

"I'm not descended from Charles Darwin." I said, having found an appropriately innocent lie to come clean about.

"Why did you say you were?" Gideon took a sip of tea. He didn't, I was relieved to notice, seem very perturbed.

"Your mother was telling me how she was descended from the Royal House of Stuart, because she was a Stuart with a u, not Stewart with a w. Do you remember?" I explained.

"Of course I remember." Gideon said.

"Your father said this was rubbish. He'd done some research on her family tree and her great something grandfather changed the spelling because he was a Jacobean."

"Jacobite," Gideon corrected me.

"Potato, potarto, who cares? Anyway, your mother was a bit annoyed about this." I say annoyed, I thought she was going to rip Malcolm's head off using nothing more than her bare hands and the cake fork she was gripping very tightly at the time. "So I thought it would be a good idea to change the subject. I was trying to defuse the situation."

"So you thought lying about being descended from Darwin was a good way to end a row between my parents?" Gideon asked.

"Yes," I said. "And it worked. I meant to say Charles Dickens but once I realised I had said Charles Darwin it was too late to go back on it without looking stupid."

"I didn't believe you anyway." Gideon laughed as he recalled the conversation. "It just sounded hugely implausible and you didn't seem to know the slightest thing about Darwin. You thought his ship was called the Bagel."

"It could have been." I said. "The captain might have been Jewish."

"He might have been." Gideon replied, clearly not convinced. "So why were you going to say Dickens? Do you know any more about him?"

"I know all the words to all the songs in Oliver." I replied.

"That's pretty much the same thing I suppose," he agreed.

"I'm glad you can see that." I said.

"Yes, yes I can. I would suggest, though," Gideon went on, "that you give up lying from now on as you are clearly very bad at it."

"All right," I agreed, "seeing as it is not one of my top skills I will never lie to you again, I promise." This was a lie, obviously, but one told with the best of intentions.

"The thing I don't understand," said Gideon, "is where this all is coming from. Mum, I mean, saying she doesn't trust you. I thought everything was going really well with you two. I think," he continued, "that she must be a bit unbalanced at the moment." Gideon looked thoughtfully into his tea. "I don't think we should take anything she says too seriously for the time being," he continued after a long pause. "She's sick and scared and it's making her behave badly. And I am going to marry you, just not, it seems, this Thursday."

Chapter 26

'Cat now' said the text I had just received from an unknown number. What cat and why now? I wondered. I was on the point of deleting the text when Gideon (who had been marking essays in his study) came into the sitting room. I was glad of the interruption as it meant I didn't have to go back to the book on science I was supposed to be reading. Gideon had given me it to me to read instead, he said, of my usual idiotic trash. He is simply mad for science, but I would happily have left this book where I had thrown it on the floor. If only it had been a little bigger I might have been able to conceal a magazine behind it and everyone would have been happy.

"Read this," he said, laughing as he handed me his phone. 'Call me he you hate time' it said.

"Huh?" I asked.

"It's from Mum. She's got a really old phone and no idea about predictive text. It's supposed to say 'call me if you have time'."

It wasn't very funny, but I knew Gideon was trying to make things seem normal after Marjorie's recent 'I have cancer and you can't trust Eve' bombshell.

"Oh, right." I said, not laughing. I couldn't find it in myself to find anything Marjorie did amusing at the moment. "Are you going to call her?"

"Not right now, I don't hate time." Gideon threw his phone down on the footstool next to me. "Fancy a coffee?" he asked.

"I would absolutely love one!" I responded, just a tad too enthusiastically. I had just realised that Gideon's phone might hold the answer to the cat riddle. As soon as he left the room I grabbed it and, as I suspected, the text was from Malcolm. He was telling me to act now.

"And what, Eve, are they?" Marjorie was glaring at me from what I supposed was her sick bed. She was propped up on a huge pile of pillows, a large box of chocolates open by her side. I had gone round as soon as I could manage after getting Malcolm's text.

"Hello Eve," Malcolm had said when he opened the front door, "I suppose that you have come to see how Marjorie is."

"Yes, Malcolm, that is the sole purpose of my visit." He didn't, as he had promised, acknowledge that anything about our relationship had changed. And now I was standing at the end of Marjorie's bed shaking a set of keys at her.

"These, Marjorie, are keys." I said.

"Thank you Eve, I can see that," Marjorie replied. "Why are you standing at the end of my bed waving keys at me?"

"I am returning them to you, Marjorie."

"What, Eve, do those keys have to do with me?"

"They are, Marjorie, the keys to your home." I replied.

"The what?" she exclaimed. Fifteen love. I had not only surprised her, but she had been the first to drop the use of the other's name in every sentence.

"Have you been spending a lot of time in bed recently, Marjorie?" I asked.

"I am unwell, as I'm sure Gideon has informed you," she replied while reaching for a chocolate. She didn't offer me one.

"Comfortable, is it, Marjorie?" I asked.

"Is what comfortable?" she asked in return, the chocolate still in her hand.

"Your bed, Marjorie." I said.

"Yes, it is. It is a very expensive mattress." Even with her nemesis jangling her own house keys at her from the end of the bed, Marjorie still had the energy to brag. "The Queen sleeps on one of these," she added.

"I'm sure she does. So, here's a question," I replied. "Do you think the Queen would notice if something were to be slipped under her mattress? Or," I paused for dramatic effect, "something were to be taken from under it that she had been keeping there? Although I don't suppose the Queen keeps secrets under her mattress, do you, Marjorie?"

For a supposedly sick woman Marjorie leapt from the bed with lightning speed and, throwing the now slightly melted chocolate back into the box, began rummaging around under the much discussed mattress. Having flailed her arms around under it for a few moments in a fruitless search, she realised that her precious folder was no longer there.

"What do you want?" Marjorie hissed. She had recovered herself enough to try to quell me with an intimidating look. Unfortunately her look, intimidating though it was, was undercut by her attire. It's hard to quell someone with an intimidating look while dressed in a pair of pyjamas covered in little love hearts and a pale pink bed jacket.

"What I want is for you to back off," I hissed back. "That, Marjorie, is what I want." I might, I'm afraid, have let my amusement at her discombobulation show. It's not often, after all, that anyone gets to see their sworn enemy under quite such undignified circumstances.

"I don't know what you mean." Marjorie attempted to look down her nose at me imperiously. As she was considerably shorter than me she had to tilt her head back quite a long way and so only succeeded in giving me a good view of the underside of her chin and the inside of her nostrils.

"I think you know very well what I mean, Marjorie." I replied. "Since I met your son or, to be more precise, since I met you, you have done everything in your power to destroy my relationship with Gideon. I want you to leave me alone. I have something of yours," I continued. "I think you know what it is, and what it would mean if I were to share it with Gideon." I felt about ten feet tall at this point, such was my advantage over Marjorie. How, I thought, could this go wrong?

"You wouldn't dare!" She all but screamed. "You can't possibly believe he would side with you against me. Me!" she cried thumping her chest in a 'Me Tarzan' like way. She was trying her best but we both knew the game was going very much my way. "And if he knew what I know about you..." she continued.

"We'd neither of us come out of it very well, would we Marjorie?" I replied, satisfyingly calmly. My heart was going like the clappers and I felt a hot flush travelling over my entire body, but I was holding it together pretty well despite these physical symptoms of stress. "I might well lose him," I continued, "but you'd have a lot of explaining to do yourself, wouldn't you? It's called..." What was it called?

"Mutually Assured Destruction," Marjorie almost spat at me. "That's what you're suggesting isn't it? If I tell Gideon what I know about your...your past, you will reveal things that you believe you know about me."

"I don't believe that I know them, I do know them, and I have evidence, while you only have speculation. But," I went on, "if you were to stop interfering in my life, there would be no reason for me to interfere in yours, would there?" Had I been holding a long haired white cat I'm pretty sure I would have stroked it menacingly at this point.

"You can't believe for a moment that my son would ever turn against me, not after all I've done for him." Marjorie wasn't going to take this lying down.

"Maybe he would, maybe he wouldn't." I mused. "Does what you've done for him cancel out all that you've done to others? The question you have to ask yourself is 'do I feel lucky?' Well do you, punk, I mean, Marjorie? Do you feel lucky?"

"You really are a piece of work," Marjorie hissed.

"Well thank you Marjorie. I'm glad that you ..." I have no idea where I was going with this but luckily Marjorie interrupted me before I had to work it out.

"I don't have much choice do I?" she hissed. "I will give into your blackmail, and make no mistake, that's what it is."

"Blackmail is an ugly word, Marjorie, but you of all people know that, don't you?" I replied, which was probably over egging it but I blame the adrenalin rush I was now experiencing.

"I will agree to your demands on one condition," Marjorie continued, ignoring my comment.

"Do you really think you're in a position to make demands?" I countered.

"Yes, I do." Marjorie sounded very sure of herself. "I could have you sent to prison, and I don't suppose you'd like that, would you?" She was clearly unaware this wouldn't be a novel experience for me.

"I don't suppose I would." I said nonchalantly. "But how would you achieve that?"

"By reporting the theft of my ring. The ring that you stole." Marjorie pointed an accusing finger at me. Bloody Meg, why'd she have to take the damned ring? "You have already proved that you're a common thief," she continued. "But don't you think taking the ring was going a bit far, even for you?" As it happens, I did, but I couldn't tell her that Meg had taken it without revealing my connection to Marjorie's twin, and I didn't feel that this was the right time for any more revelations.

"I didn't take it," I said, "but if I can ensure that it's returned to you, do we have a deal?"

"You expect me to believe that you were not the thief, and yet you can ensure the return of the ring?" Marjorie sneered at me. I really didn't like the inference, or rather the outright assertion that I was a common thief. I am many things, but I am not a thief.

"I don't care what you believe." I said. I did, inasmuch as I didn't want her to think that I was a thief, but overall I didn't. "I repeat, do we have a deal?"

"Yes, I suppose that we do." Marjorie conceded ungraciously. "I have to say though," she continued, a nasty little smirk on her face, "it'll be a relief in some ways."

"Look," I said, taking this as a conciliatory gesture despite the smirk, "all I want is for everyone to get on. I really do love your son, and I will do my best to make him happy. I don't want us to be enemies."

"How very touching, although I'm not sure that you know what love is," she replied. Perhaps I hadn't until I met her son, but it wasn't worth telling her that, she wouldn't have believed me. Marjorie resumed speaking. "I was referring to the fact that I won't have to spend any more time listening to your appalling brother moaning on about his dreadful life in order to find out a few snippets about you that might prove useful."

For a moment I was ready to spring to Dominic's defence, it seemed a little harsh to call him appalling, but then I realised what it was that Marjorie had just said.

"It was Dominic? Dominic was your source?" I let out a hoot of laughter. "Really, you must try harder, Marjorie. Dominic can barely see beyond the end of his nose. He's certainly never taken much interest in my life. He would be the last person I would go to if I wanted to find out about me." That didn't really make any sense, but I'd said it now.

"He knows enough," Marjorie replied, clearly smarting from my comment, "and he certainly shares my feelings of distaste for you. What a lovely pair you make, and now I am to be forced to accept you into my family, god help me."

"Yes, god help you indeed. Now," I said, "I think I'll be on my way. I'm so pleased that you seem to have made such a miraculous recovery. I'm sure you'll be back to your usual self by the time my wedding day finally comes around."

"Yes," she said, "I'm sure I shall." With that she turned away from me. The urge to make one last zinger was strong, but as she was as keen as me to get the last word the exchange might have gone on indefinitely and I had other fish to fry.

Chapter 27

"So I was right," said Claire. "I did tell you, didn't I?" she continued, only just stopping short of wagging her finger at me as if I were a naughty child. I adore Claire. She is my oldest and best friend and easily the cleverest person I know (not that I have mentioned this to Gideon) but she can be insufferably smug at times, and right now was one of those times.

"Yes, you were, and you did," I agreed, displaying none of the annoyance anyone might naturally have been expected to feel on being talked down to by Mrs Smug McSmugface. "I should have listened to you. Aren't you pleased though, that it was all in my mind? I certainly am. Can you imagine what kind of monster Marjorie would have to be to behave as badly I imagined?"

I had just finished telling Claire, at whose kitchen table we were sitting having just finished lunch, about recent developments. A slab of Claire's homemade bread sat reproachfully on my plate. It was the kind of bread that made you realise why we evolved wisdom teeth (all those hours reading that science book hadn't been totally wasted), as too much of this stuff and even the strongest molars would undoubtedly be ground to dust and need replacing with shiny new ones. It looked like a buttered paving stone. I had managed one piece only because it had been served with soup which meant I could saturate it to the point where I felt my teeth would survive the encounter. I wasn't about to risk another slab however, now that I was soupless.

"Are you finished?" Claire looked reproachfully at the uneaten bread. I hate wasting food but I think Claire actually sees the face of a starving child imprinted into every uneaten morsel. She is a very, very much better person than I am.

"Yup, that was delicious." I was only half lying, the soup had been very nice.

"So following the health scare she sought a rapprochement with you?" Claire asked as she cleared the table.

"That sounds disgusting," I replied, "but I don't suppose it means what I think it does."

"It means that she wants to establish harmonious relations with you." Claire attempted to clarify.

"Like the von Trapps?" Why couldn't Claire just speak English like a normal person?

"What?" Claire said, rather sharply.

"You know, the von Trapps." I said. "The Sound of Music. Harmonious relations."

"Oh do shut up, you know very well what I meant."

I had been telling Claire how, having been given the all clear following a second opinion (funny that, how she went from deadly, unspecified cancer to the all-clear in just two appointments), Marjorie had invited me over for a little tête-à-tête. Once there, or so I told Claire, Marjorie apologised for all that she had said to Gideon regarding my lack of trustworthiness. She had, so she told me, (in my narrative to both Gideon and Claire at least) been on some very, very strong painkillers and they had interfered with her thinking, making her somewhat paranoid. She couldn't express how sorry she was and asked, no begged, for my forgiveness

(Gideon had particularly liked that bit) and we were now as thick, somewhat appropriately, as thieves.

Claire is not easily fooled, or at least not as easily as most people, which is partly why I value her friendship so highly. She knows as much about me as anyone ever will, but there are limits, even with Claire. Fortunately even she is not immune to that most powerful of deception techniques, flattery. In many ways the enormous size of her brain is both her greatest asset and her greatest weakness. It can make her just a little too sure that she's right because usually she is. She also has a very strong belief in the essential goodness of people. She was therefore more than happy to believe that Marjorie had shown herself to be a decent person after all. It fitted in much more neatly with her world view than the idea that Marjorie really was a conniving, vicious, unprincipled ... person.

I didn't enjoy lying to Claire, but I felt that things had moved beyond the point when I could, any longer, involve her. I had no idea what might happen next but I was quite sure that, despite what Marjorie had said, she was not about to give up on her goal of getting me out of Gideon's life. Having seen the evidence of what she was prepared to do to get her own way, the idea that she would meekly accept defeat was not realistic. What I needed to do, therefore, was to make it clear to Claire that there was nothing untoward going on in my life, and therefore no need for her to examine it any further.

Gideon had been even more delighted than Claire with his mother's volte face regarding me, and hadn't expressed the slightest suspicion over her equally abrupt return to full health.

"Unbelievable, isn't it?" Gideon had said, holding a bottle of champagne aloft as he came home the evening following Marjorie's having risen, Lazarus like, from her bed. I could only wholeheartedly concur that it was, indeed, quite unbelievable.

"I knew there must be something more to it, you know," he had continued after I had explained the 'very strong painkiller' story. Yes, there must, I had again concurred. So, in Gideon and Claire's world at least, everything was just peachy.

"Hi Rich," I said. "I wasn't expecting to see you, but I'm really glad you're here." Claire's husband Richard came through the kitchen door just after Claire had poured us each a mug of mint tea.

"Oh, are you? Why?" Richard looked at the ground about a foot in front of me. He never looks directly at me, or anyone else for that matter, but then he is a computer programmer.

"Because I have a favour to ask." I continued. "I hope you don't mind."

"Mind? Doing you a ... a ... a favour?" Rich's gaze shifted from the floor to the table a few feet to my right.

"I'm sure he doesn't mind, do you Rich? All you have to do Eve, is ask, isn't that right Rich?" Claire was laughing as she spoke. Rich glared at her from under his brows. Goodness knows what was going on.

"So you'll do it? That's great. So the thing is ..." I left not long after, my favour secured and Claire's concerns regarding Marjorie and me well and truly quelled, so that was two jobs, at least, done. And on to the next.

"But you must give it back, you have to!" I implored Meg as we sat in the cold winter sun under the watchful eye of the Buddha of Battersea.

"I damn well don't have to. My sister has been making me do what she wants all our lives and this is where it ends. I won't do it, and you can't make me." Meg was proving every bit as intransigent as I had feared she would be.

"But if you don't give the ring back, or at least give it to me to give back, she's going to report me to the police." I implored again.

"They can't prove anything can they?" Meg replied. "You don't have the ring, you didn't steal it. Why on earth would anyone believe that you had? It would make her look dotty." What Meg said did have merit. I wasn't very concerned about Marjorie's threat to call the police. No one had broken into her house and the spare keys had been returned to their spot in the shed. How Marjorie intended to convince the police that a crime had been committed was beyond me. It was far more likely that Marjorie had simply lost the ring than that someone had taken it. What I couldn't see, however, was what purpose was served by not returning it. It was the only loose thread in an otherwise fairly tightly wound conclusion to recent events and I was reluctant to leave it dangling. Loose threads can be pulled at, but I could only tie it up with Meg's help, and she was utterly unmoved by my appeals. As there was nothing more I could do for the moment I left Meg on the park bench, hopefully contemplating how her intransigence would go down with the Buddha, and made my way to an altogether less salubrious part of town.

Despite not having spoken for several months, it had been the work of a single phone call to arrange a meeting with my brother. Dominic is, he would be appalled to know, very easy to play. His Achilles heel is that he is totally unsuspicious of anyone's motives. This might seem surprising given his penchant for conspiracy theories, but is actually a direct result of that mindset. He frequently refers to anyone that doesn't believe the same things as him as 'sheeple' and thinks we are pretty much beneath contempt. That any of the 'sheeple' could fool him is therefore unthinkable, which means that we, the sheeple, can fool him pretty much any time we choose. And so here I was in his frankly disgusting flat in one of the grimmer parts of east London, planning on fooling him and pretty sure I would succeed.

Looking around at the piles of magazines and newspapers, the plates of half eaten food, the mugs stained so brown you could have made a reasonably strong cup of tea simply by filling them with hot water, it occurred to me that he probably hadn't invited Marjorie here.

"You don't know what this means to me Sis." Dominic said, gesturing for me to take seat. He only calls me Sis when he wants something from me and I am complying. "I couldn't imagine my life without Pixie in it," he added.

"And you'd bring her to live here?" I enquired, having perched myself on the very edge of the nearest chair while glancing as uncensoriously as I could around the room. No wonder it had needed fumigating last Christmas. Now, nearly a year on, it looked as if it was well past its due date for another going over.

"I'll move somewhere else, somewhere more 'socially acceptable'," he said, throwing himself into a dilapidated armchair. "I'm only here because it's near to Pixie." And it's only a pigsty because ... ?

"Something has happened," I had said when arranging this meeting, "and I think that you might need my help." And now I was here, ready to help.

"I knew you'd realise I was right, given enough time," he now said. "I mean we should stick together shouldn't we? I am all the family you have, after all."

"Yes, Dominic, you are." I concurred. The concept of family is a very fluid one for Dominic. His idea of who comprises his, or my, family changes depending on what he wants at the time.

"Yeah, each other, that's all we've got," he continued. "I have your back and..." and you'll stab me in it if it suits your purposes, I thought as he looked at me with his soft brown eyes. I have been guilty of giving Dominic the benefit of the doubt far more times than I care to remember and so I am partly responsible for his shortcomings as a human being, but even so he's bloody annoying.

"We have each other's backs and no mistake," I said, "which is why I'm here. So," I continued, "it seems that Sophie is quite prepared to say that you're not Pixie's father if it means it will help her case against you. I just felt that I had to tell you." I looked deeply into Dominic's eyes, making sure that he could see that mine had become quite moist, tearful almost. "And if she says Pixie isn't your daughter, then it follows that she's not my niece. And I couldn't bear..." I chose not to make what it was that I couldn't bear explicit. Dominic could imagine whatever he wanted. "I know we've had our differences over this," I concluded, "but I just thought you ought to know."

"I don't believe it!" Dominic exclaimed, slamming his arms down on the arms of the chair, and sending up great clouds of dust as a consequence. "That is utter crap!" He conveniently forgot that he had, on more than one occasion, suggested the very same thing. "She can't get away with this. What should I do?" He looked at me, his face that of someone who hasn't the faintest idea how to proceed.

Dominic is chock full of conspiracy theories about virtually everything from Roswell to the death of Diana. He justifies these beliefs on the basis that he has worked out what no one else (except for every other nut job conspiracy theorist with access to the internet and too much time on his hands) can see. But, at the same time, he is totally incapable of thinking for himself, but then again perhaps the two things may not be as unrelated as they appear.

"I think you should do a DNA test." I said. "Just to make sure you don't lose your rights completely."

"Too right," he said, leaping up in a fever of self-righteousness. I couldn't help noticing that there was a pizza box where one might have more reasonably expected there to be a cushion on the chair from which he had just leapt. "I bloody should. In fact," he continued, "I will! That'll show Sophie. She won't like that!"

"No, I'm sure she won't," I agreed. "If you call her bluff by proving you're Pixie's father then she'll have to respect your rights, won't she?"

"So, where do you get a DNA test from?" he asked. I frequently have to remind myself that my brother is a teacher. He is allowed to teach children, children who might one day be adults (he works at a very rough school). He is responsible for shaping young minds. But then I further remind myself that he teaches geography and even he can't do much harm when all he has to do is tell young minds about deserts and rivers. And glaciation. That was all geography seemed to be about when I was at school and I don't suppose it's changed all that much. Geography doesn't, does it?

"I've got one right here as it happens." I said. Knowing that if the DNA test were to be taken I needed to strike while the iron was hot I had brought one with me. Dominic is possibly the most indolent person ever to have lived. Left to his own devices he would get all fired up about taking the test and then not bother to do it because he had got side tracked by a mole on his leg that he hadn't noticed before and which might be a melanoma, or a listening device placed there by the government (this has actually happened before, his believing such things that is, I am not making this up). Luckily one can obtain DNA tests very easily over the internet and although they cost a few quid it was, I thought, money well spent.

"Brilliant!" Dominic exclaimed as I handed him the device, which looked rather like a pregnancy test kit. "What should I do?" he asked. "Pee on it?"

"Best not as you have to use it to take a swab from the inside of your mouth." I explained. "The instructions are here," I handed them to him. "I've filled it all in for you. You just need to take a swab and I'll stick it in the post on my way home."

"What about Pixie though? How will I get a sample from her?" he asked.

"You don't need to worry about that," I replied. "Just leave everything to me."

"You are the best sister ever," he said, giving me a big hug. Aren't I just?

Chapter 28

Christmas was coming around again and the weather was bitter. It had begun snowing unseasonably early and it had settled, causing London to come to a virtual standstill. Puddles froze over, pavements became impassable, and snow lay in dirty great heaps all over the place. A Frost Fair on the Thames began to seem like a distinct possibility. I was therefore already feeling cold to my bones even before Gideon sent a bitter wind through to my very marrow.

"Dinner at Mum and Dad's tomorrow, OK?" he said cheerily, wandering into the sitting room where I was watching the Breaking Bad box set I'd bought for Dominic the year before, and which he had left behind. It was quite good as it happens.

"OK," I replied, non-committally. I knew I was going to have to see Marjorie again, but I had assumed that she would be as reluctant as I to have a cosy family get together so soon after our last conversation. Marjorie was obviously playing this very differently to me, but I supposed it had to be done as, as far as Gideon was concerned, everything was hunky dory, tickety-boo, top hole, so what possible reason could there be for not dining with his parents?

⚜ ⚜ ⚜

"This looks..." Even Gideon couldn't summon up a suitable complimentary adjective for the dish his mother had thrown down (or possibly up, it was that bad) in front of us that evening. It was, according to Marjorie, a vegetable curry with paneer. Never having used paneer before, Marjorie had grated it over the curry, much as one might grate parmesan over pasta. It looked, if one was being kind, like a cowpat crawling with maggots. The truly astonishing thing was that it looked better than it tasted.

"Wow, that's..." Gideon was again lost for adjectives. It tasted of chilli, lots of chilli, and had the consistency one might expect from an actual cowpat if one was ever desperate enough to eat one. Malcolm, Gideon, and I soldiered on, but I noticed that Marjorie ate very little of hers. She also spoke very little.

"The Palmers are moving out," she announced at one point. "Downsizing," she hissed, as if this was akin to having been convicted of people smuggling. "They can't afford to stay. No pension," she pursed her lips into a censorious sneer, "but she would have that yacht, well it was more of a dinghy really, even though it gave her terrible seasickness. I expect she's feeling pretty sick now!"

"Who are the Palmers?" Gideon asked ignoring, or perhaps not noticing, the hoot of unpleasant laughter Marjorie had just let out.

"You know the Palmers. Eric and June." Marjorie snapped.

"Never heard of them." Gideon replied.

"Of course you have." Marjorie said categorically.

"If he says he's never heard of them, he's never heard of them." Malcolm chipped in. I have always wanted a family, but this one? Perhaps I had been very bad in a previous life, and the Buddha had decided that this should be my reward.

We all munched on in silence (not that the curry offered much resistance, being essentially mush) until Gideon decided, bless his heart, to draw attention to the elephant that only he, it transpired, was unaware was in the room.

"Where's your ring Mum?" he asked, possibly to give himself a few moments break from the slurry on his plate.

"Well," said Marjorie, putting down her knife and fork in such a way as to indicate that she had finished eating, "there's a funny story behind that. A few weeks ago," she continued, "your father and I went to a do at the golf club and I noticed once we were there that I hadn't got it on. I was worried that I had lost it as I couldn't remember having taken it off. So we went home early, which was no loss as they have let some very odd people join that club recently." She mouthed the word 'immigrants' while quite deliberately catching my eye. I looked back at her, my face a mask. She was getting nothing from me. "So I looked by my side of the bed," she continued, "which is where I would have put it. It's always been perfectly safe there, and we have an alarm, so no one could possibly get into the house. Unless, of course," Marjorie looked meaningfully at me, "it was someone who had keys and knew the alarm code, but, apart from your father and I, who could that possibly be?" I always inwardly sneer when people pretentiously say 'and I' when it should be 'and me'. It shows that they are both snobbish and ignorant, which summed Marjorie up perfectly. "But it wasn't there!" Marjorie threw her hands up as if to illustrate how very mysterious the ring's absence was.

"So it's been stolen?" said Gideon, aghast.

"Well, no, not according to your father." Marjorie now directed her gaze at Malcolm. "I looked everywhere I could think of for it. It was only when I told your father that I couldn't find it that the mystery was finally solved. Wasn't it Malcolm?"

"Wasn't what?" Malcolm either hadn't been listening or was feigning deafness.

"The mystery of my ring, Malcolm," Marjorie said as if talking to a particularly dim child. "Do keep up. It was only solved when you told me what you'd done, wasn't it?"

"Err, yes, I suppose it was." Malcolm looked at me. Nothing in his look betrayed his feelings, but I could imagine.

"Your father had, you see," here Marjorie waved a hand towards Malcolm as if to ensure that Gideon knew who she meant, "taken my ring to be cleaned. Thoughtful of him, don't you think, Eve?" Marjorie gave me a penetrating look. "How many husbands would notice that their wife's ring needed cleaning? Not many, I'm quite sure."

"Why didn't he mention this when you said you wanted to go home to find it?" Gideon asked, not unreasonably.

"Ah, well," said Marjorie, "he misheard and thought I'd lost my.... thing." How had this hopeless creature managed to create such havoc in so many lives? She gave lying a bad name.

"So where is it now?" Gideon asked, ignoring the 'thing' comment.

"It was, so your father assures me, so filthy that it needed to be sent away and it still hasn't returned. Has it Malcolm?" She placed her hands, palms together and fingers lightly touching, just above her plate and gave Malcolm a penetrating stare. I had a sudden déjà vu, but a real one. I remembered back to that very first lunch when I had momentarily thought she was going to say grace. Whatever I had thought of her that first day, I really hadn't seen any of this coming. For the best really.

"You must be pretty annoyed, having it gone so long," said Gideon, snapping me back into the present. He couldn't seem to shut up about his mother's bloody ring.

"Oh, I am," said Marjorie. "I adore that ring and if I don't get it back soon, very soon, heads will roll, believe you me, heads will roll." So now she also knew, or at least suspected, that Malcolm was in cahoots with me. On the one hand this was not good, but on the other, did it really matter? She had been blackmailing Malcolm to do as she wished for nigh on half a century, how much worse could her behaviour get? It was when Gideon and I returned home that I found out.

"What is that awful smell?" I asked as I entered the bathroom.

"What do you mean?" Gideon asked.

"The bathroom smells funny. It's like damp, but worse."

"Haven't you ever smelled that before?" he replied.

"No, what is it?" I waved my hand under my nose in an attempt to dissipate the unpleasant and unfamiliar smell.

"That, my dear, is asparagus wee." Gideon explained. I have since learnt that not everyone's wee smells this way after ingesting asparagus. Mine never has which is why I had no idea what the smell was or where it was coming from. "We must have eaten asparagus," he continued. "There must have been some in Mum's curry, not that you could taste it, or see it for that matter. That was bad wasn't it, even by my mother's standards."

My pleasure at the fact that Gideon had at last acknowledged that his mother was a rotten cook, and therefore not perfect, was rather tempered by the knowledge that she had just tried to murder me believing, as she did, that I had a deadly allergy to asparagus. This was not a turn of events that, I must confess, I had anticipated.

Chapter 29

I awoke the next morning from a fitful night's sleep, during which I had struggled with a mixture of thoughts and emotions. My life has not been without incident and I have found myself in some difficult and even dangerous situations on occasion. To my knowledge, however, no one had ever tried to murder me before. It was a new and wholly unpleasant experience. I was unsure how to proceed. What does one do when someone has tried to murder one and yet one is still alive? Does one simply wait around for the potential murderer to try again? Does one try to turn the murderer into a murderee (there's no such word, but there should be)? Or does one simply hope that the potential murderer has got it out of their system and one is now safe?

In addition to worrying about my own safety, I was also mystified as to why Marjorie should make an attempt on my life right now. She wanted her ring back and she thought I had it. Why get rid of me when I offered the only hope she had of seeing her ring again? I was still pondering these questions when, around midday, I got the answer to one of them at least.

"She knows I've got it." Meg hissed down the phone. She had quite fallen in love with the mobile I had bought her when we had carried out The Great Inheritance Fail as I had come to think of it, and had even gone so far as to suggest that everyone should have one.

"How do you know she knows?" I hissed back.

"She was just here." Meg explained. "At my flat."

"What happened?" I enquired.

"I can't tell you over the phone," Meg said. "But we must meet. And soon."

"Yes, I suppose we must." I replied. "But I have to work this afternoon."

"We must meet today," Meg insisted. "We have to stop her, or who knows what she might do." She might try to kill me again, I thought.

"All right. All right," I acquiesced. "How long would it take you to get to Richmond Park? I will be going through there on my way to work in a couple of hours. We could meet there and then I could head off."

"It's a bit close to Mar... her house, don't you think?" Meg said.

"She never goes there," I assured her, "she told me. She has literally never been to Richmond Park even though it's just around the corner from her house."

"How strange," said Meg, "I'd go there all the time if I were her."

"Mmm," I said. I wasn't terribly interested in Meg's feelings about Richmond Park. I was more worried about the risk we were taking. But Meg had handled Melissa's grandmother so well, and the situation was so desperate that I decided it was a risk I would have to take. Marjorie clearly knew that Meg and I were in this together, and had already made an attempt on my life, so being seen in a public place with Meg would hardly register on the riskometer right now.

"All right then," said Meg, "I'll see you there in an hour, by the White Lodge."

❧ ❧ ❧

"She tried to kill me, the ... the ..." Meg seemed more annoyed than scared as she related her encounter with her murderous sister. I had not even got off my bike when she launched into her story.

"What a coincidence, she tried to kill me too!" I replied. Two attempted murders in as many days. Marjorie was obviously quite angry. "What did she do to you?" I asked.

"She tried to throttle me, but I managed to fight her off." Meg explained. "She just kept screaming at me to tell me where her ring was. 'Give me my ring, give me my ring,' she bellowed as her hands tightened around my throat." To ensure I understood exactly what she meant Meg grabbed her own throat and made a croaking noise, as if she was being throttled. "It was very unpleasant. Look." Meg pulled the neck of her coat back to reveal some light bruising. It didn't look that bad. "How," she asked, "did she try to kill you?"

"With some asparagus." I replied.

"Really? Asparagus?" Meg looked puzzled. "That doesn't sound very dangerous. She had me by the throat and ..."

"Yes, I know," I said as Meg began miming being throttled again.

"Unless it was in a tin. Was it in a tin?" Meg asked. "Did she bash you over the head with a tin of asparagus?"

"Of course not." I replied. "She thinks that I'm allergic to asparagus. I once had reason to tell her that it might kill me if I were to eat it."

"So why did you eat it?" Meg asked.

"I'm not actually allergic to it." I explained. "And anyway she had hidden it in some horrid ... look the details don't matter. She thinks asparagus could kill me and she fed it to me in disguise. That's pretty damning, don't you think?"

"Yes, yes I suppose so," Meg reluctantly conceded, "but she didn't actually attack you."

"This isn't a competition Meg." I said. It was a competition and I had clearly won it. Marjorie's attempt on Meg's life was very half hearted, and Marjorie would have known she couldn't get away with it. I was pretty sure it was only a feint. Her attempt on my life was an altogether more serious affair. "Marjorie has tried to kill both us," I continued, mainly to mollify Meg. "What we have to do is work out how to deal with it."

"We have to stop her." Meg slammed a fist into the palm of her hand.

"Duh oh!" I exclaimed. "I'm not about to let her finish me off, and I don't suppose you want to die either. What she wants is her ring and she knows that you have it. What we have to do is use it as a bargaining tool. There's a cafe over near Roehampton Gate. Let's go there and warm up, and perhaps we can come up with a plan."

The bitterly cold weather had continued and there was still a lot of ice and snow on the ground as we made our way across the park. I had the extra problem of having to wheel my bike across the rough ground so it was some time before I could wrap my frozen hands around a warming mug of tea.

"What we need to do is find a way to ensure that she knows she can't get the ring if anything happens to either of us." I said. I was thinking as hard as I had ever thought before and it did actually hurt a little.

"So Mar…." Meg began.

"Shhh. Don't say her name." I warned Meg in a hushed voice. "I know it's not very likely, but we don't want anyone to hear anything that might…well, you know. The thing is," I continued, "we need to make sure that she needs both of us alive if she's ever to get her ring back. And," I continued, "that she knows that she needs both of us alive. But how... how...?" I mused. Then suddenly it hit me. "What," I asked Meg, "exactly did you say to Mar..."

"Shhh!" hissed Meg.

"Oh, oh yes." I lowered my voice. "What exactly did you say about where the ring was?"

"I told... her," Meg explained, "that it was somewhere she would never get it, not if anything happened to me, at least."

"Good, good." I think I might have rubbed my hands together at this point, but that might have been on account of the cold. "And where actually is it?"

"Right here," said Meg, pulling the great rock from her pocket. "It was in my cardigan pocket the whole time!"

"Put it away." I said, very firmly. "Right, this is what we are going to do. Are you listening carefully?" Meg nodded her assent but it still took me about half an hour to explain my relatively simple plan before she got it, and even then I wasn't entirely sure she understood what she had to do. She assured me, however, that she did.

"But why won't she just forget about the ring and try to kill us anyway?" Meg asked.

"Because," I explained, "she hates to lose, so she won't give up trying to get her ring back. She might have tried to kill... both of us, but my hunch is that she wants her ring back more than she wants us dead." I very much hoped I was right or it might cost both me and Meg dear. "And in the meantime," I continued, "we will be working on another plan to make sure that we have her trussed up like an oven ready turkey."

"So this isn't the end?" Meg looked rather crestfallen.

"I'm afraid not." I said, resignedly. "We can never let our guard down, not against a foe like Mar… like her. And now I'd better go or I'll be late for work."

"What is that you do, really?" Meg asked. "You're not an actress are you?"

"No, I'm not. I'm an estate agent, so you can see why I keep it to myself." I'm not an estate agent, but I did once work for a letting agent so it was almost true.

CHAPTER 30

"I don't see what possible purpose can be served by our meeting." Marjorie said, rather haughtily, when I called her. She seemed rather taken aback to hear from me but she must have realised that I hadn't died as Gideon might have thought to mention it to her.

"Perhaps you should come along then, and be enlightened." I replied.

"I can't imagine anything on which you could enlighten me," she continued in the same haughty manner.

"Perhaps that says more about the limits of your imagination than it does about my ability to enlighten." I replied, or at least that's what I choose to recall that I said. I may not have been quite so eloquent in the heat of the moment. "But don't come if you don't want to," I said, calling her bluff, "it really is up to you."

She clearly knew by now that I was not only in cahoots with her husband but also with her twin (I was cahooting pretty indiscriminately by this point). She also knew, or suspected, that her twin had her precious ring so she had no choice but to meet me. This, however, didn't prevent her from acting as if she had some agency in the situation. The upshot of all this verbal sparring was, predictably, that Marjorie did agree to meet me but insisted that she should choose the venue (an expensive hotel on

Richmond Hill, and I doubted she'd be picking up the bill) and the time (when I should have been at work). So it was going to cost me on all sorts of levels to meet the hateful woman.

"So what is it that you have to say to me?" Marjorie said as we sat opposite each other, a tower (literally) of afternoon tea on the table between us. From the large window to my left I had a spectacular view of the snow covered water meadows that border the Thames at Petersham. Its beauty was not my main concern right now, however.

"In many ways, Marjorie, we want very different things." I began. "Our desires are, one might say, diametrically opposed. I want to live..." I let that hang in the air for a moment, "happily ever after with you son. You would rather I did not."

"My only concern is for the happiness of my son." Marjorie had taken a scone from the tea tower and now proceeded to cut it in half before slathering each piece with jam and cream.

"That scone looks huge," I said. "I don't suppose you'd like to share."

"No, I would not." She cut one of the halves in half again and shoved it into her mouth. "I don't like sharing," she added threateningly, although her threatening tone was undercut by the fact that she was speaking with her mouth full.

"No, you don't, do you?" I observed.

"I like to keep my things to myself," she continued, having swallowed the scone. "Perhaps if you had had the misfortune to be born a twin you might understand."

"I would like to live happily with someone that I love." I replied. "Perhaps if you had had the misfortune to be orphaned at the age of six you might understand."

"I suppose you think I should say touché. If I thought for a moment that you loved anyone but yourself I might." Marjorie shovelled more scone into her mouth. If only it would choke her.

"But let's not waste our time talking about the past." I said brightly. "We're here to talk about the future."

"Ha!" she exclaimed with such vehemence that a little bit of scone shot from her mouth and landed on the crisp white table cloth between us.

"We are," I said, pointedly ignoring the crumb, "going to talk about how things are going to be from now on. You see, in addition to your nasty little folder, I also have your ring."

On such a cold winter's day it was hardly surprising that we were the only people having afternoon tea. It was therefore only the waiting staff, all of whom were far too discreet to raise so much as an eyebrow, who witnessed Marjorie trying to grab for my bag and in the process come perilously close to toppling the tea tower.

"Not on me, obviously." I added, having saved the tower with the loss of a single strawberry macaron. "I have put both items somewhere safe. The folder is with a solicitor friend of mine, with instructions that should anything untoward happen to me he, or she, should forward it to Gideon. It'll give him something to read while he's grieving my untimely... well, departure. And who knows? It might just shake his faith in you."

"And the ring?" Marjorie replied.

"Ah," I said, "the ring."

I was quite pleased with my ruse to control Marjorie's behaviour through the medium of the ring. It involved placing the ring in a safe deposit box which could only be opened using two keys at the same time. Each of these keys would be placed in its own safe deposit box, and each of these boxes could only be opened by two keys. I would know the whereabouts of one of these secondary boxes, Meg the whereabouts of the other. We would then each take one key from each of these boxes for safekeeping. This meant, effectively, that the ring could not be obtained without the consent, and presence, of both of us. The price for the return of the ring would be Marjorie's good behaviour. If she was prepared to supply me with a written confession detailing her past sins, to be lodged in a safe place, then we would return the ring. But if anything happened to either of us the ring would be lost to her forever. I was pretty pleased with the plan, if I do say so myself. I had, I thought, stitched her up like a kipper.

"So how many boxes are there?" Marjorie enquired after I had explained my plan in some detail.

"Three." I said.

"And how many of them have keys in them?" she asked.

"Two." I replied.

"And only you know where all are?" She looked at me quizzically.

"No," I said slowly, "I only know where two of them are."

"But you know where the box with the ring in is, so what stops you from taking it any time you want?" she asked.

"I can't because Meg has the other key." Goodness she was being as slow on the uptake as Meg.

"To the box with the ring in it?" Marjorie asked.

"No to the box with a key in it." I said, as patiently as I could manage.

"What's the point of locking a key in a box?" Marjorie looked puzzled.

"Look, I'll write it all down for you." I reached into my bag for a pen and paper. I thought perhaps a diagram might help, but I seemed to have come out without any writing implements, which was probably just as well.

"I've had quite enough of this nonsense," Marjorie suddenly announced, "I'm going home." And with that she leapt up and stalked off.

"But..." I called after her retreating back. I was as happy as she was to have this horrendous tea party come to an end but I wasn't at all sure that she realised that I had, quite literally, boxed her in. As it turned out, the events of the next few hours made Marjorie's understanding of my master plan (and on reflection it may have been a little too Moriartiesque) null and void.

Marjorie stalked out of the hotel leaving me (as I had anticipated) to pay the bill. I presumed she would be long gone by the time I was ready to leave about ten minutes later. It hadn't taken that long to pay the bill, but my heart was beating quite fast (and not just because of the size of the bill) and so I had taken a few minutes to calm myself. I used the time to look at the beautiful view and wonder if I would ever, while Marjorie was in my life, have a moment's real peace. Was Gideon really worth all this? Why, I pondered, didn't I just up sticks and move on?

The truth was I couldn't. I was far more attached to Gideon than I had imagined possible. I was also determined not to be beaten by Marjorie. And I sensed that time was increasingly against me. I couldn't keep moving on indefinitely, and I was unsure that I would be able to settle so well with anyone else now that I had Gideon as a comparison point. All these factors conspired to bind me to the situation in which I found myself. I was, I decided, going to have to make it work, come what may. I am very much one of life's optimists and so, my resolve strengthened, I headed out to face whatever the future might hold.

I don't know exactly what I expected to encounter once outside, but it certainly wasn't the sight that met me in the car park. The weather had ensured there was no one around, which was just as well because I have no idea what a spectator other than me would have made of the scene. Meg and Marjorie were locked in physical combat. Each had hold of the other's hair, and Meg, or it might have been Marjorie, also had a grip on Marjorie's, or it might have been Meg's, arm. They were going round and round tugging at each other, their free arms flailing about as each tried to land a blow on the other. And the language! If words really could produce colours the air around the pair would have turned very blue indeed. I made my way over to them as quickly as I could (the car park had been gritted but it was still treacherous), and managed to pull them apart.

"Give me my ring!" the one who must have been Marjorie bellowed. They were both dressed in startlingly similar outfits and even up close it was almost impossible to tell them apart.

"I will not!" Meg screamed back.

"She hasn't got your bloody ring," I said, positioning myself in front of Meg and shielding her from Marjorie.

"She bloody has!" Marjorie retorted furiously.

"Oh yes I have, you bitch." Meg replied, waving the aforementioned ring at Marjorie from behind the safety of my human shield.

"Why is that here?" I demanded to know. Meg had promised faithfully that she was going to deposit it, as per my now tattered plan, in a safe deposit box.

"I wanted to see her face when she saw I had it," said Meg, slipping the ring on her finger and taking a moment to admire it. "Suits me doesn't it?" It was the admiring glance that was almost her undoing as Marjorie lunged and almost grabbed Meg's hand. All she managed to do, however, was dislodge the ring slightly. Meg pulled her hand back as hard as she could causing the dislodged ring to fly off and skitter across the ground, where it bounced off a largish piece of grit and pinged under a parked car. All three of us threw ourselves to the ground in pursuit, but it was Meg who was quickest. Grabbing the ring she leapt up with an agility I would not have expected of a woman her age, and headed off up the very steep lane that connected the hotel car park to the top of Richmond Hill. Marjorie and I set off in pursuit. Meg had the march on Marjorie, but being some years younger and much fitter than either of them it took me no time to catch up with Meg.

"What the hell do you think you're doing?" I demanded to know, as I drew level. "We had a plan!"

"You had a plan, but you haven't had a lifetime of her getting her own way in everything." Meg was fuming.

"And how is this going to stop that?" I asked.

"I don't know. Ask her." Meg snapped back at me.

"Ask her what?" I replied.

"Ask her... about... Teddy... Claus." Meg was a little out of breath as it was a very steep hill and she was moving quite fast.

"Who?" I replied.

"Ask her!" Meg shouted again as loudly as her breathless state would allow. I dropped back to where Marjorie was struggling up the hill.

"Who's Teddy Claus?" I asked.

"Is she still going on about him?" Marjorie managed a nasty sneer despite being short of breath.

"Who is he?" I asked.

"He was her precious little teddy, and I took him for myself." Marjorie said.

"Why?" I asked, outraged on Meg's behalf.

"Because she loved him. So I took him." She looked inhumanly smug as she recounted this bit of unpleasantness from their childhood.

"Why didn't you just take him back?" I asked Meg when I caught up with her again.

"Because she destroyed him." Meg almost shouted. "She cut him up with Mother's dress making scissors."

"Why on earth did you do that?" I asked once I was back by Marjorie's side.

"I didn't want him," Marjorie said, almost nonchalantly, or at least as nonchalantly as an elderly woman walking very fast up a steep and icy path could manage. "I just didn't want her to have him."

"She really is a bitch, isn't she?" I said once I was back with Meg. We were fast approaching the gates to Richmond Park and Meg, despite her breathlessness, was still going strong. I was pretty knackered however as I not only had to cover the ground they did, but also keep running backwards and forwards between them.

We carried on across the park, Meg striding out in the snow, Marjorie huffing and puffing along some hundred yards behind. I, meanwhile, was running as fast as I could in the conditions between the two women trading a lifetime of stories of hurt and bitterness. It was as we approached Pen Ponds that Meg finally mentioned Malcolm.

"I was actually in love with him," she said, "you can tell her that. I never let her know before. I wouldn't give her the satisfaction."

"I know she was," Marjorie responded when I reported what Meg had said. "That's why I did it. It was for her own good."

"How do you work that out?" I asked.

"If he'd loved her he wouldn't have been so easily persuaded to marry me, would he?" Marjorie sneered.

"You told him you were going to send me to prison if he didn't marry you." Meg shouted her response directly at Marjorie who was now only a few feet away. We had come to a stop by Pen Ponds, not that you could see the actual ponds. They were presumably frozen and a thickish layer of snow covered their icy surface. To anyone unfamiliar with the topography of the park they would have been invisible.

"Oh come on, Meg." Marjorie bellowed. "Even you can't really believe that. He didn't want to marry you. He wanted a career and to make a lot of money, and that's what I gave him. What could you have done for him?"

"I wouldn't have been a cold hearted bitch who didn't care whether he was happy or not," Meg bellowed back. "You've only ever cared about getting what you want. Like this lovely ring. But you haven't got it now, have you? Have you?" Meg taunted Marjorie, waving the ring around above her head.

The two women had gradually moved closer to each other, leaving me unsure what I should do. I wasn't that keen on getting embroiled in another fight between the pair of them. I am pretty strong and they were a lot older than me, but I wasn't sure how long I could realistically keep them apart. They did outnumber me after all. They were, by now, almost toe to toe. They looked like prize fighters at a weigh in, each trying to psyche the other out.

"You're pathetic, you really are," said Marjorie, "if you weren't so hopeless you wouldn't have ended up with such a sad, pathetic life. Go on, keep the ring, I can always buy another one. With all that money I got from Daddy."

"You…" Meg looked at her sister, hatred emanating from every cell of her body.

"How do you think I paid for the ring?" Marjorie continued. "It was your inheritance. Your money. Just think of what you could have done with the money I spent on that ring." If I had thought Marjorie couldn't get any nastier I had clearly thought wrong.

Meg made an unearthly sound which I presumed encapsulated a lifetime's impotent fury. It was a noise of such ferocity that for a moment even Marjorie lost her equanimity. Unfortunately the moment had passed before Meg launched herself at Marjorie, who took advantage of the fact to grab the ring. I knew I had to do something so pushing myself between them I somehow managed, in the melee that ensued, to get hold of the ring myself. I have never liked jewellery, and I felt particular antipathy towards this ring, so without a moment's thought I threw it as hard and as far as I could over the heads of both women.

They watched as it flew through the air and landed with slight 'pfft' in the snow. For a moment all three of us froze but then, with a bellow loud enough to shake the snow from the trees, Marjorie launched herself after her ring. Unfamiliar as she was with the topography of Richmond Park she had no idea what was beneath her feet. I grabbed Meg's arm before she could follow her sister.

"Careful," I called to Marjorie's retreating back, "you're on thin ice." Marjorie turned her head to look at me without stopping her forward motion and began to speak, or rather to shout.

"I don't need your advice about..." Whatever it was that Marjorie didn't need my advice about I wasn't destined to know. An enormous cracking sound rent the air and she disappeared from view.

Chapter 31

"You madam, are a boney fido heroine. But if I could give you a bit of advice, it would be to stay away from open water from now on." The man I had come to think of as my own personal paramedic had come to my aid for a second time. This time, though, I was not the drowned wretch, Marjorie was. "This woman," Clive, for that was his name, turned to the assembled crowd while gesturing towards me, "very probably saved a life today."

As soon as Marjorie had entered the water a throng of previously unseen dog walkers had appeared as if by magic, drawn by the sound of cracking ice and shrieking. Most came to gawp under cover of offering help, but one or two suggested that someone should enter the water and attempt a rescue. One elderly man even went so far as to take his coat off, but I insisted, not that I had to insist very hard, that no one should follow Marjorie into the water, quoting the advice Clive (not that I knew that was his name at the time) had given me following my misadventure in the Serpentine. I think Clive was as surprised as me that we should meet again, and under such similar circumstances.

Having called the emergency services and established that the fire brigade were the go to service for getting people out of ponds, and also asked for an ambulance, both arrived in no time flat. Marjorie was hoiked from the (not very deep as it turned out) pond by the fire brigade and then Clive and his crew stepped in. Having loaded Marjorie's limp form into the ambulance, Clive had delivered his little homily in which I was, for the second time in my life, hailed as a hero. He, Meg, and I then climbed into the ambulance and we headed off, sirens blaring, to the nearest hospital. Under other circumstances I would have found the journey quite exciting. A friend of mine, who has a very boring job in Whitehall, was once whisked to RAF Northolt as part of a diplomatic cortege accompanied by motorcycle outriders. It was, she told me, one of the most thrilling experiences of her life, and not at all what she'd been expecting when she went to work that morning. Turned out she'd got in the wrong car and got in terrible trouble when she got back to the office, but it had been worth it she said, to go through all those red lights. I think the lack of windows in ambulances reduces the thrill factor somewhat anyway, but having a prone Marjorie next to me would have taken the shine off it even if I had been able to see out.

As we hurtled along, presumably running numerous red lights (not that I could see them), Clive asked endless questions. How long the patient had been in the water? Did she have any known medical conditions? Was she allergic to any medication? I seemed to have temporarily lost the power of speech, but luckily Meg took charge. It was only when Clive asked the patient's name that it suddenly struck me that there was really only one way out of this situation. I had to speak up. But the only thing I could possibly say was a lie, and it wasn't my lie to tell.

"She's my boyfriend's..." It was the first time I had spoken since getting into the ambulance. I paused mid-way through the sentence. It was as I was internally debating whether I dared tell the lie, the biggest I had ever had cause to tell, that Meg piped up.

"Aunt," said Meg. "She's your boyfriend's aunt, isn't she my dear. Her name is Mar..."

"Margaret Stuart," I completed Meg's sentence. "That's who she is. Margaret Stuart." I opened my eyes as wide as they would go at Meg behind Clive's back. Do you really think we can get away with this? I mouthed. Meg looked back at me, a little smile playing around her lips, and nodded.

"Yes, that is her name. Margaret. She's two minutes older than me you know." I opened my eyes wide again in an attempt to get Meg to stop talking. Lies are best left unembellished if they are to succeed. "We're twins." Meg added, rather unnecessarily. "My name is Marjorie, Marjorie Rowe." I put my index finger to my mouth in the internationally recognised sign for 'shut up' and glared at Meg. Too much talking can be the death of a good lie, and this was a doozy and therefore required as little talking as possible to ensure that it would shimmy through this stage unquestioned. It was going to get much harder when, as they inevitably would, Malcolm and Gideon arrived on the scene, without blowing it right now. Luckily we drew up at the hospital at that moment causing all conversation to be suspended. Marjorie was rushed off into the bowels of the building while Meg and I were led into a waiting room that was thankfully unoccupied by anyone else.

"It's the only solution," a very calm Meg explained. "If she comes round we can just say that I made a mistake and that I'm mad."

"What about me, am I mad too?" I asked.

"You can say that I misled you." Meg replied. "It's the only solution," she repeated. "She was never going to agree to your silly plan. All those boxes!"

"It was a good plan," I said, somewhat affronted.

"No it wasn't." Meg continued. "But even if it had been, this is a better one. If Marjorie falls into a pond, there's lots of awkward questions. Why were we all there? How did she come to be in the water? Did she fall or was she pushed? But if I fall into a pond, well, I'm a well-known loony."

"Are you?" I asked.

"You know very well that I am. That's what she told Gideon and Helen." Meg made a good point. "So it would arouse far less suspicion if an accident of this sort happened to me than if it happened to my sister."

"But what if she doesn't die?" I asked. Up until now I had been very much in the driving seat, plotting wise, but Meg and I seemed to have swapped roles somewhere between Richmond Park and the hospital.

"We'll cross that bridge if, and it's a big if, we come to it." Meg said decisively. This was not the slightly ditzy woman I had come to know, but an altogether savvier one. Had she, I wondered, been planning something like this all along? But that was ridiculous, she couldn't possibly have been, could she?

"But how," I asked, "will you pull it off?" If she dies, I mouthed, hardly wanting to say the words. "Can you really pass yourself off as her?"

"You forget, my dear, that I am her, to all intents and purposes. You can check my DNA if you don't believe me." Meg giggled at her little joke, which reassured me that she hadn't changed beyond all recognition in the last few minutes.

"But won't everyone realise straight away?" I asked. As if in answer to my question the door of the waiting room was flung open and Gideon walked in. Without a glance towards me he made straight for Meg, enveloping her in a huge bear hug and saying "Mum, this must be awful for you." Catching Meg's eye over his shoulder I raised my eyebrows in surprise.

"Yes, Ian, my darling, it is," she said, as cool as an especially cool cucumber. I was impressed.

The next few hours were not the most pleasant I have ever spent as Marjorie hovered between life and death. I found myself examining my conscience in minute detail. I had not done her any physical harm. I couldn't possibly have known when I threw it that she would chase after the ring. And I had done the right thing (the heroic thing according to Clive) by stopping anyone following her into the water. I had even gone so far as to warn her that she was on thin ice, although I could see how my words could have been misinterpreted in the circumstances. Still, I was left with the nagging feeling that I was responsible for Marjorie's situation in some way, and much as I had disliked her, and even in light of the fact she had tried to murder me, I had never contemplated that our relationship would end like this.

I even began to wonder if she really had been so bad after all. She had given up a kidney to a complete stranger, which must count for something, so she certainly understood maternal love despite her many faults. I had also been pondering whether there was even the slightest chance that the deception Meg and I had embarked on would work. I didn't hold out much hope.

"You OK?" Gideon, who had been sitting by what he thought was Meg's bedside, entered the family room where I had been put some hours before.

"I'm fine, but how is she?" I asked, although I wasn't at all sure that I wanted to know. Gideon sat down beside me and took my hands in his.

"She's gone I'm afraid," he replied. "I know you didn't know her but..." I think he was rather taken aback by the fact that I had burst into tears on hearing the news. It was the shock really. In an instant everything had changed, and I had no idea what would happen now. If Meg were to lose her nerve and admit to the deception I would have to say that I had been deceived by her, but was that plausible? I had been seen having a pretty furious row with Marjorie in the hotel and there must have been plenty of witnesses to the strange chase that had ended at Pen Ponds. If it came out that it was Marjorie and not Meg who was dead there would be quite a lot of explaining to do.

It was as these thoughts swirled around in my mind that the door opened again and Meg and Malcolm walked in. I held my breath, or rather I stopped breathing. My throat and chest had constricted in such a way as to make breathing impossible. The moment seemed to go on forever and I thought it was possible I might actually pass out when, finally, Malcolm spoke.

"I'm going to take your mother home," he said, directing his comment to Gideon. My first thought was can you do that, just take a cadaver out of a hospital, even if it was one of your family when alive? Then I realised that he meant Meg. He believed Meg was Marjorie. The air re-entered my lungs in a great rush. I felt lightheaded from all the oxygen and even went so far as to burst out laughing. "Well," said Malcolm, obviously slightly taken aback, "we'll be off then. If there's anything that needs signing you can deal with that can't you Gideon?"

"Yes, Dad, not a problem." Gideon replied.

"Oh, come here you two," said Meg, "I need to hug you both." Gideon and I went over to where she was standing and leant in for a rather awkward group hug. "Everything is going to work out fine." Meg hissed in my ear.

"I do hope so," I replied, equally quietly. "I really do hope so."

"I'm really glad that you and Mum are getting on so well now, especially after what's just happened," Gideon said once Meg and Malcolm had left. "She's going to need a lot of support. I know it might seem as if she isn't upset about Meg's death but they were sisters, and twins, so it won't be easy for her. We all need to be there for her."

"Yes, yes we do," I murmured. I really wasn't up to having any sort of discussion. I knew that Marjorie had died and that Meg had just left the room, but Gideon and Malcolm were so convinced by the deception that I was left wondering if it had actually happened and it was I who was deceived. I was also unsure of how to continue with the deception. I had heartily disliked Marjorie but if I was to avoid any slip ups I knew I should really start believing, like a method actor, that Meg was Marjorie. Unfortunately my feelings for Marjorie resurfaced every time I tried to do this. Just keep calm, I told myself and it will all work out fine. But I needed a bit of time to get used to the new situation and I couldn't keep my mind straight with Gideon gabbling on about supporting the loathsome Marjorie, even though I knew it was actually Meg who I would be supporting. Luckily, just as I was about to have a minor nervous breakdown, a nurse came in and said she needed a few minutes with Gideon and I was left alone.

On Gideon's return I was able to claim extreme tiredness (it was by now after midnight) and feigned sleep on the journey home. By the next morning I was feeling slightly more on top of things, although it was the strangest experience, to be with a man whose mother I knew had died the day before who was not only ignorant of that fact, but would have laughed at the very suggestion.

That day we visited Malcolm and Meg/Marjorie. During this visit I was amazed again by the coolness of Meg/Marjorie (I found that this was the easiest way to think of her for the moment). She did absolutely nothing that might arouse suspicion. She had even managed to come up with a perfectly believable version of the previous day's events, which explained the presence of all three of us and how come we had ended up at Pen Ponds. Like all good lies it stuck to the truth as much as possible.

"So there we were, Eve and I, having had an absolutely delightful afternoon tea, although I was a bit of a twit and nearly knocked over the tea stand, but you caught it didn't you dear?" Meg/Marjorie looked at me for confirmation.

"Yes, I caught it," I said before shutting up sharpish. This was Meg's show and I figured I had best leave the details to her.

"So there we were," she repeated, "making our way across the car park, when Meg suddenly appeared from behind a parked car. I hadn't seen her for several months and she looked simply dreadful. Her hair was unkempt and she was, I'm afraid to say, a little unsteady on her feet. And then she just lunged at me! It was quite frightening, wasn't it Eve, my dear?"

"Yes, yes, it was." I replied quietly, as if this might minimise the lie. The irony of the situation was not lost on me. How many lies had I told in my life? Too many to count, but this one was by far the most high stakes ever. I couldn't afford to put a foot wrong.

"And then she started raving about my ring," Meg continued. "She said she had it, and do you know what, she had!

She knew where we kept the spare keys, they've been in the shed for years, and I think we do forget to put the alarm on occasionally, don't we Malcolm?"

"We may do," Malcolm (almost) concurred. What, I wondered, did he make of all this? He knew that Meg had been there the night the ring went missing. Did he know that the woman with whom he was now sharing his home was the thief rather than the victim? And if he did, did he mind or was he happy to go along with the deception? It would increase the chances of it succeeding exponentially if he did.

"So Meg was waving the ring about," Meg went on with her story, "and, inevitably I suppose considering the state she was in, she lost her grip and dropped it. I picked it up and headed off, but she chased me. I really didn't know where I was going. I just wanted to get away, but she came after me. Poor Eve was running between the two of us trying to calm me down and talk sense into Meg. Anyway, Meg caught up with me by the pond, and made a grab for the ring. I really didn't mind if she took it, I was just terrified of what she might do to herself. So I decided that the best thing to do was to give her the ring, but as soon as I did she threw it over my head, but then she must have decided that she wanted it after all ... and well, we all know what happened next." Gideon, I could see, was lapping all this up as it concurred entirely with his view of his 'amazing' mother. How it affected Malcolm I was less sure. Only time, I supposed, would tell.

Chapter 32

"You're going to see who?" I asked in disbelief.

"The donor woman." Gideon replied. I had been clearing the table after breakfast one morning a few weeks later. If I had thought that I was out of the woods, it would seem that I had thought wrong.

"The what? I mean who, why, how?" I gabbled, unable to string a coherent thought, let alone sentence, together.

"Meg was on the donors' register, so I agreed that everything could be donated." Gideon said as if this was the most reasonable thing in the world rather than the end of it.

"But she was really old, who'd want bits of an old lady?" In my wildest imaginings about what could go wrong, this had not figured. I was furious with myself for being so stupid, but then what could I possibly have done to forestall such an eventuality?

"That's not really the point." Gideon said. "They can still take whatever is useful. Corneas, heart, lungs..." and then he said the fateful word "... kidneys."

As a rule I find breathing comes very naturally to me, it's not something that I have to put a lot of thought into, but recent events had overturned a lifetime of thoughtless breathing and left me gasping like a fish in the bottom of a boat on more than one occasion.

"I'll come with you." I said once I had regained control of my oxygen intake.

"Oh, OK, if you really want to." Gideon looked doubtful.

"Oh ... I'd love to. I think organ donation is ..." Breathe, I told myself, breathe, "fantastic."

"Yeah, you're right. OK, let's go."

"Now? Right now?" This was very little notice to get of the upcoming apocalypse. I would have liked a little time to prepare myself. I might have been able to come up with a reason for neither of us to go given enough time. But I wasn't to have any time and so off we went. As we drove to the hospital, I tried my hardest to find ways in which the situation could be salvaged. There must be reasons, other than having taken on the identity of someone who only had one, for someone to have had fewer than the average number of kidneys. I just had to come up with one. Just one, that's all I needed.

"Did you know," I said, "that some people are born with a different number of organs than normal? Sometimes fewer, or more even." I added, in an attempt to disguise my intent.

"Are they? Where did you hear that?" Gideon asked.

"I read it somewhere." I said as I stared disconsolately out the of the passenger window, fearful that my lie would be detected. It was that bad, I was losing the will to lie.

"On the internet no doubt," Gideon scoffed. "Really you mustn't believe everything you read online."

"Oh, I don't." Damn. "Have you seen those stories about people that have their organs stolen?" I tried another tack. "Didn't Meg go to India once?" Hopeless, bloody hopeless. The first rule of lying is plausibility. The second is ... well, I'm not sure exactly what the second rule is, but the first is definitely plausibility.

"Not that I know of." Gideon laughed at the suggestion.

"I must have heard it from Helen I suppose." This was desperate stuff, but I was desperate. We were about to learn where all the organs supposedly belonging to Meg had gone, and a missing kidney was bound to excite comment. But what could I do? I would just have to wait and see what Gideon's reaction was.

"Twins!" I exclaimed, as if in preparation for saying something of importance.

"What about them?" Gideon asked.

"Nothing," I said, "nothing at all." I turned my head to stare disconsolately out the of the passenger window again. This must, I thought, be very much how people on death row feel, and I wasn't even going to get a last meal.

"So," said the plump, friendly looking woman in whose hands my fate lay. "I've got some great news for you. A donor can save up to eight lives through the donation of what we call the, um, solid organs. That's the heart, kidneys, pancreas, lungs, liver and," she stopped to check her notes, "intestines. Your aunt, Mr Rowe..."

"Professor," Gideon interrupted her. "It's Professor."

"Oh. Your aunt, Mr Professor," she resumed, "was relatively elderly but we still managed to, for want of a better word, harvest enough solid organs to save," she checked her notes again, "four lives." If this was what I did for a living I'm pretty sure that I would have come up with a better word than harvest for the process, but we're all different I suppose.

"Oh, that's great," said Mr Professor enthusiastically.

"Yes, so there was a liver patient that had been waiting for several years, but unfortunately he is an alcoholic so, between you and me," she looked at us conspiratorially, "I'm not sure how that one will go."

"Oh, OK," said Gideon, rather less enthusiastically.

"The lungs, the lungs," she said riffling through her papers. "Oooh this is lovely," she exclaimed, "they went to a young woman with cystic fibrosis. We couldn't give her the heart unfortunately as it was rather atrophied." Why didn't that surprise me? "And then we come to the kidneys. One went to a teenage boy and other to a young mother. Oh my!" said the woman, while Gideon stared at me open mouthed. The reason for their reaction was that I had leapt from my chair and fist pumped the air while bellowing "Get in!"

Sensing that I had misjudged my response, I resumed my seat and said, rather more calmly, "Well, that is good news, I must say."

A huge weight lifted from me. Any guilt that I had felt over Marjorie's death, any doubts I had over whether I had misjudged her had evaporated in an instant. She had lied. She was a big fat, dead liar. She had never donated a kidney. She had not been so moved by the plight of another mother that she had put her own health at risk. She had, on the contrary, lied to her beloved son in order to exert lifelong control over him. Someone capable of such a deception was capable of anything. I felt an overwhelming sense of relief sweep through me. It was over, she was gone.

Chapter 33

The cold weather had hung on well into the New Year, and there was still snow falling in April. By May, however, the temperature had returned to around the seasonal average. It was a Saturday evening midway through the month and Gideon and I were lying in a very large, very comfortable bed in a very lovely room in the most expensive hotel I have ever stayed in. Luckily Malcolm was paying. The hotel, and the room we were in, was dead centre in the Royal Crescent in Bath, a hotel so discreet that it could have taught Claire a thing or two about discreetness (I looked it up and it turns out that Gideon was wrong, there is such a word. I'm just waiting for the right time to tell him). We had, that morning, married at a Register Office in Bath with two complete strangers as witnesses.

"It's strange isn't it?" Gideon observed. "We're the honeymooners but it's Mum and Dad that seem more like newlyweds. I hope we're like that when we've been together as long as they have."

"Mmm," I replied non-committally, knowing that in fact we had been together rather longer. It's not that I begrudge Meg and Malcolm their happiness, but they are rather revelling in each other's company. They are constantly laughing and joshing with each other and have about a million private little jokes. They go for long walks (in Richmond Park of all places) accompanied by Pookie, who Meg/Marjorie insisted on keeping despite his awful flatulence. They go to the theatre, the cinema and, rather more bizarrely, they have taken up clay pigeon shooting. The house has also undergone something of a change. Much of Marjorie's ugly and uncomfortable furniture has gone and Meg has all but cleaned out OBVAC refilling it with stuff more to her taste. They are having a ball. Only the most unobservant person could fail to notice that something had changed. Gideon, it seemed, is that person.

Helen is also a much happier woman. As I had deduced from listening to her conversations with Celeste and from reading the contents of Marjorie's folder, Celeste is Helen and Joe's daughter. Helen (who was only fifteen at the time) fell pregnant during their teenage romance but Joe returned to Australia unawares. Marjorie shipped Helen off to France and insisted she have her baby adopted by a French couple. She then used the threat of telling Joe to ensure Helen did as she wished ever after.

Having shared what I knew with Meg she had, as Helen's putative mother, told Helen that she was sorry and promised to never again hold this knowledge over her head. Whether or not Helen has come clean to Joe I have no idea, but they seem very happy, so one way or another it's all good.

Even my brother and Sophie are getting on pretty well since he dropped his custody case.

"You know," Dominic told me, "I got the results back and I decided not to even look at them. Pixie's my daughter whatever any DNA test might say."

He had, I'd be prepared to swear, opened that envelope and in it he saw proof that he wasn't Pixie's father. Except what he actually saw was proof that I'm not the daughter of Claire's husband's, Richard. Whatever the truth, Dominic dropped his custody case and everything has pretty much returned to normal, although he is rather less bolshie about demanding his rights now.

I even received another postcard from Sasha. On the front was a picture of two peas in a pod and on the back it said All's well that ends well. I think she was suggesting that the ends justify the means and while I'm not sure that is really such a good thing as a general rule, I'm very glad that things have turned out as they have in this case. It's a bit disconcerting however, to realise that Sasha seems to know exactly what happened. Perhaps Dominic isn't so wrong to think his every move is being watched, although I don't envy the person who has the job of watching Dominic's every move.

"It's great being married isn't?" said Gideon as we lay in bed following the most delicious dinner I have had in a long time. "It might have taken us a few false starts to get here, but I'm really, really happy," he continued, stifling a yawn. "There is one thing I'd like to know about my wife though, now we're married."

"And what, my darling, would that be?" I asked.

"You promise not to tell one of your daft lies?" he said.

"I solemnly promise not to tell you one of my daft lies." I replied.

"I'd know anyway. I can always tell when you're lying." He laughed at the mere suggestion that I might be able to fool him. Bless. "But I've never been quite sure what you do, for a living I mean," he continued.

"No, you haven't have you?" I replied.

"So what do you do?"

"The thing is," I began, but looking over I could see that his eyelids were already drooping. Gideon falls asleep in an instant and that instant was almost upon us. I therefore dropped my voice to a soporific murmur. "What I actually do is ... well I ... how best to describe what it is ..." As I murmured on, very much in the style of a snooker commentator, I heard Gideon's breathing change. I was by now very familiar with the rhythmic inhale and exhale that means he has fallen asleep and so, after a little more murmuring just to be sure, I fell silent.

I knew that one day I would have to deal with his enquiry, but not now, not right now. I wanted my happy ever after to last for as long as possible and telling Gideon the entire truth, not just about my occupation but about all sorts of aspects of my life, wasn't guaranteed to secure this outcome. I could, of course, lie (I hadn't promised not to, only not to tell a daft lie) and that was probably what I would have to do. But I had made a promise to myself not to lie to Gideon once we were married. I knew I would break that promise at some point, but I felt that on our wedding night, at least, he should hear nothing from me that wasn't entirely true.

"I love you," I therefore whispered into his unhearing ear, "I would do anything not to be parted from you." And I had never said anything I meant more, not to anyone.

Lightning Source UK Ltd.
Milton Keynes UK
UKHW03f0757200318
319738UK00001B/126/P

9 781786 080486